MW01109285

For Roger,
with aloha,
your shipmate,
Tom

the BIMINI BOYS

A Novel

Tom Jacobs

Represented by The Farris Literary Agency, Inc.
P.O. Box 570069
Dallas, TX 75357-0069
972-203-8804
farris1@airmail.net
http://www.farrisliterary.com

ISBN 978-0-9786305-1-5

Cover Art: *Don Quixote* by Pablo Picasso, 1955

This book is dedicated to the
Glory of God and to
my beloved wife, Linda.

CONTENTS

the BIMINI BOYS

chapter 1

NOK: None

Manning Crenshaw didn't want to get involved. He wasn't looking for it. All he wanted was a good, quiet meal. If he had stayed out of it he wouldn't have become a multi-millionaire, and his ex-wife wouldn't have signed for his cremated ashes in a FedEx box.

What happened was this: the man in the booth next to Manning's at dinner slumped sideways and came to rest with his eyes closed and his cheek on the seat back. Manning worked on his Caesar salad, pretending not to notice. After a while he glanced over. The guy looked asleep. How do you fall asleep in the middle of a restaurant in the heart of Manhattan? Any signs of breathing? Nope.

Manning looked around, hoping someone else would notice. Not likely. The man's booth hid from the rest of the room behind a projecting aquarium full of pastel fish from the tropics. After a while Manning looked for a waiter. No luck, and none expected. Manning was eating at Circa 2000, an upscale room on the Upper East Side. The décor and the food matched the prices, but with vintage New York service. Manning's waiter ("Hi, I'm Charles, I'll be your server tonight.") had come by twice chanting his mantra ("Everything all right here?") and trying to snatch Manning's half-finished salad. Manning knew that if he had been signing a client or proposing marriage Charles would be back, interrupting. Now, when he really needed someone, all the waiters had gone to wherever waiters go when it's time for the check.

Manning finally got up, went over to the next table, and sat down. No one in the room looked up. He lifted the man's head, leaning him back against the imitation leather. "Sir? Sir?" No movement. Manning looked at a peaceful and unlined thirty-something face with dark hair combed straight back from a high forehead. A narrow head, long, thin nose. . . European, maybe, or Mediterranean. Manning put his finger under the guy's chin, wishing he had paid more attention at CPR class. He couldn't find a pulse. I'm not doing this right, he thought. He thumbed back an eyelid. A fixed pupil stared straight back. Blue light from the fish tank on his new friend's skin made him look dead a week.

"I'm looking at a corpse," Manning said to himself. Expired. Unbidden, his mind went back to high school French. "Spirare," to breathe. In-spired—breath in. Expired—breath out. Was he even looking for a pulse in the right spot? He felt his own pulse. A little fast. Easy does it. He ran through his options. Lay him on the table and start CPR. . . pump, pump, in, out? Scream and shout? Dial 911? He felt for his cell phone.

The room's atmosphere discouraged all of these. People didn't just lie down and die at Circa 2000. Manning glanced over to his own table. His prime rib sat, pink and plump, untouched.

All he wanted to do was escape the week, the worst week of his life, with some peace and quiet and a good meal. God wouldn't even allow that. He looked down at his dead companion while the events of the week crept unbidden, like Bedouins, into his head.

Monday had brought a form letter from the Miami-Dade County Circuit Court of the State of Florida, finalizing his divorce. Nine months earlier Ellen had left a perfumed note folded on his TV recliner ("Manning, I'm so sorry. E.") and had driven to Florida with Skippy, their best-of-breed Pomeranian, and his almost-new, not-yet-paid-for BMW sedan.

Eric Anderson, next-door neighbor and close friend—apparently much closer to Ellen—had followed a week later. Eric's departure was followed closely by all of Manning's liquid assets and the household furniture. Since Eric was an attorney, the petition for divorce was in clear, brief English: Ellen got everything, including Skippy. Manning got to stop paying on the BMW.

Tuesday started with coffee and donuts in Manning's boss's office at Capital Aerospace. Manning's employer glued his eyes to his coffee cup and mumbled on about the demise of the Soviet Union and the collapse of the Berlin Wall. While this had been good for Civilization, his boss made it clear that it was unfortunate for military contractors and Capital Aerospace in general and for Manning Crenshaw in particular. It was simple math: the end of the Cold War equals loss of Defense dollars, equals loss of Government Defense contracts, equals loss of jobs. Manning was an accountant working in Business Management. The engineers at the firm had circled the wagons. Women, children, and engineers first, support people last. Business Management was support.

"Hell of a note, Manning. . ." his boss got up and stood in front of a company sign: "Celebrate Diversity." He was whining now, "… have you know I voted against it. . . probably just temporary. . . let's hope so, eh?" Manning had until the end of the month to clear out his cubical. His boss shook his hand and promised a first-rate personal reference. Manning got the extra donuts.

Wednesday brought a short-fused assignment, Manning's last with Capital. A software supplier in New York City was over budget and behind schedule. Manning drove down from Hartford in rush-hour traffic.

Thursday and Friday were twelve-hour days. The supplier was defensive and resistant to cost cutting. The deal was no-win for Capital. Probably why a lame duck with a pink slip in his in-box was sent down in the first place.

On Friday evening Manning stood in line to check out of his hotel, looking forward to a long drive through clogged freeways back to Hartford. At the end of the drive lay a crummy walk-up studio apartment with a bottle of vodka and a vial full of sleeping pills in the kitchen cupboard. Manning had begun to dwell on that bottle and that vial, and what he was thinking frightened him.

He watched two teen-aged boys charge out of one of the elevators. They were tall and slender with strong tanned legs under the three-quarter length Bermudas currently in fashion. Skateboards dangled under their arms.

They could have been from Mars, they looked so out of place among the worn middle-aged businessmen in the lobby. Manning looked into their fearless eyes and saw two brothers who had been just as ready to take on the world a quarter-century earlier. Those boys had carried surfboards, dashing and laughing into the water on Cape Cod summers. What was their motto? Manning smiled, remembering. "Charge the wall." The wall was the wave face—you charge it, no matter what, and you bust through and make the wave. You hang back, play it safe, the wave eats you—you wipe out.

The brothers had surfed and dreamed. They would surf forever. No desk jobs for them. Paratroops—special forces, maybe. The CIA. Why not? What wasn't possible?

The boys grew up. Dreams changed. Manning's brother stayed with his. He joined the Navy, became an elite SEAL team member. Quit that, actually went with the CIA. Maybe he still surfed; Manning didn't know. He couldn't remember what had become of his own surfboard. Manning had played it safe: an accounting degree, a big, steady aerospace company, a loyal wife. All the careful moves leading to this hotel checkout line and the shambles of a life. The wave ate him.

Manning watched the boys in his hotel bounce out of the lobby into the street. He watched rain splatter the glass doors closing behind them. A tired, pale, prematurely middle-aged man with gray hair and a gray face in a gray raincoat looked back at him from the glass—his own reflection.

"Sir? Sir?" Manning blinked his thoughts away and

looked at the desk clerk, who was waving him over. He lifted his briefcase and went up. "Yes, sir. Checking out?"

Manning picked his room key out of his pocket and looked at it, then handed it across the counter. "No. I think I'll stay overnight." He smiled at the clerk. "Maybe longer. Any problem?"

"None at all, sir." The clerk made a note, then ran Manning's key through the electronic machine that gave it a new life.

Manning took his briefcase back to his room. He hadn't yet packed. Now, he didn't need to. He walked outside, turning his collar up against the weather and dodging under awnings and balconies. The first restaurant he came to was Circa 2000. Beautiful rich people entered, laughing. To hell with it, Manning thought. I've got one last expense report, and one more week's paycheck. He walked in.

Charge the wall.

Now the fates won't even give me a last meal, Manning thought as he looked at the corpse sharing the booth with him. Time to get the restaurant involved. He raised his right hand to signal a waiter.

Strangest thing. His hand, moving with a will of its own, slipped inside the dead man's suit jacket and came away with a long wallet made of the skin of some high-priced reptile. His left hand joined the rebellion. It held the wallet, while the right hand explored its contents. Credit cards (platinum), driver's license made out to Henry Toledo, address a few blocks away on Fifth Avenue, age 55 (he looked 20 years younger), membership cards to two very nice private clubs. Three thousand in cash.

He found a medical insurance card. "NOK: None."

Manning Crenshaw's thumb rubbed the wallet's smooth exterior, while he scanned the room under his eyebrows. Were people watching him and whispering to each other? Nope... the few patrons who had a view of the booth were still safely inside their own bricked-in egos. A young couple ten feet away ignored their dinners as they discovered each other's eyes. A fat cat on a cell phone chewed out someone far away, waving a fork with his free hand. His elegant wife picked at her salad and looked neglected. Two old ladies dressed like tourists sipped white wine. Manning quietly slipped Toledo's wallet into his own jacket. He lifted Toledo's wine bottle from its silver ice bucket and poured a rich red Pinot Noir into the half-filled glass on the table in front of the corpse.

Next-of-kin: None.

He raised the glass to his lips, sipping. Excellent. A plan began to form in his mind, just an outline, details missing, but the next several moves snapping into place as clearly as if binoculars had been brought to sharp focus. He took his own wallet out and put it into the dead man's inside jacket pocket. He had joined the conspiracy of his hands.

In the next few minutes, between sips of wine, Manning exchanged the contents of his pockets with Toledo. He was careful not to attract attention, but the beautiful people around him were full of rich food and of themselves. He made one last check of the dead man's pockets and was glad that he did. Toledo's passport was in his other inside jacket pocket. Stamps from all over: Moscow, Riyadh, South America, Japan. The last imprint was for re-entry into the U.S. from Vienna. Yesterday's date.

"Everything all right here?"

Manning snapped the passport shut, startled. Charles, his waiter, was making a rare cameo appearance. Manning put on a worried look. "My friend seems to be ill."

Charles was a pro. He vanished and reappeared immediately with the Maitre d'. The two men bent over Toledo. Manning stood to his feet. "Perhaps a private room?" The Maitre d' nodded immediately. The three men carried Henry Toledo out of the dining room. They kept him vertical—a drunk, perhaps. Heads turned, but the noise level in the restaurant remained the same. Manning looked over his shoulder as they entered an empty side room. Heads were turning inward again.

Circa 2000's manager appeared. The police and an ambulance were called. Two patrolmen took down the story in little spiral note pads. Manning talked and talked. The corpse became his brother-in-law, Manning Crenshaw. Delicate heart. . . no surprise. . . terrible, terrible. "How do I tell his wife?"

Some of Toledo's three thousand dollars, spread liberally, disposed of the restaurant staff. He signed a police statement, and the cops were off to fight real crime. The corpse began its trip to the city morgue. Suddenly, simply, easily, a different Manning Crenshaw stood at the sidewalk entrance to Circa 2000. He stood again in the rain, but this time he lifted his head to let the water wash his face. It felt clear and cold and wonderful. He felt wonderful, really alive for the first time since Ellen had left. He was a new man. A new man named Henry Toledo. He pulled out his wallet, checked his new address, and took off walking.

Toledo's address was a tall brownstone at Fifth and 77th Street. A brass plate next to a red entrance awning intoned "Burrough House." It was one of the elegantly reconditioned condominiums circling Central Park. A doorman stood guard under the standard green awning. Manning stood across the street, along the fence to the park, out of the rain, watching. In half an hour three couples entered the building, and an old woman came out. The couples nodded to the doorman and entered with a key. Manning crossed the street.

The doorman turned a bearded face toward Manning, head wrapped in a turban. A Sikh. Weren't all Sikhs named "Singh," after their founding prophet? "Evening, Mr. Singh," he said to the doorman. "Wet."

"Evening, sir." The doorman gave him a cool look. Manning felt only excitement. He was ready with another line of baloney. . . friend of Toledo, staying a few days. He had a hundred in his pocket for emergencies. But the doorman turned back to face the street.

He found Toledo's key ring and searched for a key that fit the lock in front of him. Too many keys. He could have sorted keys across the street. This was taking too long. He glanced over his shoulder. Mr. Singh still had his back to him. Three gold and black keys each with an engraved "B. H." filled the ring. He tried one. Didn't fit. The second was clearly too small. Manning fumbled with the third key, eying the doorman. Mr. Singh was watching him now, hands behind his back.

Come on, dammit! Mercifully, the key found its way home. Turn to the right. Nothing. To the left. Nothing. Mr. Singh walked over. "Trouble, sir?"

"Damned key. . ." Manning Crenshaw, master criminal, twisted the key back and forth. "… won't work."

Mr. Singh stood next to him now, looking at his face. Manning turned away, as if that helped. The doorman gently took the key. He pushed the door inward and twisted the key at the same time. The door unlocked.

"Sometimes it sticks," Mr. Singh said. "Just push the door fully closed."

Manning nodded furiously. "Thanks."

"My pleasure, sir." The doorman walked back to the street. Manning scuttled into a high-ceilinged alcove and pulled the door shut, leaning against it with his eyes shut. He realized that his shirt was damp with sweat.

Thirty-five polished brass mailboxes lined the lobby. Manning found one marked, "Toledo." No apartment number. A problem. A second smaller gold and black key opened the box. The second envelope was addressed to Toledo at Suite 1601.

Excellent, like the wine.

He punched the "16" elevator button. The elevator opened onto a small hallway with four heavy wooden doors. The first gold and black key opened Number 1601.

Suite 1601 was a penthouse. Manning looked around with wide eyes. He stooped to take off his shoes and stepped from the marble entry onto thick Oriental carpeting. A large living room was decorated in hand-carved oriental rosewood furniture with tapestry pillows. He closed the heavy front door and sat on a brocade sofa. A hundred thousand city lights winked at him through floor-to-ceiling glass that lined one wall. He realized that he was sucking in short, rapid breaths between his teeth. NOK: None.

He walked in stocking feet into a study complete with ornate desk and computer-printer-fax built-ins fit for a military command center. A giant plasma-screen TV took up a whole wall next to an entertainment center. The Knicks silently played the Lakers. A guest bedroom in soft pastels peeked out from one side through an open doorway. On the other side, across the living room, the master bedroom looked out on the same magnificent city view. A walk-in closet held dozens of tailored suits in various shades of black standing shoulder to shoulder on dress parade. A sunken tub and jacuzzi lay next door in the bath.

Manning wandered back into the living room and selected a Burgundy at a built-in bar. He swirled the wine in a snifter goblet. It stuck to the glass like red paint. The wine was smoky and smooth on the roof of his mouth. NOK: None. A sleek black cat, a Persian, stalked out of the kitchen. Manning stroked the cat's head. After a while he put a Beethoven symphony into a CD player and loosened his tie, humming along.

Just at this time a tax auditor named Audrey Cobb worked after hours at the Internal Revenue Service building in Washington, DC She loved working late.

She relished the absolute quiet, the feeling of limitless time, and the chance to do her job right, without the phone or her boss interfering.

Audrey was a perfectionist, a name she used on herself. She had organized her job and her life into tidy piles of typewritten notes with no misspellings. Hospital corners on her bed sheets.

Audrey was white, single, and thirty-two. Everyone told her that she was pretty—even striking—but she couldn't see it. Not hard to look at, maybe, she thought, but too thin. Certainly not an hourglass figure. A hundred-twelve pounds, for goodness sake. It's what Mother would say, "For goodness sake." Mama fed her high calorie stuff every Sunday after Mass, working on the hourglass, but Audrey's metabolism took it all in stride, burning carbs like straw, refusing to let her move beyond Size Three in the "Petite Miss" section.

Mama. Audrey smiled. Mama weighed 110 pounds herself. They were both five-six, Mother watching fat content, proud of her own figure. Relax, Mama, it's in the genes.

Audrey punched a key to wake up her computer screen. Interesting case: an old man reporting an income of over $450,000, taking no deductions, pushing his return through none of the usual tax loopholes. She moved her mouse. Point, click. Zzup. The guy's W-2s came up—except. . . hmm. No W-2s. Only 1099s, and lots of 'em. Audrey's pigeon had absolutely no income from salary or pensions last year. No social security? Almost a half million, and it was all from dividends paid from seven different financial institutions. Audrey brought up Page Two. He paid the maximum tax, not even itemizing deductions. Just a patriot? Audrey shook her head at the screen. Her experience and her gut told her that she had a snake in the woodpile here. This guy was filing a beige return, hoping for no audit. He had something to hide.

Step one was to look for unreported income... Forms 1099 or W-2 not listed in his return. Audrey highlighted the guy's social security number and executed an IRS software program to check that number in detail, including all reported income. A flag came up:

ACCESS TO THIS FEDERAL SOCIAL
SECURITY NUMBER NOT AUTHORIZED.
EXECUTIVE ORDER 917009.

Audrey sipped lukewarm coffee. She had never seen this flag before. She tried again. Same flag. Executive order? Which executive? IRS Director? Presidential? Audrey computer-searched all IRS directives. Executive Order 917009 didn't exist. She tried White House directives. Almost immediately a memo told her: "There are no current presidential directives that affect IRS procedure or policy."

Audrey stood and stretched. She walked to the window. Below, Constitution Avenue glistened in the steady rain that was forecast to blanket the entire East Coast for the weekend. She looked at her wrist: 10:15 p.m. Time for bed? Try again Monday?

Audrey the Perfectionist prevailed. This looked like a

tough nut. They cracked best late at night when she could apply constant pressure. She sat down and pulled the guy's previous five years. Same SSN. Same flag. After another hour she was still stalled.

She tossed her cold coffee and drew a hot cup, thinking. She looked at the guy's birth date. August 1st, 1920. Eighty years plus. Making a half mil. Why wasn't someone that old, making that kind of money, drawing social security? Probably working since at least 25. . . since 1945. Tax returns that old were still hard copy. No way to access them with her computer. They weren't even in the building. They had been transferred to a federal records warehouse in Rockville, Maryland. It wouldn't open until Monday. She chewed on a knuckle of her index finger. She had chewed on that knuckle since childhood, when her mother told her she couldn't suck her thumb any more.

Audrey left a note on her boss's chair:

> Winnie,
>
> Got to go to Federal Records in Rockville
>
> Monday A.M. Be in the office late morning.
>
> A

Winnie wouldn't care. He'd assume she needed to do it. Audrey did a good job. She was a perfectionist. Besides, they were dating. Audrey turned off the coffeemaker. Round One goes to this guy, whatever he was hiding. She'd get him, though. She made a note of her pigeon's name and SSN before she turned off her desktop.

Henry Toledo.

Manning Crenshaw awoke early Saturday morning wondering where he was. Then he remembered: he was rich. Delicious. Like the wine. He wiggled his toes in the sheets. Egyptian cotton, high thread count. The bed's pillow-top mattress felt impossibly soft, and the bedroom filled with sunlight and with the silence that money was able to buy even in the heart of the City. Since Ellen had left, Manning had slept restlessly on a second hand mattress in a crummy walk-up in the seedy part of Hartford. He looked forward to never visiting that apartment again. He remembered his wife screaming at him: "Get a life!" Well, he got one. He showered and padded naked to look into the medicine cabinet. He found a headache powder for his slight wine hangover and a new toothbrush still in the wrapper. Pill vials lined the cabinet shelves. Manning looked at the labels. Several other headache remedies, antibiotics of several flavors, minerals, vitamins, and other health supplements. Most of the medicines dated from this week, from an apothecary in Vienna, Austria. Manning remembered the visa stamp from Vienna. He looked at the name of the prescribing physician. Herr Doctor Hermann Steinmetz.

Audrey the Perfectionist awakened early in suburban Arlington, Virginia, on Monday morning. She'd beat the Beltway traffic to Rockville, have breakfast there, then open the Federal Records Building at 8 A.M. The gray Middle Atlantic day promised more rain. She put on a bright red raincoat over a blue dress to counterpoint the morning's somber mood. A perfectionist, maybe, but she had lots of sap running, too.

Ed, the Records Curator, led her to the 1940s Section. Audrey decided to pull Toledo's 1948 tax return. That would make him 28. She would see what she could find, then work forward. It took 20 minutes, but she found what she was looking for on microfilm. She fed it into one of the building's readers, wishing that Ed provided coffee with the machine. She smiled at the return. A total of three pages in those days. Amazing.

Also amazing was Toledo's income for 1948: $98,144. Almost a hundred thousand, in 1940 dollars, and it was still all in equity dividends and interest from bonds. No paychecks. Rich family? Maybe. Something illegal? Not much drug trade in 1948. And Toledo not yet 30. Audrey glanced at the birth date on the return, then looked again: 1885. He had changed birth dates. That made the guy 63 in 1948. It made him 122 today.

chapter 2

"?Mira, Que Tal?"

The City Coroner's office opened at 9 A.M. Monday morning. Manning was first in line. He sat across from a middle-aged clerk in a shapeless dress and Adidas running shoes who seemed much too large for her tiny typist's stool. Manning's face wore an expression of extreme strain, some of it genuine. He ran through the same story, smoother now with practice. ". . . my brother-in-law, Manning Crenshaw. Heart attack. So sudden. Chain smoker. Warned him. Need to make arrangements. . . for the family. . . my sister. Oh, dear."

"Identification?" asked the clerk through a large wad of Bubble Yum.

Manning handed over Henry Toledo's driver's license. He had considered another identity but had abandoned the idea. No time. Besides, the police report already linked Toledo and Crenshaw.

The clerk looked at the photo on the license and looked at Manning. The likeness was striking. That was because Manning had spent most of Saturday building a new license with the apartment's desktop computer. Henry Toledo had thoughtfully listed his Internet address and access code in a notebook in his desk. A rogue web site posted driver's license templates for all 50 states, ready for downloading. He pasted in a photo of himself taken at an arcade photo booth in Times Square and printed the result. Then he ran it through the laminating machine at the same arcade. He did the same trick with Toledo's passport.

Manning practiced Toledo's handwriting all day Sunday, especially the signature. He listened to the short clip of Toledo's voice on the greeting message on the apartment's answering machine. All afternoon he talked like Toledo. Slight accent. Maybe Italian. He'd have to read up on Italy.

The clerk was asking about disposition of the remains.

"Cremation, please." Manning handed her a large brass urn purchased Sunday at the Little Saigon Bazaar. "It's the family's wish. Only. . ." He pasted on a worried look, ". . . only I must have the ashes quickly. Very quickly. I leave for Europe tomorrow." He made a long face at the clerk. "Can it be done. . . today? I'm more than willing to pay. . . the city. . . for expedited service."

He passed the remainder of Toledo's cash under the clerk's nose. She sat back, considering. "There is a way," she said. "A fee. . . two hundred and fifty." Manning kept smiling, nodding. "Then there's a borough tax."

"I completely understand, very good of you." Manning ripped off his worried look and pasted on a smile. He was laying hundred dollar bills in front of the clerk. "Will a thousand cover it?"

The clerk's hand passed across the desk. The money

was gone. "Will you need a receipt?"

Manning recognized the coded message. "No."

The clerk nodded. The deal was struck.

Manning took a taxi to a spot two blocks from the hotel room he had rented the previous Wednesday and walked the rest of the way. He climbed three flights of stairs to his room and let himself in with the computer-coded key card that he had foresightedly kept. He stood inside, careful to touch nothing, looking around. Several notes from the hotel had been slipped under the door. The management was probably wondering why Mr. Crenshaw hadn't checked out. A garment bag hung in the closet with his extra suit and some dress shirts. His briefcase lay where he had dropped it. A toothbrush and deodorant decorated the bathroom countertop. He had told himself that he might need something, but now he realized that he just wanted to say goodbye to these odds and ends of his previous existence. Get a life. He dropped his key on the desk, turned, and left, listening to the door click shut behind him.

Listening to his old life click shut behind him.

Manning phoned Miami that afternoon from a pay phone. "Hello?" It was Eric, husband-in-law.

Manning visualized a wide, soft face under a completely hairless head. Friendly grin. Firm handshake. "Hello. Is Mrs. Crenshaw there?"

"Ellen, it's for you." Goodbye, Old Friend.

"Yes?" Ellen's voice.

Manning lowered his voice an octave. "Mrs. Crenshaw?" He spoke through a handkerchief. Did that help? He remembered it from an old black-and-white film.

"It's Mrs. Anderson now."

Manning smiled grimly. Ellen was making this a lot easier. "Sorry. Mrs. Anderson. My name is John McKinley. McKinley and Sons Mortuary. New York. I'm afraid I have some bad news." He read from a handwritten script, trying to sound like a professionally concerned mortician. It's your ex-husband, Mrs. Anderson. Very sudden. Heart attack." The phone gasped. Manning paused. An absence of sobs. He went on. "We, all of us here at McKinley and Sons, are so very sorry. Phoning to notify you of the arrangements." He gave her the ID number of the Federal Express package containing her ex-husband's urn, ashes, and personal effects. He waited for the reaction he knew was coming.

"Wait a minute. Ashes? I don't. . . Manning always wanted. . . we have a gravesite paid for. . . in Connecticut."

Manning smiled again. Ellen was so predictable. He read the carefully worded clincher, keeping his voice concerned, bureaucratic.

"Mrs. Anderson, I should advise you that we have cremated your ex-husband and forwarded his remains in strict compliance with the laws of the State of New York, using state funds allotted for that purpose. Any desires that you or the family of Mr. Crenshaw may have to the contrary will of course be considered, but you should understand that any increased cost will be borne by you."

There was a long silence. Manning could feel Ellen chewing on the words "increased cost." Finally she said, "Well, of course... if it's already... you said the... package. .. will be here tomorrow?"

Predictable.

Manning slept late Tuesday morning. He was beginning to enjoy the movie he was starring in. The doormen at his building nodded now and smiled when he passed. He got up and opened the refrigerator. Eggs, bacon, fruit. He made breakfast and poured some milk for the cat. He had named the cat Leonard after an uncle who had always looked slightly feline. He went into the walk-in closet off the master bedroom. Toledo's suits were a close fit. The pants were a bit tight, the jackets a bit loose in the shoulders. Manning would have preferred it the other way 'round. He punched the Yellow Pages for a tailor who looked expensive and set up a measurement appointment for the next day at his condo. Then he looked through Toledo's desk and found a bank statement:

Checking:	$12,292.33
Savings:	$ 5,000.00
Money Market:	$97,505.01

Nice. He lifted out a thick portfolio labeled "Equities." Fourteen accounts were listed with three different brokerage firms, totaling, Manning guessed, about three million dollars. He found a safety deposit box key but nothing to identify its location. A black leather book listed access numbers and addresses for Swiss accounts. Manning poured himself another cup of coffee. He was a multi-millionaire, and he'd only been looking for 30 minutes. He spent the next half-hour looking through Toledo's drawers. Odd thing: he found no personal correspondence. He expected at least some letters or cards that would give some background to Toledo's life. Nothing, not even a photo. He took the coffee to his balcony. Central Park was a green wooded patch in the sunlight. He could see joggers and strollers below. They looked small. They were small, starting today.

The phone rang. Without thinking, Manning picked it up. A man's voice said, "Amigo? Mira, que tal?"

It was Spanish. There was a long silence. "Enrique? Como?"

Manning fought down his panic. He spoke in falsetto, in what he hoped was the slow drawl of the deep South. "Sorry, Sah. Mistah Toledo ain't heah. Dis de cleanin' lady."

"I see," said the voice slowly, in perfect English. "When do you expect Mr. Toledo?"

"Sorry, sah. Ah jus' doan know."

"I see. Sorry. Goodbye." The line went dead.

Manning wiped sweat from his forehead with an index finger. Have to take all calls on the answering machine, he thought. He sat at the bar gulping coffee and staring at his reflection in the glass door to the liquor cabinet. Manning Crenshaw, accountant, looked back with haunted eyes. Was he crazy, thinking he could crawl into someone's life and persona like a hermit crab? The phone's voice mail blinked with one unheard message. Manning listened to a different voice speaking more Spanish. Or was it? Manning had taken four years of Spanish in school. This sounded familiar, but somehow different. Portuguese, perhaps? The message went on for 30 seconds before the caller rang off.

Winston Churchill sat up straight in an Orthopedic Executive Form-Fit Chair in his Director of Investigations and Audits, Personal Returns office at the Internal Revenue Service Headquarters in Washington, DC. He was spotlessly turned out in a gray Brooks Brothers woolen three-button and what he hoped was this season's power tie in purple with red circles and rectangles. Winston had learned "dress for success" at the Masters in Public Administration graduate course at American University. If there were an organization entitled "Sons of the Washington Beltway" Winston would have been a chapter president.

Audrey Cobb sat across from him on the first six inches of his "visitor's chair," thumbing through ten Power-Point viewgraphs and biting her lip. She was 15 minutes early for a briefing of the Deputy Assistant Director for Audits. The subject was Henry Toledo.

Audrey had never briefed the Deputy before. She was nervous. Winston had briefed the Deputy many times, and he had a bad feeling about this one.

"Maybe I should go in and test the overhead projector," said Audrey.

"There are two," said Winston. "One doesn't work,

the other does, don't worry about it. Instead, ask yourself why the Service cares about screwed-up birth dates. We're gonna be cut off after the first slide."

Audrey shook her head, still biting her lip. "Mr. Toledo is hiding something. No one is a hundred-twenty-two years old."

"They've got Armenians, in Armenia, one-thirty," said Winston. "National Geographic did a piece."

"Are those Armenians changing their dates of birth every other decade?" asked Audrey. She reached across Winston's desk suddenly and took his hand. "Look, roll with me on this, will you? All I want is to drive up there, hear what he has to say, fish around. Nothing bites, I'm back down to DC. The trip costs a thousand bucks, a week, tops. All the Deputy does is nod, we're out of there."

Winston looked into Audrey's china blue eyes and felt her soft dry fingers on his hand. He was absolutely in love with her. They were dating discreetly. The Service didn't like fraternization in the hallways, but it wouldn't say anything. Don't ask, don't tell. Winston and Audrey would walk over after work for a drink at the Willard Hotel bar and dinner in the District. Sometimes they drove to Kennedy Center or Wolftrap for a show. It was experimental, arms-length, platonic. Too slow for Winston, but he was being careful.

Winston made a career of being careful. He worshipped rules. He viewed life as an endless staircase to be approached one step at a time, no skipping stairs. Success was a clean desk at the end of the day and lots of lined-out items on his to-do list. Washington's bureaucracy fit him like a diver's wet suit.

Winston Churchill labored under the burden of his name. His father, an Englishman, was distantly related to the original. His mother, a history major, simply couldn't resist when he was born. By the time he was a teen he was introducing himself as Winston and telling classmates to call him "Church." Everybody called him Winnie.

Winston's roommates in college found out that he kept two toothbrushes in his medicine cabinet in the belief that rotating them daily allowed them time to dry, extending their life forever. His roommates secretly wet the dry one each night. Winston never tumbled. He got up to five toothbrushes, wondering why they all stayed so wet. Life is like that for the Winstons of this world.

"Let's go in," said Audrey.

"You look wonderful, Darling," Winston said, pushing the envelope for endearments.

"Very sweet. Thank you," said Audrey, rereading her opening viewgraph.

chapter 3

". . . Dangerous Men."

Manning closed the door to his apartment, whistling to himself, and cha-cha-stepped to his terrace. There he opened a FedEx package that the doorman had handed him. Inside was a new Visa card with his name and photo on it. He had applied through the Internet for two new credit cards a week before—ones featuring a photo of the cardholder. He had e-mailed as a digital photo one of the pictures from the Times Square photo gallery. And his re-tailored suits were back. He was steadily assuming the plumage of Henry Toledo.

His answering machine doused his mood. "Mr. Toledo, my name is Audrey Cobb, of the Internal Revenue Service. I must advise you that we have some questions concerning your Federal Income Tax return for last year. Please be so good as to contact me in Washington, DC " The voice gave a number and extension.

Manning played it again. He went to the desk. Toledo had his returns for the past seven years carefully filed. Manning had been an accountant for 15 years. He knew what he was looking at. Toledo's return for the last year looked clean. How could the federal government argue with almost $180,000 in taxes? He poured some coffee, looking at all the angles. In the end he picked up the phone.

"IRS. Cobb."

"Ms. Cobb, this is Henry Toledo. Returning your call." Manning had debated Outrage or Victim, and had decided on Good Citizen.

"Yes, Mr. Toledo. I. . . ah, we. . . have some questions about your tax return. Returns, actually. I was wondering. . . can you make yourself available sometime for an interview? Soon?"

"What sort of questions?"

"It's. . . ah. . . a question of continuity of information. May I ask you to bring your returns for the past five years?"

"I don't keep my returns," Manning lied, thinking: the IRS doesn't have my returns on file?

"I see. Well, anything you have, to document your returns. . . I can be in our New York office let's say. . . tomorrow?"

"I have another call coming in," said Manning. "May I put you on hold?" He sat drinking coffee. This was nuts. He knew a fishing expedition when he saw one. The woman on the other end sounded young and unsure of herself. He knew auditing. He would probably learn more from a face-to-face meeting than she would. He put the phone to his ear. "Sorry about that. Overseas call. Sure, tomorrow is fine. Why don't you come to my place in the city. . . Three P.M.?"

Ms. Cobb sounded surprised. "Three P.M.? Oh. . . fine." Manning gave her directions.

When he hung up he found a juicer in the kitchen and threw a lot of fruit and some carrots in. He took his glass to the terrace and sat in the warm terrace sunshine developing a bad case of cold feet. His plan had seemed so simple in the beginning, before reality got in the way. Put on Henry Toledo's persona and life like putting on his trousers—perfect fit. NOK: None. No relatives, no questions, no sweat. Except that life is always richer than our imagination. Like strange voices on the phone speaking a language Manning can't even recognize, much less answer. Like the IRS, so interested in his taxes that they don't ask him to fax some record or other, Oh, no, they airmail an agent all the way from Washington.

Manning swirled the juice in his glass and shook his head. I'm in way over my head. Time for Plan B. Look at the places where Henry keeps his money. Pick off the low-hanging apples—the easy money, easy to move, easy to convert to cash, that no one will miss for a while. Then, catch a train out of town. Change identities. Fly to somewhere warm and sunny. Watch the bridges burn.

Except. . . Manning had become a different man the evening he lifted Henry Toledo's wallet at Circa 2000. He was on a high wire, working without a net, and he loved it. He was having the time of his life, and he could pull it off, he knew it. Maybe Plan B was inevitable, but not yet. He would decide later. Maybe after he listened to what Audrey Cobb had to say.

Charge the wall.

Manning opened the door to his apartment the next afternoon. Audrey Cobb, IRS investigator, stood there looking nifty in a business suit that accentuated her slim figure. Pale yellow chemise top, pearls. She juggled her briefcase and extended her right hand. "Mr. Toledo?" Her fingers were small and soft. So was she. Manning led her to a small coffee table next to the windows. He had coffee, cheese, and crackers spread out. Manning had always been good at customer relations.

"I'm a little early," Audrey Cobb said. She was 20 minutes early. "I wasn't sure how to get here, wanted to leave time." She walked to the glass windows, trailing Coco by Channel. "Is that Chicago I see in the distance?" She turned toward him, impressed.

"It's nice, isn't it?" Impressed was what Manning wanted.

Audrey wandered over to look at an old mandolin that hung by a dark leather strap on Manning's wall. "This is wonderful," she said. "It's Italian, isn't it? Spanish?"

"Portuguese," Manning lied. "Seventeenth Century." I've got to find out more about my toys.

"I play twelve string guitar," said Audrey. She sat on the sofa and held up a coffee cup. The atmosphere was friendlier. Manning liked his prospects.

He poured for them both. "What's all this about, Ms. Cobb?"

Ms. Cobb put on her bureaucratic face. Her blue eyes looked a couple of sizes too large for her face. "We have some irregularities to resolve, is all."

"Ms. Cobb, I pay my taxes. I'm a good private citizen.

What irregularities?" Henry Toledo, innocent taxpayer.

"How old are you, Mr. Toledo?"

Manning stared at her. He had no idea. "I am. . . how old?"

"It's a simple question. Most people know the answer."

"It's on my return," he said carefully.

The girl spread three returns on the table, facing Manning, like a croupier dealing Blackjack. "Here are your tax returns for last year, 1960, and 1948. Each lists a different birth date. Your age seems variable, Mr. Toledo. Your return from last year makes you eighty. Here's your return from 1960, makes you ninety-five. Here's 1948. Makes you one-twenty-two today." Ms. Cobb sipped coffee. "Which is it, Mr. Toledo?"

Manning maintained eye contact while his mind raced. What are you doing to me, Henry Toledo, Manning asked the ashes in the urn. "I've got a perfectly reasonable explanation," he stalled.

Audrey Cobb picked up the most recent return. "Let me read to you the certification you signed on this,"

> Under penalties of perjury, I declare that I have examined this return and accompanying schedules and statements, and to the best of my knowledge and belief, they are true, correct and complete.

She leaned back in her chair, smiling. "Is that your signature, Mr. Toledo?"

Manning jerked his head up and down, mind blank.

Audrey nodded. "Our handwriting analysts have certified that all three signatures are the same. You look, oh, late forties to me. Maybe fifty, tops. So why do your tax returns, legal documents, remember, make you somewhere between eighty and a hundred-twenty-two? Go ahead, Mr. Toledo. What's your 'perfectly reasonable explanation'?"

Manning took a deep breath. The "late forties" remark hurt. He was only thirty-nine. It was the gray hair. "Better gray than no hair at all," Ellen had been fond of telling him. That was before she ran off with a man as bald as a basketball. Audrey Cobb was tapping her pencil eraser on the coffee table, waiting for his answer. The Manning Crenshaw of last week would have thrown in the towel, extending his wrists for the handcuffs. But this lady was up against Henry Toledo, master of the high wire.

He gestured with an open hand to show his guest his condo. "Ms. Cobb, look around. Do you think I'd jeopardize all of this for the sake of some glitch on my tax return? What do you think I'm up to, here?"

Audrey Cobb took another sip of her coffee. "I'm working on a premise that you've got something to hide, Mr. Toledo. So far, you're doing a good job of confirming my premise."

Manning shrugged. "Good Citizen" wasn't working. He decided to mix in some "Benito Mussolini."

"Ms. Cobb, my returns, the tax I paid, it's all there, right? I didn't cheat on my taxes, right?"

"Right, yes. But your birth dates. . ."

"I sent you carnivores a hundred-eighty-thousand last year. If I pay my taxes, what do you care about my birth dates? That's my business, right? Lots of people lie about their age."

"Not to the Feds they don't." But Audrey's face was clouding up. "I mean, it's a federal offense to. . ."

"You people have a long history of bullying the little guy."

Audrey waved her own hand around to indicate Manning's apartment. "You're hardly the little guy, Mr. Toledo." But her voice had lost some steam. She bit the knuckle of her right index finger nervously.

"Horse manure." Manning raised his voice and mixed in some outrage. "I seem to recall your director making promises on TV, no more IRS abuse. Okay I'm feeling abused. Also folded, spindled, and mutilated." He rose and stood over his guest. "There is a perfectly good explanation for those birth dates. But I'm damned if I'm gonna explain it to you."

"I can get a subpoena, Mr. Toledo."

"And I can get a shredder." Manning walked to the front door and opened it. "Good day, Ms. Cobb."

Audrey put her coffee cup down with an angry clink. "I'm notifying you of a formal tax audit at the New York office of the IRS, in Manhattan, this Monday at eight A.M.

"I'm gonna need that in writing, Ms. Cobb."

Audrey Cobb stuffed papers into a blue leather bag. "You'll get your damned letter!"

Manning pointed to the tax records on the coffee table. "May I keep those?"

Audrey stood, nodding briskly. "They're copies." She tapped out the door in her heels, looking straight ahead.

"Phone any time," Manning called after her disappearing back.

He sighed. She looked as good walking away as she did bow-on. Manning wondered if the new Henry Toledo had enough of the right stuff to date beautiful women. Maybe beautiful IRS employees.

Enough. He picked up the tax returns and read through them. The birth date problem was obvious, and just as Audrey Cobb had described it. The Henry Toledo that Manning had seen at Circa 2000 was young. . . maybe in his forties, but more likely mid-thirties. Manning played some scenarios in his mind. The only one that didn't bounce had a long line of Henry Toledos in it with the most recent one corking off at Circa 2000. Father-son-grandson perhaps. Maybe a great-grandson too. All those Henries would "inherit" without paying any taxes by simply becoming the previous Toledo. Now I'm the latest Toledo, Manning reminded himself, for different fiscal reasons.

He picked some crackers from the dip tray he had set out for Ms. Cobb and walked out to the terrace munching and thinking. The wind, always brisk on the 16th floor, tossed his hair and blew his tie into his face. Scenario A didn't explain why handwriting pros called all three signatures the same on the tax returns. He, himself, had practiced until his rendering of Toledo's signature would pass most inspections, but he doubted that it would fool an expert. He watched the city in motion below him. Maybe there was a computer somewhere that copied exact handwriting—surely there was—but not decades ago. Anyway, why risk exposure by blandly changing birth dates every generation or so? Why not simply "lose" the money into a Swiss account? Money could always be laundered, even in the Roaring Twenties.

Manning was getting cold feet again. The IRS was on Toledo's case, and probably with good reason. The guy was hiding something. How long before Audrey Cobb was replaced by an FBI agent? What was really going on? Manning was clueless. He sat at Toledo's desk absently rummaging drawers, looking for a Rosetta stone. He found a key chain with what looked like two electronic car keys attached—the kind he used to own before Ellen took the BMW. He pressed a small button on one. Sure enough, an ignition key flipped open like a switchblade. Manning got up and took the elevator down to the parking garage. He needed a diversion.

Late model cars sat in rows in the cement underground reflecting the fluorescent lights. Lots of spaces were empty. People were at work. The stalls were not identified by apartment number. Manning pointed the electronic keys at each car and blazed away. A black Mercedes E300 winked a green light at him. Very nice. He pointed the second key at the car. Was it a duplicate? Nope, the red convertible next stall over winked green. Mercedes SL500. Even nicer.

Manning got into the convertible.

He started it up. The engine awoke with a throaty rumble like a big cat. Manning had never even been in a Mercedes. He fiddled with the sound system. A CD player began Gershwin's Rhapsody in Blue. Speakers everywhere gave the music three dimensions, maybe more. Manning sat in the leather seat, his leather seat, with the wonderful car trembling under him while his cold feet warmed. To hell with the IRS. I'm gonna pull this off. He went back to his condo and opened the Yellow Pages to "Universities."

The next morning Manning drove his new black Mercedes sedan out to Hofstra University on Long Island. Traffic was light at mid-day, a Saturday. Manning cruised east on 495 at 70, enjoying the speed and the car's magnificent engineering. He found the college at mid-afternoon—five minutes late and no parking in sight. After a couple of wrong turns he parked in a handicapped space at the Languages Building and found Professor Iturbe in the Latin Languages Section. He had chosen Hofstra for its language department, and Iturbe in particular as an expert in the Spanish language.

Iturbe was free of classes for the weekend. They shook hands. "Please excuse me, I have a terrible cold," Iturbe said through blocked nasal passages. Manning smiled and wiped his hand on his trouser leg.

Iturbe led Manning into a cramped cubbyhole filled with books on shelves, on desktops—so many that the professor had to lug them off of a chair so that Manning could sit down. The little academic offered some warmed-over metallic coffee that still tasted good.

"You have a request, sir?" Iturbe had a rich Mediterranean accent that matched his dark eye sockets and olive skin.

Manning had phoned to set up the meeting. "I assume that you will act as a consultant for me on a language matter, for a fee," he said. The professor nodded. "I have a taped conversation that I want you to hear."

"My rates are one hundred an hour," Iturbe began, but Manning was already counting out five twenties on top of a book in front of him.

"Here's a hundred," he said to the professor. "This won't take an hour." Manning laid a hand-held tape recorder on Iturbe's desk and thumbed it on. The professor listened to the short voice mail message, taking notes.

"He's asking Enrique if everything's all right," Iturbe said. "He says, 'This is Pablo.'" Iturbe took a minute to blow his nose into a neatly ironed handkerchief. "He asks, 'Are you coming to Paco's for Easter?' He leaves a number." Iturbe handed Manning a slip of paper with a phone number on it.

"What is it? Basque?"

Iturbe shook his head. "Spanish."

Manning stared at Iturbe "I took four years. It didn't sound like Spanish to me. Some words, maybe."

"It's not the modern idiom," Iturbe said. "It's old."

"How old?"

Iturbe walked to his window. "You are lucky," he said, looking at maple trees outside. "My doctorate was on Cervantes."

"Cervantes. . ." Manning was uncertain. "The statesman?"

Iturbe gave him a smile he probably reserved for the illiterate. "Cervantes the author. Don Quixote. The phrasing on this tape is very old. For example, he uses a phrase that means, 'May the Good Lord keep you safe in His hands.' The subjunctive form of the verb 'to keep' indicates uncertainty. That phrasing hasn't been used in Spanish for some time."

"Before the war?" asked Manning.

Iturbe turned and smiled at his guest with watery eyes. "Yes, before the war. Before World War II? Yes. The Spanish Civil War? Yes. World War I? All yes." He held up the small tape. "If you had given this to me without comment, I would have taken it for a reading from a 19th Century Spanish manuscript." Iturbe shook his head, still smiling. "Mr. Toledo, I think maybe that someone is playing a trick on you."

Manning drove back to the city thinking about Iturbe and the tape. His phone's voice mail was blinking again when he got home.

"Hello, Mr. Toledo. My name is Talmud. Isaac Talmud. We've not met, but let me assure you we have a lot to talk about. Can you give me a call?" The caller left a local phone number. Deep voice, every word pronounced with care, as if the speaker was foreign. But no accent.

Manning sat on his expensive recliner in his elegant living room staring at the wall. All the air went out of him again. After a while, he dialed the number left on the recorder.

"Talmud."

"Mr. Talmud, this is Henry Toledo."

"Mr. Toledo, how good of you to return my call. How has your day been?"

"I've had worse," said Manning. And better.

"Wonderful to hear it. I hope I'm not imposing. I have some information that I think you will find interesting."

"I will find interesting. . ." Manning used an old trick—when stuck for something to say, repeat what you've just heard. Finally he tried, "Let's hear it, Mr. Talmud."

"Not over the phone, I'm afraid. Can we meet? I don't want to impose. I promise you, you won't regret hearing what I have to say. Can we meet for lunch tomorrow? My club?"

After a long minute, Manning agreed and wrote down Isaac's directions. He hung up feeling even more depressed. He would be walking into this meeting ice cold. He thought again about punching out, finally deciding to keep the luncheon date. Maybe he would be able to put some of the missing pieces into the Toledo puzzle. But unless life as Henry Toledo became a whole lot less complicated, he would empty Toledo's bank account, draw what cash he could from his credit cards, computer-construct a new identity and passport, and try life as an ex-pat in South America. They had Mercedes dealerships in South America.

The Peter Stuyvesant Club was in an old brownstone near the UN Building, unmarked except for a brass plaque with the street number on it. Beautiful people in thousand-dollar suits that matched the ones in Henry Toledo's wardrobe posed in a lobby that dated from the beginning of the last century. A blond receptionist gave him a brilliant smile at the name "Talmud" and pointed to one of the sitting rooms that circled the main lobby.

"Mr. Toledo?" A tall, slender, elegant looking man rose to meet Manning, smiling. "I am Isaac Talmud. A pleasure."

Manning tried on a copy of Toledo's smile. They shook hands. Talmud led the way through the club. They wound up in a wood-paneled dining room that smelled of old leather and old money. A white haired waiter, as old and distinguished as the décor, bowed and nodded them into a booth. "Mr. Talmud, good afternoon. So good to see you, sir." He smiled at Manning. "Drinks?"

"Drinks indeed," said Manning's host. "Charles, isn't it?" he said, shaking hands with the waiter. "Good to see you, too."

Isaac looked at Manning, who hesitated, said, "Beer, please. Corona?"

"Of course," said the waiter. "Mr. Talmud, the usual?" Talmud wiggled his fingers.

Manning took a long look at Isaac Talmud, who seemed to be about his same age. He wore the elegance of his private club as gracefully as he wore his perfectly tailored suit and custom shoes. His black curly hair and narrow curved nose made him look Middle Eastern or Mediterranean European.

"Talmud. Is that Jewish?"

"Yes."

"So you're Jewish?"

"Used to be. I'm Christian now."

"I didn't know you guys could do that.'

"Why not? Jesus did."

Time to change the subject. Manning rubbed his hands together. "It's cold in here."

Talmud smiled his agreement. "Some of the members think it impedes the aging process."

Their drinks came with the speed of light. "Nice club," Manning said, looking around.

"You should know," said Talmud with a wide grin. Manning looked at him, trying to hide his panic. Am I a member? Am I up on my dues?

Isaac Talmud ignored the look and picked up his drink, a white wine. "I have known Henry Toledo for a long time. For a long, long time. Who are you?" He laughed out loud at Manning's face. "Look, your secret is safe with me. I have secrets enough of my own. You have stolen the persona of my good friend, Henry Toledo. Fine. Hello, Henry Toledo. Look, what is your real name?"

Manning was silent. Talmud nodded. "You're careful. That's okay, too. Very well, Mr. Toledo. May I call you Henry? I don't know your game, but I can make a pretty good guess. You have nothing to fear from me. For all I care, you can be Henry Toledo until you die. You can keep Henry's money, the equities, the apartment here, the villa in Cote d'Azur. . . all of it. I need only to know how Toledo died."

"What villa?" asked Manning.

Talmud smiled a prosperous smile. "You have much to discover, Henry Toledo. Most of it will be very pleasant." The smile switched off. "How I envy you the wonder of discovering everything for the first time. Everything new.

The world will open for you as it does for a small child." He laid a hand on Manning's arm, serious now. "Toledo. How did he die? You were there? How did he die?"

Manning downed a large gulp of Corona. He was going thirty in an eighty-mile-per-hour world. He glanced across the table. This guy probably had some answers. . . maybe some solutions. What did he have to lose? "Perhaps we can help each other," he said carefully. "I'll tell you what I know. In return, I need some answers. And some help."

Talmud smiled his congenial grin and raised his glass. "Fine. I will do what I can. Now, what were the circumstances of Henry's death?"

"Forgive me," said Manning. "Perhaps I should ask some questions first."

"No, forgive me," said Talmud. He stared at his guest, and his dark eyes could have been fashioned from anthracite. "You are in way over your head, my friend. Soon, if you can be patient and can listen, you will understand what I mean. Again, what were the circumstances of Henry Toledo's death?"

The man's smile never wavered, nor did the eyes. There was no give to him. Manning told the Circa 2000 story. "Just laid his head down and left the planet. Like everything just. . . shut down. I thought he had fallen asleep."

"Yes. Yes. But from what? Any autopsy? Any forensics?"

"None."

Talmud was silent for a moment, thinking. "We must exhume. Where is he interred?"

Manning didn't look at him. "He was cremated. Immediately."

"I see." Talmud's eyes darkened, and his smile died. "Before he died, how did he look? Sick? Old? You saw him."

"I told you," said Manning. "He put his head down and just went to sleep. No fuss, not a sound. He looked. . . fine. He looked remarkably fit and young for a man who. . . may have been much older." Manning thought of Audrey Cobb.

The waiter brought a second round of drinks without being asked. Talmud ordered lunch for them both. Roast duck. Then he lifted his glass in another salute. "To Enrique Toledo. It's very important," he continued, "did anyone touch him? Even slightly. . . for a moment?"

"Didn't see it."

"What he was eating, drinking? Could it have been. . . tainted?"

"You mean poisoned? His food, I don't know. I finished his wine for him. I'm here."

"Yes. You are here." Talmud tapped his index finger on his water glass. "This is an important matter. I can't stress how important. I must know how Enrique died. There are perhaps clues to the matter in his apartment. A medical report, or some records. Something."

"I'll help you all I can," said Manning. "Are you willing to help me?"

"Help you how?"

"I'm in tax trouble. The IRS came to see me yesterday. Some woman. An auditor. She showed me some of my tax returns. She thinks I'm older than I look. Maybe seventy years older. Toledo goes back a long time. His tax form ten-forty birth dates go back even farther."

The man across the table widened his eyes. "That qualifies as a lot more than tax trouble. What did you tell her?"

Manning laughed nervously. "Tell her? What can I tell her? She had me. The birth dates on Toledo's returns were all over the map. I stalled, gave her some Spam about IRS harassment. I bought myself some time."

Talmud looked at the ceiling. "That's all right then. We should have time enough."

"Enough for what?" Manning leaned away as the waiter served soup. He waited until the waiter left. "You're worried, but you're not surprised that the IRS has heartburn with Toledo's birth dates. What's going on?"

Talmud's secret smile was back. "Mr. Toledo, my dear old friend, the IRS is right. You are older than you look." He waved his hand in a circle. "Like this club. This room has been redecorated several times, but the club is much older. Founded right after the war. The first war, I mean. In 1919. Where were you in 1919, Mr. Henry Toledo?"

"In 1919... I wasn't even born. My father wasn't alive. What's that got to do with... "

"You were right here, in this room, when the club started. You're a founding member. I was at the same table. There were twenty of us, all solid citizens of the city."

Talmud smiled at Manning's expression. "Mr. Toledo, Mr. Whatever-your-name-is, you made a choice that night at Circa 2000. You could have told the nearest waiter that he had a corpse on his hands and walked. You could have lifted Henry's wallet and walked. You could have become Henry for a couple of days, looted his bank account, charged to his credit cards, maybe, and walked. You made a much bolder choice. Also much more dangerous. Was it the right choice? The answer depends on what you do next. You can become. . . remain. . . very rich. . . beyond your wildest dreams. I can help you. You must help me, too."

"How?"

"First we need to. . . neutralize the IRS. Tell me what you know about this woman. Everything you can."

Manning fumbled in his pocket for a sheet of paper. "Her name is Audrey Cobb. Here's her hotel in town, her phone number. I don't know much more than that. What do you mean, 'neutralize?'"

"There are some things about you. . . about Enrique. . . that must be kept private, you understand? Enrique's true age is one of them. He was careless with records. He always was." Talmud seemed to be talking to himself. He winked at Manning. "Don't you wonder how you got away with all of this? Why hasn't someone. . . the doorman. . . some friend of Toledo's, found you out? It's because Enrique kept himself from people. He was a hermit, a secret man. The most secret of men. He hid from the world, my friend, because he kept a great secret. We all do."

"Who's 'we?'" Manning asked. Talmud didn't reply. Manning sipped his soup, shaking his head. "You're gonna tell me Toledo was really over a hundred, aren't you?" He raised an eyebrow. "Aren't you? Makes you over a hundred too, right? I'm gonna swallow that, right? Well I'm not buying it. I'm not even renting with an option to buy."

"I suppose it's a lot to imagine all at once," Talmud said.

"You suppose that, do you? Mister, you're as young as I am. I'm looking at a fifty-year-old, tops. And Toledo was younger than you are. Listen, I've leveled with you. You've got Miss Cobb's address, her number. You level with me. There's an explanation for Toledo's different birth dates and it's not old age."

Talmud put down his drink. He hadn't touched his soup. He bowed his head, seeming to retreat into himself as a hermit into his cave. No, Manning thought, more like a baron into his castle, taking his drawbridge with him. After a long moment he raised and angled his head, so that his narrow, curved nose pointed directly at Manning.

"My friend, you don't know what you're talking about. But like most of your generation you go on talking anyway. My age, Enrique's age, that's not important. Work with me, I beg you, or suffer the consequences."

"And what consequences might those be?" Manning asked.

"You are a player in a game where you hold no cards. You don't even know the rules. You don't know the names of the men who make the rules. . . dangerous men."

"Why don't you tell me the rules?"

"They can't afford to allow you to lurch around New York City unsupervised. Cooperate, and you will realize the life you hoped for when you became Henry Toledo. Refuse, and you're in grave danger."

"My money or my life, huh? No, Mr. Talmud, or whoever you are. . . Methuselah, maybe. I'm doing okay by myself."

Talmud stood just as the entrée was served. "Forgive me, my friend. Henry? I'll just call you that. I must act on the information you've given me." He shook Manning's hand. "Bon appetit." He turned his back and walked away.

Manning looked after his departing host. He and the waiter exchanged glances. The waiter removed Talmud's plate.

The roast duck was excellent.

chapter 4

"Happy Easter"

Late on Easter Sunday morning, the private yacht Isabella, with lettering on her stern identifying her homeport as Palma, Spain, dropped anchor in the roadstead at Monaco. She was not the biggest nor the most expensive ship present, meaning that she was only 65 meters long, cost only seven million, and boasted a crew of only eight.

Isabella lowered her motorboat immediately after anchoring. The small boat made its way through the crowded harbor to stone steps leading from the oily water to a quay wall. Seven men in their thirties stood at the top of the wall, chatting. They could have been the Monaco Junior Chamber of Commerce: clothes casual but tailored, shoes at $300, haircuts by someone who used tiny scissors. The seven looked up as an eighth man joined them. He was taller than the others, who were all rather short. His thin face and large hooked nose gave him a sleek hawk-like look.

Each of the others circled him with embraces and laughter. One of them pointed to Isabella's small boat, which was tying up to the quay wall. "You just made it, Isaac."

Isaac Talmud smiled. "Timing is everything."

The eight men boarded the motorboat with a nod to the coxswain. They were aboard Isabella in eleven minutes.

Paco Rivera, Isabella's owner, met them at the top of the companionway ladder. Paco was a large round-faced, round-bellied man who used his bulk to convey prosperity and good fellowship. He was dressed for the festivities in white sailor's ducks and a Navy blue blazer, with a soft black yachting cap that matched his fierce mustache. Like his crew, he was barefoot. He greeted his guests like old friends. The oldest of friends.

The nine men seated themselves on the fantail in a soft spring breeze, under a bright sun. A smiling black man served each one the drink of his choice without inquiry. Paco nodded to the black, who withdrew.

When they were alone the men smiled to each other. "Feliz Pascua," said one. "Happy Easter."

"Feliz Pascua," the rest answered.

Paco heaved himself to his feet, glass raised. "Salud. Por Don Juan."

His guests stood. "Por El Jefe." Revel's Bolero drifted in to them from an invisible sound system.

"You are all looking well," said Paco in English. "But then, you always look well." He smiled to himself at some private joke. He looked around. "And where is Enrique?"

"Where indeed?" said Talmud.

The tiniest of wrinkles furrowed Paco's smooth forehead. "Is there a problem?"

"Yes, a problem," said Talmud. "I phoned Enrique a

week ago. His. . . housekeeper answered. She knew nothing."

"Enrique has no housekeeper," commented a square man with broad shoulders whose name was Pablo Cisneros.

"Exactamente," said Talmud.

"Can he be. . . hurt? In hospital?" asked Paco.

Talmud shrugged. "I made. . . inquiries. Some time ago he cancelled his Visa and American Express credit cards. No reason given. That same day he withdrew ten thousand from his bank."

The men sat sipping their drinks and listening to the music. Their mood had darkened, as if a rain cloud had crossed the sun. "There's more," said Talmud. "Enrique's social security number was queried by computer. Twice. The access denial block that we have in place did its job. But the query was from a section of the U.S. Internal Revenue Service."

"Madre de Dios." Paco's face lost some of its roundness. He crossed himself.

"There is a further complication, one that has taken precedence," Isaac continued. "An American, is masquerading as Enrique. He has moved into his apartment, has taken his name. . ."

"Dios mio," said Pablo Cisneros.

"Have you dealt with him?" asked Paco.

"I had dinner with him," said Isaac. "He has a story to tell. He claims that Enrique is dead."

"How did it happen?" asked Paco.

"One cannot say," said Isaac. "Enrique was at dinner.

One moment he was alive and well, the next he was gone. The American sat next to him. He took Enrique's identity."

Paco walked among his guests, refilling glasses as they all considered this news. Finally a chubby and completely bald cherub named Esteban spoke. "We should do something."

"The man is. . . resistant to advice," said Isaac. "To threats. To offers of wealth."

"Such a man could be dangerous," Pablo Cisneros said.

"Such a man is already dangerous," Isaac answered.

"Who is this one playing Enrique?" Paco asked.

"I don't know yet," Isaac said. "The waiter at my club in Manhattan is in my employ. He thinks he got a good print off of the man's water glass. We'll soon know."

The nine men sipped their drinks, not looking at each other. Their holiday atmosphere and camaraderie were gone. Each seemed isolated in his own thoughts. Finally a small man named Juan Carlos spoke. "We must act. . . again, as we always have."

"Can you leave him to me?" asked a man sitting by himself. This one was dark, all black from his polished shoes to a fine clipped beard and long ebony hair. Wide-spaced eyes across a broad rounded forehead and snubbed nose gave him the look of a lizard.

Or a snake.

Tomaso was his name. Hermano Tomaso. Brother Thomas. He smiled, teeth flashing white in all that darkness. A smile that didn't travel to his eyes.

"I agree," said Martinez quickly. "We cannot trust this man's motives. We can only trust ourselves."

"Y yo tambien," said Paco. "Me too. Bring in the best. I want the best there is."

"Por su puesto," Tomaso said softly. "Of course."

"Por su puesto," Isaac repeated.

"There was something to do with the Internal Revenue Service," said Esteban Romero.

"They are investigating Enrique," Isaac said. "He was careless with the birth dates he reported to them. Some auditor, a young woman, caught it. She went back to the forties. She has gone to New York City to investigate. It's a mess."

"Enrique is—was—a fool," said Cisneros. "He refused to change identities all these years, or to move his assets into a trust, something he could control invisibly. He changed birth dates instead. I tried to tell him. He was in love with his own name."

"They must not complete this investigation. Silencio," Esteban said. The others nodded.

Tomaso spread his hands in front of him. He alone smiled. "You may leave that to me as well."

The others nodded again, except for Isaac Talmud, who sat looking at the mid-day sun. "Y tu, Isaac," Tomaso spoke with an easy, conversational voice. "?Que quierres decir?"

Isaac's eyes returned to his friends. "Nada."

Paco smiled massively. "My friends, we cannot let this spoil our Easter. We have, after all, dealt with problems such as this for a long time. Come. A wonderful meal awaits us. I have prepared it myself. It will be like old times."

He stood and led the way to lunch.

chapter 5

The Great Man

Andrew Trotter drove his seven-month-old Porsche Boxster into the Hollywood Hills, top down, humming a little tune. He always drove with the top down unless it was actually raining. It never rained in Southern California. Anyway, if it did, the car was leased.

He was driving to the Great Man's estate. Trotter had worked for the Great Man for five years. Before that he had been one of a large crowd of "dealmakers" who populated the Los Angeles Basin. A dealmaker represented one side of whatever deal two or more parties were trying to make. The job required good business sense, a fat-cat network, and the instincts of a pit bull. Trotter had been doing well in his chosen profession until he met William Jennings McKinley. McKinley was a medium-sized player in electronics. He had found a couple of aerospace engineers who had patented an electronic filter and surge suppressor that ran much faster and quieter than the current state of the art. Trotter represented McKinley in a deal to market the device. Halfway through the deal McKinley invited Trotter to lunch. "These guys are bozos," McKinley said during dessert. "We challenge the patent, present one of our own, they're looking at years of court action. We make them an offer, buy the patent, we're rich."

So that's what they did. The deal was so sweet and sure, that Trotter violated the First Rule of the Dealmaker and put in his own money. He threw in all his liquid assets and took a second on his house. That's when they found out that the Great Man was a silent partner of the two bozos. They found it out when lawyers and government agents came after them the way tornadoes search out trailer parks. When the smoke cleared William Jennings McKinley was in county accommodations for fraud and tax evasion, trying to raise $200,000 bail, and Trotter was looking at the shambles of his once-solid finances.

The Great Man called. He liked the way Trotter operated. No hard feelings. Since then Trotter had knocked down mid-six figures annually and charged to an indulgent expense account, while he looked for profitable ways for the Great Man to venture his capital.

Trotter was driving to the Great Man's estate to tell him about a new deal. He was humming his tune, because it was just what the Great Man was looking for. He turned right on Mulholland Drive and drove 200 yards to a hidden turnoff. He sat idling in front of a high black iron gate, while a TV camera digested his license plate. The gate slid smoothly open. He drove another quarter mile up a winding road to the main house.

The Great Man lived alone in a stone and glass building cantilevered over a view of West LA. Trotter let himself in the front door, which was unlocked. He stood patiently smoking, looking out of full-wall windows at Beverly Hills and the Pacific glinting in the distance, wondering how long it would take him to score a similar view. Soft music oozed from hidden speakers. After twenty minutes a slim Hispanic in white duck trousers and black silk shirt open at the neck led him downstairs to a poolside lawn.

The Great Man was in the pool on a cell phone. Trotter waited with some more patience just out of earshot. The Great Man gestured with his free hand as he talked. Someone somewhere in the world was catching hell. The Great Man was without the modifying presence of female companionship, since he was in the middle of another divorce. Trotter was in the middle of it with him. Trotter had broken the soon-to-be-ex-wife's code just three days before. She was okay with the financial settlement, which was what the pre-nuptial specified, no more, no less. She simply wanted the Great Man to eat some crow. That was easy. Trotter had laid out a deal where the Great Man would grovel in the LA Times and on Larry King Live, and the ex would retire in triumph to the house in Palm Desert. So the lawyers had it now, and they would end it as soon as they squeezed out their fees. Meanwhile, no girls around. That might look bad in People Magazine.

The Great Man finished his call. He waved Trotter over. "Andy, you look wonderful, how are you, have a drink." Trotter shook his head. His employer never had time for the social stuff no matter what he said.

The Great Man sipped from a poolside glass, some green liquid. He was into squeezed wheat grass and chopped spinach. "So what's up?"

"There was a very hush-hush meeting at IRS headquarters in DC last week. Three people. Deputy Director, the Audit Review Chief, an investigator named Audrey Cobb."

"Is it me?" The Great Man didn't seem concerned.

"Not you. Guy named Toledo, from New York. This Cobb lady had tossed his returns from last year and then going back here and there all the way to the '40s."

"Shouldn't cheat Uncle. Unpatriotic." The Great Man smiled indulgently. He had paid over three million in federal taxes the year before.

"No, the taxes were legit. Guy's personal data bounced. His birth dates were screwy."

"Birth dates? Deputy Director wants to be briefed on birth dates?"

"Guy's birth dates kept getting earlier, the further back they looked. Go all the way back, he's way over a hundred, now."

"Is there a headline here somewhere, Andy?" The Great Man's eyes wandered back to the cell phone. Wondering who to call. Trotter was losing him. He picked up the beat. "Sir, I think this guy Toledo really is over a hundred. Way over."

"So?"

"So he reported a half million income last year. He's still a player. Still walking, talking. He's a healthy guy."

The Great Man was interested now. "So you think. . . what? He's got something to hide? Something interesting? How old?"

"Sir, I think he's way over a hundred. Maybe almost two hundred."

The Great Man stared at Trotter, turning things over. "No one's two hundred."

"The IRS looked at his returns way back, the signature. Two of their experts say it's the same."

"They can screw up."

"I got copies," said Trotter. "I put three handwriting guys on it. Guys I know, pros. They say the same. The signature from fifty-two years ago is the same as last year's."

"So he's. . . maybe a hundred. Where's two hundred coming from?"

"There's a document in the archives of New York City. Police Report from 1880, a mugging. Victim was Henry Toledo. Same signature, boss. There's a bloodstain on the form. I got the form. . . borrowed it. I got someone into Toledo's apartment, got some hair from a brush."

Trotter laid an envelope on the tile next to the Great Man. "This is a DNA analysis. DNA's the same. Same guy. We snapped his photo coming out of his apartment. It's in the envelope. He's forty. . . fifty. The police report from 1880 is for a guy fifty. Makes Toledo, today, one hundred seventy years old. At least."

"So he's got a way to stay young." Trotter had the Great Man's full attention. The Great Man looked at the liver spots on the back of his hand. Trotter knew what he was thinking. He was thinking what Trotter wanted him to think, that he was pushing 70. He worried about it, Trotter knew. He had standing instructions to pull the string on any deal that held the promise of life extension. Trotter thought of a bumper sticker he had spotted on Santa Monica Boulevard that morning.

"Keep going," said the Great Man. "Where he is, where he eats, his friends, family, business, everything."

"How much?" asked Trotter.

"As much as it takes."

"Yes, sir," Andrew Trotter said, and walked back into the house. This would be fun. And who knows where it would lead? He was 47 himself.

chapter 6

"I Will Tell You What To Do, And You Will Do It."

Audrey Cobb left her hotel room two days later on the way to the New York City IRS branch office. She was tired. She had spent the weekend and most of the last night at that office searching Henry Toledo's tax records. She waited for the down elevator with her mind stuffed full of Toledo. She knew a lot more about him, and most of it didn't make sense. The guy apparently never worked a day in his life. His income was all from investments and trusts. This was true for as far back as she could go on her computer. Audrey needed more info. She'd get Winston to FedEx copies of Toledo's pre-computer, hard copy tax records to New York. How to get that computer block of his Social Security Number removed? The elevator door opened. A man stood facing her. "Ms. Cobb?"

Audrey was startled. "Yes?"

"What a coincidence! I was on my way to tap on your door. My name is Greenway. James Greenway. I have information concerning Henry Toledo that will interest you. Can we talk?"

Audrey felt disoriented. Who was this guy, suddenly in her face, telling her about an ongoing, privileged investigation? "Talk?"

"I assure you, you need to know what I have to tell you. Shall we go to your room?"

Audrey hesitated—the man noticed. "Of course. Who would want a strange man in her hotel room? May I suggest a cup of coffee? The hotel cafeteria? Better yet, the lounge in the lobby."

They rode the elevator down. The man was Audrey's age, small, with a broad, friendly face. His pug nose and short black beard reminded her of Tubby, the Pekinese Mama had found for her when she was six. When Daddy was still with them. The memory was a warm one. Still, how did this stranger know her room number? Hotels are careful about giving them out.

The bearded man led her into a seat at a small marble table in the lobby. Audrey was still on edge. "Mr. . ."

"Greenway."

". . . Greenway. I have a full schedule today. I'm already late."

"I can make this short." A waitress showed up. Greenway looked at Audrey, then smiled at the young lady. "A pot of coffee, please? Then we really will need some privacy." His teeth couldn't be that white naturally. Caps, maybe.

When the waitress left Greenway turned back to Audrey. "You have an investigation under way on Mr. Toledo. He mentioned it to me. He's very concerned. Ms. Cobb, I've known Henry Toledo for a good many years. I can assure you, he's done nothing illegal. Not even unethical. I've come to try to persuade you to drop all this."

Audrey felt disoriented again. A stranger comes out of nowhere, out of an elevator, to tell her how to run her investigations? Things were moving too fast. "Mr. Greenway, who are you, and who do you think you are, influencing an IRS audit, a Federal matter. . ."

"I guess you can call me a friend of the court." That smile again. "Really, I'm just trying to be helpful."

"You can help your friend by going back and telling him to stop stonewalling and answer some simple questions." Audrey stood. "I'm already late." She was trembling.

Greenway stood too, smoothing her back into her seat. "I've upset you. I'm so sorry. How can I convince you to cooperate, Ms. Cobb?" Greenway brightened. "I know! I can introduce you to a really horrible man." He pulled a sheet of paper from his inside jacket pocket and unfolded it. "This is an Interpol bulletin on an assassin. His name is Andres Chamineaux. French father, Algerian mother. He kills for hire. Twenty-three suspected victims. Some shot in the back of the head, some in the kneecap, some missing all of their fingers. Not a very nice man, do you agree? No photo, do you see? He has never been photographed, never fingerprinted. Remember the name, eh? Andres Chamineaux." Greenway opened his cell phone and pressed a number. "Put her on," he said into the phone. After a moment he said, "Hello? Just a moment." He handed the phone to Audrey. "It's for you."

"Hello? Oh. . . Mamma?" Audrey looked at Greenway. "What's wrong?"

"Audrey, my dear," her mother chuckled. "I love you,

but why must you go through life assuming that something is always wrong? I'm perfectly fine. More than fine. I have a new caregiver, Darling. He started today. Dolores can't come any more. Illness or something, I don't know. Anyway, I couldn't be more delighted. This man is absolutely wonderful! Charming."

"Mama. . . that's wonderful." Audrey glanced at Greenway, puzzled.

"Ask his name," said Greenway. "Go ahead."

"Mother. . . what's his name?" asked Audrey, knowing the answer.

"Andy," said her mother. "Andy something. I don't know." She giggled. "Something French. . . I don't know. He's French."

"Andres? Mamma, is it Andres Chamineaux?"

"My Dear, you're behind this, aren't you? However did you find such a charming man?"

Audrey laid the phone down in front of her. She couldn't speak. Greenway picked it up and carefully closed the mouthpiece. "Your mother is fine," he said. "Safer than ever, in fact. No harm will come to her with Andres around. Now, are we clear? I will tell you what to do, and you will do it."

Manning was looking at a three-color brochure on Caribbean cruises, wondering when he could safely take one, when the phone rang. It was Audrey Cobb. "You son of a bitch!"

"Pardon? Ms. Cobb?"

"What have you done with my mother? You bastard!

Oh, you're toast, Toledo. I'm gonna fry your butt like a pork chop! How can you threaten me?"

Manning held the phone at arm's length and took a long breath. What now? Audrey Cobb was still yelling out of the receiver. He waited for a moment of silence. "Ms. Cobb, I have no idea what you're talking about."

"Like hell you don't! Your friend Greenway has been to see me, you. . . you. . . vampire! Kidnapping is a felony, Toledo. You're going to jail!"

"Kid. . . Ms. Cobb. . ."

"Shut up! I'll be up there in five minutes!" The line went dead.

Manning made some coffee and washed and shaved while it perked, thinking: how much time do I have before this house of cards collapses completely? He cut himself with his razor. I am going 35 in an 80-mile zone.

Audrey took 20 minutes to arrive. She was red-faced and red-nosed, out of breath. Manning smiled. He couldn't help himself. "Did you take the stairs?"

"Shut up!" Her eyes were bugging.

It wasn't true, Manning thought. Women aren't more beautiful when they're angry. "Sit down, please." He eased her into a Chinese silk brocade sofa. "Okay, now. From the top."

Audrey hissed like a snake, "You've got my mother, you bastards."

"I haven't got your mother, Audrey. Please trust me."

"Trust you. . ." Manning watched, astonished, as Audrey crumpled, sobbing, into a ball. "I don't trust you, but I don't have anyone else to turn to. I can't go to the police.

He'll kill my mother."

Manning found a box of facial tissues. He mopped up the tears and let her cry. Finally, between sobs, she told him about Greenway. When she finished, she looked up, red-eyed. "You're behind this, Toledo. You're hiding something, something evil, or you wouldn't try this."

"Sounds like something a friend of mine might have arranged," said Manning gingerly.

"'Something a friend might have arranged,'" Audrey repeated in a singsong voice. "Did you tell your friend about me?"

Manning was silent.

"You did didn't you, you weasel! You knowingly put my mother's life in danger to blackmail me. You. . . you're going to federal prison, Mr. Toledo, for a long, long time."

Manning took her hand. She jerked it away. "Ms. Cobb, believe me. I told someone about you, yes. Nothing illegal about discussing a tax audit. I had no idea what he would do with the information. What did this Greenway guy tell you to do?"

That stood her on her feet again, voice rising. "He told me, drop the audit. Tell my boss it was just a father and son and grandson trying to avoid inheritance taxes. Told me you would provide death records, would pay back taxes, pay penalties. Told me to keep it low key, turn away any inquiries, make it go away. If I do that, I get Mama back. If I don't. . ." Tears ran once more down Audrey's cheeks. "I don't, he said, 'You wouldn't want what will happen to your mother to happen to anyone.'" She sat back down with her hands over her face.

"Ms. Cobb, please."

Audrey looked up with swimming eyes. "How can you? How could anyone?"

"It'll be all right," Manning lied. "I can fix this. I'll do it now." He poured some coffee. "I need to make a call. Give me a couple minutes." Audrey looked at her coffee cup but reached for the Kleenex box instead, watching Manning pick up his cell phone.

"What kind of a man are you, Mr. Toledo?"

Manning walked onto his terrace and closed the glass door without answering. What kind was he, anyway? He punched the phone.

"Talmud."

"This is Toledo, Talmud, or is it Greenway?"

"Ms. Cobb has spoken to you."

"You bet she has!"

"Henry, there is no reason for you to be involved. She was told not to say anything to. . ."

"I am involved, dammit!"

"I can fix this. I'll call you. Work with me. Come on."

"You kidnapped an old woman and scared the sap out of a young woman based on information that I gave you. . ."

"Henry, believe me, Ms. Cobb's mother is in no danger."

"Believe you? Believe you? Believe which part? That you can help me? That 'dangerous men' control my life? That you're a hundred-fifty years old?" Manning slammed the phone's flip-top shut, breaking the connection. He stood in the morning sunlight, thinking. Finally he looked at his wrist. Five minutes gone. He would have to tell Audrey something. How much?

Audrey had used up the tissues and her tears. She turned when he came back in, wide-eyed. "It's okay," he said, smiling, nodding, lying some more.

"Is Mama safe?"

Manning nodded again, lying again. "She's safe. I've talked to my friend. He'll talk to Greenway. Nothing will happen to her."

"Thank God." Audrey closed her eyes. "When can I get her?"

Here comes the tough part. "Not yet. She needs to stay where she is."

"Stay where she is?" Audrey swung her legs to the floor, blue eyes wide. "She's with a serial killer!"

Manning took her hand again. This time she let him. "Listen, Audrey, you and I are in grave danger. We have to move carefully. That's all I can say for now." Manning thinking, you bet that's all I can say. I'm only a half page ahead of her. And who knows, we might actually be in grave danger.

Audrey wasn't buying. She pulled her hand away and made a fist with it, bouncing it against her other hand. "Mr. Toledo, I'm a federal employee. Someone is threatening me. He's holding my mother." She leaned into an end table and picked up a phone. "There's an answer for all of this. It's nine-one-one."

Uh, oh. "Audrey, think this through. What's first priority?"

Audrey's eyes shifted to the window. "Mama."

"Right. We can't do anything to put her in danger. Right now she's okay. We're okay. Give me some time. I'll find your mother." J. Edgar Hoover speaking.

Audrey put the phone down. "Twenty-four hours."

Manning exhaled. Time enough to extend that later. "Go to your hotel. Get some rest. I'll call you."

Audrey stood up. "Twenty-four hours. That's all. Give me something."

Manning saw her out. He went to his terrace and watched her walk down Fifth Avenue. She looked small and vulnerable. Also wonderful. What did he do to put her mother in danger? Was he, or was the IRS probe, driving things no matter what he did? But he had told Talmud about the probe in the first place. Manning shook his head. His ninth grade Science teacher, Miss Peacock, had had a sign on her classroom wall, "Wisdom is knowing what to do next." He had no idea what to do next.

chapter 7

Jimmy Foster

Manning spent the next day searching through all of Toledo's records, looking for clues. He had nothing to go on except the unbelievable stuff from Audrey Cobb and Talmud about Toledo's old age. At three in the afternoon he arched an aching back and rubbed his eyes. Toledo was a singularly private character. His files covered his finances in detail but the man seemed to have no personal life: no letters from friends or family, no photos, no diary.

Manning found a receipt for a safety deposit box from Citibank's Manhattan branch. He opened the middle desk drawer and pulled out the key he had found earlier. Time to open the box. He put the safety deposit key in his pocket and took the elevator.

He paused in front of his building to get his bearings. Citibank was only a few blocks away. He would walk. The afternoon was perfect for it: cool, dry, and full of pedestrians taking the fresh spring air. Violin music came from somewhere. A dog was barking. Four very small girls played jump rope on the sidewalk, two turning, two jumping. They sang a jingle to the slap of the rope:

Surname, dear sir
Have I none,
Use my first name
I've got one.

Some leadfoot was goosing a car engine up the street. Manning decided to cut through Central Park. He stepped into Fifth Avenue between two parked cars, jay-walking. The car engine's noise wound up like a jet turbine. He looked left, looking at taillights. He was new to Fifth Avenue, he kept forgetting—it was one-way headed downtown. He looked right. A black TransAm a half block away leapt toward him with smoking tires. Manning was flat-footed in its path.

Deer.

Headlights.

Right then, Jimmy Foster saved his life.

Manning, his brother, Adam, and Jimmy Foster had lived on the same block in New Haven. Manning and Jimmy sat next to each other in third grade. They did best-friend things together: rode skateboards, traded baseball cards, read each other's comic books. One Tuesday in springtime, just about this time of year, maybe May, maybe just before summer vacation, they had run home from school playing tag. Jimmy was a little faster and maybe a little smarter, so Manning was "it." Jimmy danced just out of reach, laughing, in control of the game. Manning was frustrated and getting mad. Jimmy skipped backwards into the street between two parked cars with his eyes on Manning. He looked to his right. Manning could hear the screaming of braking tires.

Manning ran toward his best friend. He ran for what seemed like a long time. Jimmy stood in the street all of that time, that long, long time, frozen, looking right, mouth open, not smiling now. Then a car blurred past the parked cars and Jimmy was gone.

"It's not your fault," Manning's mom told him. Jimmy's mother said the same thing: "It's not your fault." Manning nodded and went to Jimmy's funeral, and maybe it wasn't his fault, but he couldn't sleep at night except maybe for an hour, and then Jimmy was there looking to his right for a long, long time while Manning ran on and on, and finally Manning was sitting up in bed in the darkness, shaking.

They tried the usual stuff. Manning's mom held him close until the shakes stopped. Manning drank warm milk at bedtime and then tranquilizers and then a kindly old therapist once a week. After a long time, Manning cured himself by changing the dream. He made Jimmy look right, crouch down, take two running steps, and leap over a parked car just as the squealing tires sped by. Then he made Jimmy sit up on the grass on the safe side of the parked car and blow air out of puffed cheeks and smile and wink. Then the dream ended, and Manning slept until his mother woke him for school.

So when Manning looked at the TransAm bearing down and heard the whining engine he crouched, turned, took two running steps and vaulted over the hood of a parked Honda Accord just like he made Jimmy do in his dream. The TransAm, really coming now, just missed his heels as he kicked his feet up. It careened off the parked Honda with a scream of tearing metal. Then the car was gone around the corner at the end of the block, and the whining engine and squealing tires were gone with it. Manning lay face down feeling the sidewalk cool and fuzzy against his cheek, feeling a delicious silence after the TransAm noise, feeling his heart thudding in his throat, feeling alive.

His doorman helped him to his feet. Manning moved his left shoulder in a circle. He had landed on it, and it felt broken. "Did you get a license number?" asked the doorman. Manning looked at him blankly. He was amazed to be alive. The doorman was holding him upright with his hands under Manning's armpits. "Some kids," said the doorman, angry now. "Spics. Two a' them. Lookin' back at ya. Crazy kids."

The doorman looked at Manning with a new respect. "Hey, were you a gymnast?" he asked. "Vault?"

"What?"

"The way you cleared that car, man."

"A friend taught me," Manning said. He thanked the doorman and walked in the park until he could walk normally and his shoulder felt better. He felt better, too, exhilarated at being alive. He took a taxi downtown to Katz deli and ordered two pastrami sandwiches in a row. The rich hot meat had never tasted so good.

chapter 8

"Drink Your Milk Now, Dear. Promise?"

Manning awoke before dawn the next morning with a bruise covering his whole left shoulder and a stiff back. Last night's exhilaration had dried up, and the condo seemed lonely and sinister in the dark. Was yesterday an accident? He was an accountant, in over his head. He made some coffee and sat watching the sunrise define the tall buildings around Central Park, while he calmed himself. Maybe the hit-and-run attempt wasn't premeditated. A car can't sit on Fifth Avenue forever waiting for Henry Toledo to leave his condo and cross the street. Can it?

He poured himself another cup, brooding over Audrey Cobb. How in the hell could he find her mother? Sooner or later she would blow the whistle on him. He gingerly rubbed his shoulder and went to the bathroom for some aspirin.

Manning's intercom buzzed just as he took the pills. He pressed the talk button at the front door. It was Cozmo, the black doorman. He was the Tuesday and Thursday guy. "Your aunt is here to see you, Mr. Toledo."

Manning stood by the intercom trying to think of something to say.

"Mr. Toledo?"

Manning was silent. He didn't have an aunt, did he? NOK: None. "Send her up," he blurted before he could stop himself. For five minutes he stood by his front door waiting, palms sweaty. The doorbell sounded a three-tone tune. The old woman on the other side of the peephole could have stepped straight from the Saturday Evening Post. Kewpie cheeks and mouth, gray pinstripe hair, thick glasses that made her look like Bill Gates, and a shapeless dress made of something resembling mattress ticking. Whistler's mother up from her rocker. She was clearly someone's aunt. Manning opened the door.

The old lady swayed across Manning's living room marble on low heels. She opened her mouth, and elevator music came out in an unbroken stream. "Nephew! Lovely place who is your decorator and a park view of course how magnificent how can you keep those patio doors open in this heat but of course it's cooler up here isn't it Chinese how refreshing to see Oriental things." She paused for oxygen, then rattled on. "You must give me your decorator's name is that Canton Roseware in the dining room let's sit here!" She settled onto the brocade sofa like a parachute, skirt spread over crossed ankles, smiling at Manning. "Now you talk my Darling give your Aunt Dot a kiss." Her gravelly voice didn't match her matronly figure.

"You're not my aunt," said Manning.

"Well my dear of course not, but you're not Henry Toledo either." Aunt Dot crinkled her mouth up and started a cackle that ended with a nicotine cough. "We'll want to chat about that but first let's observe the customs of Western Civilization you may offer me some tea hot tea which would be absolutely perfect shall we both have some let's do."

Leonard the Cat jumped into her lap and immediately went into a purr. "Look," Manning said uneasily, "you can't just come in here. . ."

"We're getting off to a frightfully bad start, Dear," said the woman. Her speech slowed. "Let's start over, shall we?" She curled on the sofa like a larger version of the cat in her lap. "You begin. Offer me a cup of tea."

"Look, miss. . . lady. . . I don't know you, I don't have time for you. . ."

"Henry Toledo has lots of time, dear. More time than you can imagine. Hot tea, that would be nice."

Manning strode into the kitchen muttering to himself. The old bat was getting the upper hand. He pawed through the pantry until he found a carton of herbal tea bags. He heated a cup of water in the microwave and looked over at his coffeepot. Empty. Manning poured himself a glass of milk. Damned if he was going to balance a teacup on his knee. He bounced the hot water and teabags in front of the old bat.

Aunt Dot took her time, lifting and inspecting each bag. Manning walked to a window to look out. He was climbing out of his skin. Finally the woman found the perfect blend and dunked it. She sipped and sighed. "How wonderful a green tea so kind of you won't you join me so nice on a hot day isn't it warmer than usual in the city for spring?" She reached way down into a ten-gallon handbag and produced a brand new pack of Camels. That's where the Bogart voice comes from, thought Manning. The old lady flared an old-fashioned wooden match with a practiced flick of her thumbnail and lit up. "Ash tray, please?"

"Use your saucer, Auntie." Manning had no idea where Toledo kept his ashtrays. He had given up smoking five years before. Now he hated the smell. Ellen had insisted on smoking in the house. "Please tell me what you want with me and leave," he said. "I've got a very busy schedule today. . ."

The old woman held up two fingers like a bishop bestowing a blessing. "We all have timelines, Nephew. I have my own. Just tell me what happened to Henry, and I'll be on my way."

"I don't know who you are. You haven't told me. I've told you, I'm Henry Toledo."

"Henry Toledo speaks Spanish like a wetback," said Manning's aunt. She used a paper napkin to dab the corners of her mouth. "Habla Espanol?"

"Un poco," Manning replied. Aunt Dot gave him a mean look and let loose a torrent of Spanish like a Gattling gun. Manning was silent.

"Thought so," said his aunt. She blew smoke at Manning. "Who are you?"

"You know my name, Auntie," Manning said.

"You lie like a Cossack," the old lady said. "Look, we have no interest in you. You stand here in Henry's condo, in his Gucci shoes. You're in this for his money, right? Certainly. You can have it, Dearie. You can walk away this afternoon, back into whatever hole you crawled out of, with more money than you dreamed. I can become your fairy godmother. First you shall answer some questions for me. Who are you, Dear, and what happened to Henry?"

"I've had enough," said Manning, his voice shaking. "You come uninvited, unannounced, to make accusations that you can't prove, asking for information that makes no sense. Did Talmud send you? I think he did. This sounds like his line. Doesn't matter. Time you left."

Aunt Dot let out a cackle. Her eyes were bright. "Fine. You tell me what I want to know, I'm out of your life. You can continue to be Henry, or anyone else you want to become, we don't care."

Manning walked to his front door intercom. "Cozmo? Mr. Toledo. My aunt is ready to leave now. Will you send Security up to escort her out?"

He turned back to the living room. His "aunt" fingered another cigarette from the pack, looked at the Camel still burning in her saucer, and put the second one back. "You're no help at all," she said to herself.

"That's right," Manning said. He poured his milk into the saucer, putting the cigarette out. "I'm no help. I have no intention of being a 'help.' Here you are, uninvited, stinking up my apartment. . ."

"Toledo's apartment," corrected the woman.

". . . My apartment, with your nicotine habit and your storm trooper attitude. . . I don't even know who you are."

They sat eyeing each other in silence for a few more minutes. The doorbell chimed again. Security stood there in the form of a young man in suit and tie with a coiling phone wire that disappeared into his right ear. Manning wondered what he was plugged in to.

"Mr. Toledo?" Security was puzzled. He wasn't usually called upon for escort duty.

"All right, I'm going," said the old woman. She heaved herself out of her seat with a delicate grunt, spilling Leonard the cat. "You be very careful, Nephew," she said with an index finger in the air. "This is a dangerous town, especially for newcomers."

"You be careful too, Auntie. It's a federal offense to make vague threats to blood relatives." Manning offered his cheek to be kissed.

Auntie took his hand instead. "We'll talk again," she whispered.

"Don't bet large sums of money on it," said Manning. He handed her to Security, who still seemed puzzled.

"Drink your milk, now, dear," said the old lady as she exited. "Promise?"

Manning closed the door on them. He walked back into the living room, wondering what had just happened. He eyed the empty teacup. Was there a way to trace her fingerprints? He shook his head. Who ya gonna call, CIA? And suppose they dust up your prints, Manning Crenshaw? He carried the two cups to his kitchen. Life as Henry Toledo was becoming more complicated each day. He looked toward the coffee table. Leonard the cat sat on his haunches, lapping up milk from the saucer.

"That's full of cigarette ashes, idiot," said Manning. "You'll get lung cancer." He tossed the cat onto the carpet, walked to his terrace, and looked down. The old woman was getting into a white Ford Bronco. O. J. is probably driving, Manning thought.

He sat at Toledo's desk; going through more files, but after five minutes gave it up. That screwy old lady had rattled him. He got up and took the fire stairs all the way down to street level, he was so mad. He handed Cozmo two twenties. "Give one of these to Security for me, will you? He did me a favor. Do me a favor, too, will you? Don't let that old bag into the building again."

"Your aunt?"

"My ex-aunt. I'm excommunicating her." Manning walked three blocks to his favorite deli and had a Reuben.

When he got back to his apartment Leonard was lying on his back with all four paws up and a thick black tongue protruding from a grotesque grinning mouth. Manning picked him up. He was already stiff. Manning looked immediately at the milk in the ashtray. What was it Aunt Dot had said? "Drink your milk, now, dear. Promise?" He had had his back to her while he was talking to Security on the intercom. Manning wrapped Leonard in a black garbage bag and sailed him down the hallway's garbage chute. Then he poured the remains of the milk into a fruit jar and left the apartment. He took the elevator down this time. He knocked on Security's office door in the basement.

"Mr. Toledo. Listen, thanks for the twenty. You didn't have to. . ."

"It's okay. Thanks for getting rid of that woman. What's your name?"

Security pointed to a nametag on his chest. "Wilson. Donald Wilson. Donnie."

"I need a chemistry lab, Donnie. Someone who can analyze things. Know of one?"

Donnie opened a small address book. "I know a guy, runs a lab. . ."

Manning had a better idea. He set the fruit jar on Wilson's desk and opened his wallet. "I want you to do me a big favor, Donnie. I want you to take this sample to your friend. I think, I don't know but I think, that there's something in here that. . . that's deadly. Poison. . . something that kills people."

"Kills people?"

"Something like that. Get him to analyze this stuff. It's got cigarette ash in there too. Forget that. Cigarettes kill people, too, of course, but I'm looking for something more sudden. When he's got the results, let me know. Give me a call, call my apartment. Leave a message. . . no, don't leave a phone message, I guess. If I'm not in, just leave a note." Manning gave Wilson three one-hundred-dollar bills. "Here's a down payment. I'll give you two hundred more when the results are in. You figure out how much to give your friend. Okay?"

Wilson slipped the money into his wallet. "Okay. Sir."

"This is between us, Donnie?"

"Yessir."

Manning went up to his condo and got out Toledo's list of securities. Two murder attempts in two days. Time to collect some money, as much as possible, as fast as possible, and scoop it up. Time to catch that train.

Donnie Wilson was at the front door the next morning to give Manning a three-page report from his friend.

"Mr. Toledo, no, please." He put his palm up when Manning opened his wallet. "You were very generous before." Manning tried to press some twenties on him but he danced backwards towards the door in a little jig. "I read this thing, Mr. Toledo. This is some mean stuff. I don't want to get involved." He disappeared.

Manning sat down at his desk to read the report. It was typewritten on letterhead paper:

Hudson Biochemical Analysis
And Compounding, Inc.

The letterhead also listed an address in Brooklyn. A laundry list of New York state, city, and borough licenses made Hudson Biochemical look very legitimate.

The report told Manning what he needed to know and little else. Aunt Dot's milk had been laced with Palytoxin, a very lethal and rare poison derived from seaweed. The pages also listed trace amounts of two insecticides and three steroids from the milk that would probably kill over a longer period of time. But Leonard the Cat had apparently been done in by the Palytoxin, which, the report helpfully noted, "depolarizes all excitable tissues thus far studied."

The report was signed by "A. Hedberg." Manning dialed the phone number listed in the letterhead and asked the girl who answered for Mr. Hedberg. "Tell him it's a friend of Don Wilson."

"Axle," a voice said, sounding like the man behind it was big and beefy.

"Mr. Hedberg, you don't know me. . ."

"This the guy wanted that milk analyzed?"

"Yes. Thanks very. . ."

"What's your name, mister?"

"I'd rather not give that out. . ."

"You bet you wouldn't pal. You got someone tryinah nail ya. I wrote that report as a favor to Donnie. What I shudda done was make it a police report. I tol' Donnie, get away from that guy. Stay outa blast range."

"I've already notified the police," Manning said, lying some more. "They'll be here soon, meanwhile I'm trying to find out as much as I can about Palytoxin. . ."

"You tell the cops to phone me, I'll give 'em a standard toxicology form. Standard rates."

"I was kind of hoping you'd give me some information over the phone. I'm willing to pay much more than the standard rates. Donnie can bring it over. Cash. You wouldn't have to. . ."

"How much?"

"Say. . . a thousand?"

Greed carried the day. "Waddaya wanna know?"

"Well. . ." Manning groped for a beginning. "You wrote that it came from seaweed. What kind?"

"Palythoa genus. It's where Palytoxin gets its name. Grows like crazy in the Caribbean. Pacific, too. Central Pacific. Hawaii. Pacific islanders used it on their spears, hunting, fighting each other."

"So it's old?"

"Old, sure. Been used a long time. Hundreds a years. New to toxicologists, though. Wasn't isolated until the late sixties. We hadn't mapped its structure until the seventies. It's a very complex molecule. . . the most complex outside of some carbohydrates, some proteins."

"How does it. . ?"

"Snuff you?" The voice on the phone chuckled. "It depolarizes almost all muscles in the body."

"Depolarizes?"

"Look, maybe you can understand this way. Palytoxin neutralizes the muscles so that they don't respond to electrical stimuli any more. Eyelids? Don't blink. No big deal. Heart? Forgets to beat. Big deal. Does other stuff too. Screws up the nervous system, ruptures red blood cells. Enough of it, you're in a deep hurt locker."

"Was there enough in that milk sample?" asked Manning, thinking of Leonard.

Axle chuckled again. "Enough to kill Tyrannosaurus Rex." The voice became serious. "Listen, Mr. Whoever-you-are, you ain't no dinosaur, except you could become very extinct."

Manning was writing furiously in a spiral notepad. "One thing more, sir. Is it easily detectable?"

"You mean as a cause of death? Most forensics would miss it. Me, Donnie tol' me to look for poison, even then I had a tough time." Axle sounded proud of himself.

"Thanks. You've been a big help."

"Yeah, well, let me help you one more time, Mr. 'I'd rather not give my name.' Don't forget the cops on this. These guys are not playing 'spin the bottle' here."

chapter 9

Henry Toledo's Last Will And Testament.

Adam Crenshaw answered his phone in Arlington, Virginia, on the second ring. "It's me," said Manning.

There was a long silence. "You're dead."

Manning smiled. "'Those rumors are greatly exaggerated.'" He was taking a chance. He had thought about some kind of oblique approach with a phony name and disguised voice and rendezvous but finally decided the hell with it. Adam would keep his mouth shut.

"What's going on? We had a service at the church, everything. What are you doing to your family?"

"Got to talk to you, Adam. It's important." Manning set up a meeting at a motel near Dulles Airport in Virginia. Adam lived nearby. "Can you keep quiet about this until then?"

"Of course. Better be good."

Adam was Manning's younger brother. Three years younger and inside-out different. He had kept the dream they shared as teenagers. Navy SEAL for four years, college on the GI Bill, then into Central Intelligence. Then out of the Agency three years ago—Adam didn't say why, and the CIA wasn't talking. Now, Adam taught Karate and

Tai Chi to plump bureaucrats as a personal trainer in the DC area. He was perfect for what Manning needed. He was also family. That was good, and it was bad.

They met in Unit Six at a Best Western on Route 95. Adam looked at his bother without shaking hands. "What the hell's going on? I went to your funeral."

"Where?"

"Hartford. Where do you think?"

"Well, maybe Miami. Ellen never liked to fly."

"That's a bit dark, Manning. She was grieving. So was Mom. Start talking. What's this all about?"

Manning told him. It took an hour. Adam had lots of questions. Manning didn't have all the answers. When Manning was through talking Adam sat on the queen-sized bed staring at him.

"I know it's a little off the wall," Manning said.

"Off the wall? You're walking around in another guy's skin. You're rich. You're a hundred. Some Jew is also a hundred. They're after you. Who is? A beautiful agent from the IRS. Aunt Dorothy. A TransAm. What's off the wall about that? An average month for an accountant."

"I'm not an accountant. I'm a multi-millionaire."

"You're a crook," said Adam. "You're stealing some stiff's estate. What are you doing?"

Manning got up from the only chair in the room and walked around. "I'll tell you what I'm not doing. I'm not spending the rest of my life as a bush league accountant with a busted marriage whose big moment each week is Monday Night Football. My life was over. A new life showed up, I took it. Charge the wall, remember?"

"Don't give me 'charge the wall,' surfer boy." Adam watched his brother pace the room while he pulled at his nose. "Okay, let's say I swallow all this, which I'm not," he said. "Why am I here?"

"I need protection. You can do that. I trust you."

"A bodyguard?" Adam was already shaking his head. "Thanks anyway, I've already got a life. Get one yourself, your own, not someone else's. Look, you told me a minute ago you can always walk away from this mess with this guy Toledo's loose change. Do it. Disappear."

Now Manning was nodding his head. "Just what I'm gonna do, except it takes a couple weeks. The best I can scrape up now is a couple hundred thousand. Two weeks, I can move two million plus into an account in Manhattan. And, I got Audrey Cobb into this. Her mother. I got to get 'em someplace safe." He sat back down. "Two weeks, we can put 'em someplace. Two weeks, I've got two million. That's a half million for you, baby brother."

"Are you alive in two weeks?"

"That's where you earn your money."

Adam stretched out on the bed with his hands behind his head. "This stinks, Manning. We're gonna play Dungeons and Dragons with some guys out there in the dark, we don't even know their names. Are they trying to kill you or Henry Toledo or Audrey Cobb or all three? Do I look like Schwarzenegger? You feel like Bruce Willis? You were always the cool one. Mr. Maturity. Mr. Nine-to-Five. You don't walk the wild side, big brother. Neither do I, any more."

"Adam, there's no risk. I don't go back to New York,

not the city, not the state. I can work the money from here using a phone, fax, and the Internet. I've got four brand new, untraceable, cell phones, just picked 'em up. Leased under some other name. Two for you, two for me.

"And I sit around and keep you alive?"

"Nope. I don't need protection until we go for the money." Manning handed his brother some computer printouts. "Here's everything I got on Audrey Cobb and her mom. You were a spy. Get a line on Mama. Figure out how to get her out of where ever she is. Don't leave any fingerprints. I promised Audrey her mom would be safe. She's safe as long as no one knows we're after her."

Adam looked through the papers. "You can promise whatever you want. I'm no gumshoe. I was S&T with the Agency. . . Science and Technology. Overhead stuff. . . satellites and photo imagery."

"You started out on the dark side, though. HumInt —Human Intelligence. Agents. You told me."

"I told you too much. Anyway, we just ran the agents. Held their hand and slipped them money. I didn't slither through second story windows between laser beams."

"Come on Adam. You can do it. You know you can. I don't have anyone else."

Adam covered his eyes with his hands with his head still on the pillow. "Maybe. A weak maybe. Why should I? For a lousy half million?"

"Let me rephrase that," Manning said. "One million."

Adam laughed out loud. "You son of a bitch!"

Three hours later one of Manning's new cell phones rang. Only two people had the number. Adam was one. Audrey was the other, and she was on the line.

"Henry? It's important that I see you right away." She sounded breathless.

"What's the matter?"

"I can't talk over the phone. Please. It's vital."

Manning thought it over. He had promised Adam he'd stay out of New York. But he needed to get Audrey out of town and into someplace safe sooner or later. Besides, he wanted to see her.

"Okay. Coffee shop on the corner of 81st and Columbus. Le Café. Across from the Natural History Museum." Audrey didn't know Manning was out of town. He worked out travel times in his head using the United Shuttle from Reagan National Airport. "Three o'clock. Don't be followed."

"Thank you, Henry."

Manning hung up smiling. She had never called him Henry before.

He walked into Le Café right at three. Audrey Cobb was at a corner table with two middle-aged men. She didn't move or look up as Manning sat down. She was chewing on her knuckle again, and she hadn't said anything about company. Manning didn't like it. "Are you IRS too?" he asked the nearest man.

The man turned his mouth up at the corners. "No, Mr. Manning. I'm in business for myself." He lifted his napkin to show Manning the barrel of a handgun. The muzzle looked as big as the Holland Tunnel.

The man put the napkin and the gun under the table. "Did you see that? It's for killing people. Don't believe all that NRA stuff about deer hunting and self-protection. Now, we're all going to go up to your place. No fuss. Any fuss, you die right now. Ms. Cobb first. Am I clear?"

"Yep," said Manning. Did every single body in New York City want to kill him? He helped Audrey to her feet. She looked as if she were drowning.

The gunman put a twenty on the table, and all four walked out of the café into brilliant sunshine. They walked east toward Manning's condo, cutting through the park. A uniformed patrolman passed them walking the other way. Manning felt the gun barrel in his back. Didn't the cop have eyes?

They waited at Fifth Avenue directly across from Burrough House for a long time, before the traffic let them into the street. The two gunmen didn't seem to mind. They didn't talk or fidget, just standing waiting patiently for the avenue to clear. Like they'd done this a dozen times, Manning figured. That scared him more than anything.

Finally they crossed to Manning's entrance. The doorman smiled at Manning. It was Mr. Singh. "Good morning, Mr. Toledo." Manning rolled his eyes at him in circles. "Yes. Hot. Sure is," said the Sikh.

They rode the elevator up, everyone still silent. When Manning unlocked his door the first gunman pulled him back, while the second man went inside with drawn pistol. The gun barrel had a long cylindrical extension. Silencer, thought Manning. He could feel his pulse in his temples. After a minute the second gunman stuck his head back out. "Clear," he said, in a high-pitched, almost feminine voice.

They all went in. Manning reached for Audrey's hand to squeeze it. The first gunman jabbed the barrel of his handgun into Manning's stomach, hard, down low. Manning wasn't expecting it. He fell to his knees hard, doubled up in pain and surprise.

"That's for trying to signal that Arab," the man said pleasantly. "Next thing you screw up I do the girl. I don't need her any more. You want to see her die? Just screw up one more time." He seemed to enjoy the sound of his own words.

Manning looked up from his carpet at Audrey, who looked back with stricken eyes. "He's Chamineaux," she whispered. "Andres Chamineaux. The killer who has my mother."

Wonderful. Manning got to his feet, holding his stomach. Just stay calm, he told himself. That's the ticket. Stay cool, play along until these two nice men put holes in our foreheads with their howitzers. He suddenly needed to go to the bathroom, bad. He told Chamineaux that. The man nodded, still smiling. "Take him in, Howard," he said.

Howard stood behind Manning as he relieved himself, rubbing his solar plexus where the silencer on Andres' gun barrel had done its damage. When they came back into the living room, Chamineaux had spread legal-looking documents on the glass coffee table. He motioned Manning into a seat across the table from him and handed

Manning a black pen. "Please sign these," he said. "Howard, here, is a notary. He has already certified your signature." Manning looked over at Howard. Did he look like a notary? He had watery blue eyes magnified behind coke-bottle eyeglasses. He also had a mean looking pistol. No, Howard looked like a killer.

The papers were four copies of Henry Toledo's last will and testament, leaving everything he owned to something called the Tannenbaum Trust at an address in Zurich, Switzerland. The notary's signature and number were already filled in. Howard Sergeant.

Manning looked into Andres's smiling eyes. As soon as I sign we'll get it, he thought. The will isn't any good to them with me alive. And they're making no effort to hide Howard's or the trust's identities. Andres gestured again, and Manning signed Toledo's name but used his own handwriting.

"Fine," Andres said when Manning had finished. "Now let's get going." He stood up.

"No good, Andres," said Howard in his squeaky voice. He was holding up one of the wills, comparing it to another paper. "Toledo's signature doesn't match."

Andres' smile never wavered. He pulled Audrey close with his left hand behind her head, the silencer under her chin. "You remember what I said? About screwing up? Now I'm gonna let fly right here, her brains all over your carpet." Same quiet, modulated voice.

"Let her go," said Manning. "You let her go, I'll sign the right way. I don't care what you do to me."

Andres stood for a long moment with his gun at Audrey's head. "Yes," he said. "This one time. Get another set, Howard." To Manning he said, "You sign, she walks. You have my word."

Manning tried for a sincere look. "All right," he said. "I'll take your word. I'll sign." Going nowhere with this. Stalling for time.

Howard opened the front door. "I'll print out some more and notarize them," he told Andres. He left.

Andres closed the door. "Now then," he said to Manning, turning into the room. He opened his mouth to say more when Audrey hit him full force on the back of his head with the "Portuguese" mandolin she had admired the week before.

Andres dropped his gun and fell into Manning's arms, but he was quick. He moved like a cat behind Manning and pinned his arms in a hammerlock. Manning's head was forced down onto his chest painfully. All he could see of Andres was his three-hundred-dollar Oxfords. He stomped on one with his heel with all his might. He heard Andres grunt, and he was free.

The two men crouched, facing each other. Both were breathing hard. "Ahem," said Audrey. She was pointing Andres's own gun at him.

Andres straightened. "You won't use that."

Audrey squeezed her eyes shut and let a round go. The gun made a sound like a tree branch snapping, and Andres doubled up with a low moan. He clutched at his right thigh with both hands, while bright red blood oozed between his fingers. Manning kicked him in the head. He let out a sort of a sigh and folded face-first onto a blue-green Pakistani rug. Audrey stood above him, wide-eyed, breathing in fast, shallow gulps.

Manning picked up the mandolin. Only the strings held its two broken halves together. "This was at least three hundred years old," he said.

"Is he dead?" asked Audrey. She sounded proud of herself.

"You shot him in the leg." Manning rolled Andres over. "He's breathing. That was a nice swing."

"I played field hockey in college," said Audrey. Andres's leg was bleeding onto the carpet. Manning put a pillow under the leg. The wound didn't look serious.

He took Andres' pistol from Audrey. It was a compact automatic. Manning held it carefully by the silencer, between his thumb and index finger. He hated firearms, was afraid of them. "Let's wait for Howard," he said.

"Right." Audrey looked around. "I'm gonna need another mandolin."

"Calm down, Mad Dog," Manning said. "I'll think of something."

Howard was back in twenty minutes with a new set of documents. He leered at Audrey, who was sitting at the coffee table with arms and legs bound in plastic cord. His face wrinkled as he realized that she was alone. When he looked around, there was Manning standing behind him. Manning had overcome his fear of firearms enough to point Andres's pistol into Howard's face.

"Just take your gun from your belt with your left hand, Howard," he said. "Careful. Slow." He tried to sound like Clint Eastwood.

Howard did as he was told. "It was Andres," he whined in his soprano voice. "I just came along to notarize this paper, is all."

Audrey stood up and stepped out of her bindings. She smiled at Howard. "No knots," she said. "How many notaries in the greater New York area carry a gun to work?" She was recovering her old smart-alecky self, Manning thought.

Howard kept his eyes on the gun in Manning's hand. "No. Andres. . . this was his play. I help out sometimes, is all. This gig. . . I just drew up and notarized the will." Howard looked up at Manning. "So help me, I didn't know this was a rough toss."

"Horse crap. You knew this was a contract job," said Manning, pretending he knew what he was talking about. "You knew we were gonna take a slug at the end of the day. The contract, who put it out?"

"Who knows?" said Howard. "Andres, he sets everything up. It's what he does. Best in the business." A touch of pride crept into his voice. "Fifty grand, what he gets. Tol' me this one was double. Double the money. Never talks about the client. Poor form to discuss the client."

Manning held up a copy of his will. "The Tannenbaum Trust, what's that?" he asked.

"Jesus, I don't know. Just a name he gave me, he wrote it down, I put it in the will."

"Your wallet," Manning said, pointing to the coffee table. He went through it with his free hand, keeping the gun and most of his attention on Howard. Everything was in the name of Howard Sergeant, including a notary public license certified by Nassau County on Long Island. Howard had some business cards for an accounting agency on the Island. Manning kept the business cards and the ID. "You show up in my life again, and the police get this," he said, waving the ID at Howard. "Give me your car keys."

Howard handed them over. "What is it?" Manning asked.

"Tan Cadillac, 1998."

"Parked where?"

"In front. Down the street."

"I'll keep it for awhile. I'll phone you, tell you where it is when I'm through with it. Go on, down the elevator, out of the building. Get out."

Howard took a minute to realize he was off the hook, then hurried to the door to the hallway. He opened the door and turned to look at Manning and Audrey. "Thanks," he said.

"Thanks," Audrey gave a good imitation of Howard's soprano voice as the door closed after him. "That clown tries to kill us, you let him walk away."

"Somebody has your mother, remember?" said Manning. "I think it's the same somebody who hired Andres. You want to turn Howard in to the police and get your mother killed?"

"Don't worry. My mother. . . that's what's keeping me here." Audrey walked to the balcony and looked down. "There goes Howard in his tan Caddy. I guess he had another set of keys. What next, mastermind?" She came back into the living room and bounced down on the sofa. "How about you? What keeps you so quiet while they set you up?"

"They've got something on me too."

"What?"

"Something," said Manning. He walked into the small guest bathroom off the living room. Andres lay on the tile floor, trussed up between the toilet and the washbasin with some bungee cords Manning had found in a clothes closet. A bath towel was taped around his leg wound. He was still out cold. Manning pulled him to a slumped sitting position and lifted an eyelid. The pupil constricted, and the other eye opened. Manning let him see his own pistol.

"The contract on me," Manning said. "Who ordered it?"

Andres didn't answer. Manning stuck his pistol barrel hard into Andres' solar plexus. "Remember that?" he asked. "I do. It hurts. I can do that all day. Who hired you to put little holes in the girl and me?"

Andres stayed silent, looking at Manning. Manning jabbed him again harder. After the third jab Andres said, "He used a go-between. I don't know who he is."

"Who was the go-between?"

Andres shook his head. "Voice on the phone. I don't know. It's a code word."

"Which is?"

"Hank Aaron. He tells a baseball story with Hank Aaron in it. I answer with a post office box location. Next day, something's in the box. Instructions and a down payment. Half down."

"How much down?"

Andres paused. "Ten grand."

Manning jammed with the gun again. "I know better."

Andres grunted. "Fifty."

"Correct," said Manning. "Let's see the instructions."

Andres paused again. Manning made like he would use the gun barrel again, and Andres said, "Inside coat pocket."

Manning found Andres' jacket on the bathroom floor and reached inside. He pulled out a legal-sized manila envelope folded neatly in half lengthwise. Inside was a photo of Manning, a long shot of him exiting Toledo's building, looking left for traffic as he crossed the street. Three typewritten pages gave some details of Manning's daily routine, Audrey's description, and her hotel address in the City. The printout told Andres how to use her to set Manning up. The last page gave instructions on the composition of the will, giving everything to Tannenbaum Trust. The last sentence was chillingly succinct: "With the will signed and notarized, eliminate Mr. Toledo and Ms. Cobb in a manner of your choice that can be interpreted only as an accident."

Manning looked at Andres, mad as hell. "How were you gonna kill us?"

Andres was silent again. He kept his eyes down. Manning let him see the pistol. "Why don't you tell me one good reason not to put the same holes in you that you planned for us?"

Andres raised his eyebrows and rolled his head. He managed a small smile. He didn't look too good, but he hadn't lost all of his starch. "Make a deal with you," Manning said. "I let you go, you let us go. Drop it. The contract."

Andres was already nodding his head. "Of course."

"Of course," said Manning. "Ah, but how do I know you'll keep your end?"

"You have my word."

"Your word. The word of an assassin. No, I have more than that." Manning opened a folded paper and showed it to Andres. Two Polaroid photos were scotch-taped to the top. They were of Andres, full face and side view, taken as he lay unconscious on the bathroom floor. Under the photos was a full set of fingerprints in what looked like brown ink.

"These are your prints, of course," said Manning. "I didn't have an ink pad, so I used your blood. You've got lots of it on your leg that you're not using." Manning held up another sheet. "Here's the best I can describe you by height, weight, that little tattoo on your wrist, and your name and address, probably false, from your wallet." Manning folded the papers. He put his thumb and middle finger in his mouth and gave a sharp whistle.

Audrey appeared in the doorway. "I wish I could whistle like that," she said. Manning gave her the folded papers. She stuck them in an envelope, gave the two men a smirk, and bounced out of the room.

Manning took the bungee cords off of Andres and stood him up, letting him see the gun again. "She's mailing those papers to someone who will keep them safe so long as nothing bad happens to Ms. Cobb and me. Something bad does happen to us, they go to Interpol and the FBI with a little note telling them what your day job is. Then what? Who knows? You've already got an Interpol sheet, but no photo. Here's a photo and DNA. Maybe if you're on a police blotter your work will suffer. Maybe not." Manning shrugged. "Best we can do."

Manning helped Andres across the living room to the front door. Andres limped silently, testing his wound out, his face set against the pain.

At the door he faced Manning. "You have nothing to fear. I shall return the contract money, saying I'm not interested. I can do that with no harm to my. . . reputation." He opened the front door, then turned in the open doorway. "They'll just put someone else on you, you know. When they finally kill you, then what? Those papers still get released."

"Chance you take," Manning shrugged. "We're taking a chance, too, letting you go. But I think you'll keep your word."

"I'll keep it," said Andres, "or I would have taken you in the last thirty seconds."

"At gunpoint?" asked Manning.

Andres pointed to the pistol in Manning's hand. "Safety's still on," he said. He smiled and closed the door behind him.

Manning looked at his front door, then down at the gun. The accountant as action hero.

chapter 10

James Bond's American Cousin

"You're letting them all go." Audrey wore a sour face. She flopped on the sofa with her legs straight out. "Andres is gonna rearm and reload and come back blazing away."

"He won't," said Manning. "He said he could have taken me just now, just after you left. He could have." Manning left out the part about the safety catch. "He promised to leave us alone. I think he'll keep his word."

"Of course. I'd forgotten the contract killer's honor code."

"Do what, then," asked Manning. "Shoot him full of holes? Wrap him in one of my Oriental rugs, stuff him in the trunk of my Mercedes? Dump him in the East River by moonlight? We're not Bonnie and Clyde, here."

"What's driving a Mercedes like?" asked Audrey with a woman's ability for non-linear thought.

Manning ignored her. He was looking through Toledo's stack of credit and club cards. "Whether Andres comes back or not, someone will. Time for us to find an off-ramp. You got a passport? On you?"

"No," said Audrey. "Not on me. Who carries their passport with them? Anyway, I don't even have one."

"Okay. Back to your hotel. Pack a bag. Pack light. Make it fast. Be back here in twenty minutes. Don't let anyone see you come or go from your hotel. Leave the key in the room. You're not going back."

"Wait a minute. Just a damn minute. Who says I'm not going back? You think I'm off to the races with a guy I hardly know, lies about his age to the IRS, his friends kidnap my mother?"

Manning put on his sincere face. "Audrey, someone's gunning for us. It's a miracle we're not dead right now. I think they've tried to kill me three times already."

"Three times. You're a slow learner."

"I've learned that the guy I told about you can't be trusted. Talmud. 'I'll call you,' he says. Next thing, here's Andres." Manning put both hands up, palms out, to stop her from interrupting. "We can't go to the cops, right? Can't jeopardize your mother. But they won't do anything to her if they think we'll tell whatever it is they think we know." Audrey snorted. "What do we know?"

"Search me. But they think we know something. It's the only leverage we've got. It's also what can get us killed. So, we disappear."

She trained her blue eyes on him and turned up the wattage. "Henry, what's going on? We're running for our lives, running with our mouths shut. I don't even know if Mama's alive. Will I ever see her again?" Her voice rose.

"You'll see your mother," Manning soothed. "I'll get her for you. Promise. First I gotta get you someplace safe."

Audrey watched him. "You'll get me safe. You'll find

Mama. James Bond's American cousin." She worked up a weak smile, shaking her head. "I'm trying to crack a nut named Henry Toledo. If I did crack it, and peeled the shell back, what would I find?"

You'd find Manning Crenshaw, thought Manning Crenshaw. Aloud he said, "I'm not that interesting."

The smile moved to her eyes. "Just what I was telling People Magazine. 'He's very rich and very old. He cheats on his taxes. He's on the run. I'm running with him.'" The smile winked out. "Never mind telling me about you. I give up. Tell me how you're gonna find Mama."

Manning took her hands and went over it again, as much to convince himself as to sell her. The need to run. The need to keep quiet. Along the way he ad-libbed an autobiography of a black sheep heir to the Toledo fortune who was just as in the dark about the attempted killings as she was.

"And your lies to the IRS about birth dates, Mr. Toledo?" Audrey kept her voice steady.

"Audrey, you're gonna have to trust me on that one. I told you, there's a reasonable explanation. For now, we've got a few minutes' lead on whoever's after us. Your hotel. Get going."

Audrey left the apartment, shaking her head. Okay, wise guy, Manning told himself, she thinks you've got a plan. Get one. He picked up a color brochure on his desk. It featured a photo of a cruise ship with decks stacked like a wedding cake. Rainbow lettering read, "Sail off into Paradise." Manning had been looking at it just a couple of days ago, wondering how long it would be before the new

Henry Toledo could take a cruise. He remembered now. It was when Audrey had called in a fury over James Greenway. How long ago was that? It seemed forever.

Audrey took 45 minutes. Manning expected that. He had been married for a long time. "I've booked a flight for us in five hours from Kennedy Airport to Paris."

"Paris." Audrey looked at herself in the mirror behind Manning's bar. "I don't have the right clothes."

"That's okay," said Manning. "We're not going. I mean we're going to Kennedy, but that's just a dodge. Really, you're sailing on a cruise ship." He smiled. "Don't tell me, you don't have the right clothes for that either."

"A cruise," Audrey said dreamily.

I'm throwing a lot at her at once, Manning thought. "No one checks cruises," he told her, hoping that was true. "People looking for us, they'll check airlines, train stations, buses. Maybe look to see if my cars are still here. Who thinks of cruise ships?"

Audrey clouded up again. "Henry, listen. I've got a job. A life. I can't just. . ."

"Can't what? Just walk away? You can. Believe me, I know. What you can't do is go home." He sat her down and sat across from her. "Your old life seems. . . safe. You're into 'safe.' What you're not into is getting killed. Never experienced that, right? You only get to try it once." He reached out and handed her the cruise ship brochure. "Look, it's gonna be all right. I'll set you up in a hotel downtown. Go to a travel agent somewhere. A small guy, an independent. Tell him a story. Your mother just died. . ." Audrey winced, and Manning started over, ". . . Anyway, you have a windfall inheritance and need to get away. Book this cruise." He pointed to the travel brochure in her hand. "This is the SS Queen of Copenhagen. It sails for the Caribbean in three days from Manhattan. Get on it. You'll get off in St. Thomas. Fly somewhere, get on another cruise line." He tried a reassuring smile, holding her hand. "Better get a lot of sun block."

Audrey was having vapors again. "I. . . I. . . can't just. . ."

Manning crossed to a large oil painting on the far wall and tilted it to reveal a wall safe. "You're thinking," he said. "Don't think. Do. We got the jump on these guys, but not for long. They're slick." He dialed the combination: 1—2—3. Nothing secure about that. He had spent a lot of money and told a lot of lies to get a locksmith to crack the safe the week after Toledo died. He opened it and took out a stack of bills. "There's about ten thousand here. After you book the cruise, go shopping. Buy what you need. No big purchases that draw attention. More than one store if you need to. Pay cash. No credit cards, no checks. You're not Audrey Cobb any more."

"Who am I?" Audrey was counting the money.

"We'll think of someone. Reminds me, there's an arcade on Broadway near Times Square. Stop by the instant photo booth, take some shots. Full face, profile. Wear your sunglasses."

"They're in the hotel." Audrey looked up at Manning, who shook his head.

"Can't go back there," he told her. "Buy some new ones. Dark, big, cover your face. Get some hair dye.

Blonde. . . blondes have more fun. Take the photos with your hair covered. Bandana or something. We're gonna reinvent you. New passport, new driver's license. Damn. You're gonna need two passports. One for the old you for the airport, one for the new one."

"You've thought of everything," Audrey said.

"Making it up as I go," said Manning. He was emptying out the drawers of the ornate desk. "I've got some experience in changing identities, though." He looked up. "Get going. Get back here in an hour. No, come right back with the photos, then go back out to book the cruise and shop. I need the photos to make up some stuff."

"You, don't you need clothes?"

Manning got up at that and pulled a suitcase from his closet, opening it on the floor. "I'm not going. I mean not with you. I gotta get these guys off our back. Can't do it and worry about you too." He held Howard's revolver out to her. "Take this. Pack it. Might come in handy on your cruise."

Audrey looked at it doubtfully. "I think I'll stick with a mandolin as my weapon of choice."

"Suit yourself." Manning threw the pistol into his suitcase. He didn't have time to argue. Who was going to teach her to shoot anyway? Not me. I can't even work the safety catch.

Audrey put the cash in her purse on her way to the front door. She put on sunglasses. "They were in my purse," she said sheepishly.

Winston Churchill answered the phone on his spotlessly empty desk in Washington. "Hi," said Audrey.

"Audrey!" Winston was enormously relieved, then irritated. "You've had me. . . us. . . worried sick. Where are you?"

"At a pay phone in the City. New York. I'm. . . look, it's too long a story to jam through the phone lines. It's not that important."

"Not that important. Oh, I see."

"You sound irritated. I'm sorry I haven't phoned."

"You're sorry. We've got a Missing Persons out on you. I'm just back from getting my backside gnawed by the Director and some teenager from the FBI. You haven't been at your hotel for days. . . and your Mother, where is your Mother? She doesn't answer her phone. So I'm checking all the hospitals and morgues in the greater New York area, and it's 'not that important!' Look, where are you?"

"Winston, just shut up for a minute, will you? I can't tell you where I am. I'm safe and sound. Mother is fine, too. . . probably. I've just mailed a letter to you. Your home address. When you get it, just keep it for me, can you? Don't open it, okay? Keep it safe."

"Listen, where are you? I'm coming. . ."

"So dear of you. Don't fret. Call off your dogs. I'll call later. G'bye."

"Audrey, I love you."

"I know, I know." The line was dead. Winston slammed his phone onto its cradle so hard that Mrs. Harris, a grandmother from the General Services Administration steno pool, got up from her desk in his outer office to look in on him.

Audrey returned two hours after her phone call to Winston with matching luggage full of clothes. She had already been back once with the photo arcade pictures and Manning had printed ID cards and passports for her: one for Audrey Cobb and one for Sylvia Trent. He stood. "Come on. I'm driving us to the airport." They went to the underground garage. Manning pointed his remote key at the black sedan. The red convertible winked back. He had picked up the wrong key.

Audrey was staring at the car. "What is it?"

"SL500," said Manning, reading the chrome figures on the car's trunk. Except for starting the car that first day he had never even touched it.

"Does the top go down?"

"You bet," said Manning weakly. He looked at the dash. A lever had an up and down arrow. He pressed it down. The roll bar in the back seat retracted.

Audrey looked suspiciously at Manning. "Don't you know your own car?"

"I just got it," he answered truthfully. He found a square plastic lever just below the roll bar switch and pushed forward tentatively. Nothing. Down, stupid. He pulled back. Through the rear view mirror he could see a deck lid open. The top unhooked with the sounds of bones cracking and slid smoothly into the opening.

Mercifully, the car was an automatic. Manning backed out and rolled onto Fifth Avenue without hitting anything.

The Mercedes handled like a racehorse. Classical music played on the high fi. "Sounds like a movie," Audrey muttered. She punched some buttons and got a CD to play Ellington. Manning hummed along with the music. The farther they got from his condo the better he felt.

They parked the Mercedes at Kennedy's short term parking with the top back up, and Manning checked them in at British Airways for the night flight to Paris. The counter clerk barely glanced at Toledo's and Audrey's passports. "How many bags?" she asked.

Manning held up their two carry-ons. "None. Traveling light." He didn't want any hassle with missing passengers and checked bags. Security crosschecked those things since 9/11.

They had some time before boarding. Manning paid for two espressos at Starbucks and found a table. He watched a tall African-American in the corner. Was he really reading Sports Illustrated or was he tracking them? Get a grip, he told himself.

Audrey made a face over her coffee. "Too hot?" he asked.

"No. I just can't catch up. We're running for our lives and I don't know if I'm going to Paris or the Caribbean."

Manning went through it again. A fake to Europe, then off on a cruise. He was still talking when they called the Paris flight.

They greased by the ticket taker, who gave their passports a nod without looking, and were in the line of tourists and businessmen in the boarding tunnel. At its end, just before entering the plane, Audrey stepped out of line, searching through her purse. "It's got to be here somewhere." Loud voice. Manning had carefully rehearsed her. He stood next to her, watching the other passengers. They glanced over and got on board.

When the stewardess just inside the plane was distracted, Manning opened a door in the boarding chute leading outside. "Come on." They ducked out.

The door led to a metal stairway down to the tarmac. They clambered down with their carry-on bags swinging. At the bottom they quick-walked back toward the terminal. Manning was breathing fast, mostly from the tension.

A flight line workman in orange jumpsuit and soundproof earmuffs watched them. Manning waved and smiled. "Can you help us?"

"You can't be down here," the worker yelled over the British Air's jets. He was very young.

Manning kept his smile. "We're coming in from Atlanta. Must have taken a wrong turn."

"You can get arrested." But the boy was smiling. "This way." He led them to a stairway. Twenty minutes later they were in the convertible headed into the city.

"Won't they find out we jumped ship?"

Manning shook his head. "Flight was only half full when I made our reservations. No one checks seats against any kind of manifest, right? Far as anyone knows, Toledo and Cobb went to Paris."

They found a two-star hotel at least 40 years old near the East River. "How many rooms?" asked the desk clerk.

"Two," Manning and Audrey said in unison. The clerk

smiled and punched his computer keys.

Manning was at the desk in Audrey's room writing in a spiral notebook. Audrey came out of the bathroom. "How do you like it?"

"I like it," and he did. She was a blonde. It went with those china-blue eyes. And with the little dimples at the corners of her mouth when she smiled, like she was doing now. Manning held a one-man conference:

Hold on, cowboy. You're married.

What do you mean? Next of kin, none, remember?

You're not Toledo. You're Crenshaw under that designer outfit.

Manning Crenshaw's not married either, any more.

He came back to the hotel room. "Want some dinner?" he asked her.

Audrey shook her head. "Too tired." She tossed her still-damp hair around in front of the dresser mirror, watching his reflection. "Henry Toledo. Can I trust you, Mr. Henry Toledo?"

Manning got up and stood behind her. He put his hands on her shoulders. "You bet. I'll get you out of this."

Audrey shook her head at that. "This is . . . crazy. A few days ago there was nothing to get me out of. I think sometimes it's all a play, written and directed by you. All these people. . . Greenway, Andres, Howard. . . they're all actors."

"It's real. Those guns were real."

Audrey looked up into the glass again. "I don't care about me. It's Mama. Say you'll get her out of this."

Manning nodded, smiling, reassuring, acting. "I will, and I'll get you safe. We'll work it out." It was easier lying to the girl in the mirror with her long neck and wide lips. Or was he lying? He wanted to work it all out, get it done. "Come on, get some sleep. Tomorrow will come soon enough."

"Tomorrow? What's tomorrow?"

"Tomorrow I stash the Mercedes. It's a neon sign. You stay holed up here until your ship sails."

The girl in the mirror opened her lips, but the woman in front of him spoke. "When will I see you?" Manning thought he heard, or hoped he heard, something in her voice.

"You'll hear from me," he said. "You'll run out of money. I'll have to refill your tank."

"How?"

"Don't know yet. Maybe a bank line of credit. Maybe a new credit card. Send an e-mail. This address." He tore a sheet from the notebook in front of him and gave it to her. "Chatty stuff, having a wonderful time. Tell me where you'll be when the cruise ends. A hotel or something. I'll get it to you."

Audrey took the sheet. Her face darkened. "My mom. What about her?"

"I'm guessing they won't harm her with you not located." He saw her look. "Don't worry. Listen, my whole life I've reacted to events. Now I'm taking the initiative. I'm gonna get her back."

Audrey looked worried. "How?"

"I've got a friend," said Manning.

chapter 11

"There's Always A Faster Gun."

Manning and Adam walked along the B&O Canal in Georgetown a week later. The canal parallels the Potomac River west of the District of Columbia and runs all the way to Harper's Ferry. Barges used it to haul cargo to the capital in the 18th and 19th Centuries. The two brothers walked along the dirt path next to the canal. Tow horses used the path to pull the barges in the old days. An occasional biker and jogger went by, but a light rain kept most people indoors. The path was perfect for private talk.

Adam didn't have much to report. He had staked out Audrey's mother's house, off and on, during the week. No sign of life. She had been moved. He had used some old Agency contacts to run a check of Andres from a photocopy of the prints and photograph Manning had taken. Adam's CIA friends had turned up nothing. The two brothers were not surprised.

"How about Sergeant?" Manning had given Adam Howard Sergeant's business card.

"New Jersey police have a sheet on him. Strong-arm stuff, ending in conspiracy to Murder Two, three years ago. Charges dropped. Witness disappeared."

"Witness disappeared. Sounds like Andres," Manning said.

"Maybe. Anyway, Howard made a career change. Filed for a CPA's and a notary's license six months later."

"And?"

"And nothing. No warrants, no sheets since then. Local police, FBI, nothing."

"So we move to Plan B," Manning said.

"Which is?"

"I've collected three million and change in Toledo's Citibank account in Manhattan. We take it. I disappear. Audrey's already out of sight. I think her mother's safe. They won't hurt her with Audrey or me on the loose. I'm gonna stay on it. Sooner or later I'll find her and get her out. They don't even know about you."

Adam hunched his shoulders against the rain and looked over at his brother with a sour face. "Too dangerous," he said. "Manning Crenshaw promises me he'll stay out of New York, remember? The same day he's in Manhattan sitting down with hired killers. You were lucky with this guy Andres. . . dumb luck. You don't know that he isn't still on the job, despite your limp attempt to blackmail him. He isn't, then someone slicker is. There's always a faster gun." Adam stopped walking and turned to face Manning. "You're day-to-day, Bro. You stay in this game, they'll sniff you out and gun you down, probability of one hundred percent. Then the girl. Then me, too, if I'm dumb enough to stay in the neighborhood. You've got a little money. Go someplace warm and sunny with no zip code. Do me a favor. Don't tell me where."

Manning bounced on his toes. "Adam, the money's there, waiting. Look, no risk. Piece of cake. We stay somewhere on Long Island, don't even go into the city until we take it. Assumed names. I know how to do that. We set it up very carefully, walk in, sign something, walk out with three million. One, two, three."

Adam made a gun barrel out of his index finger and clicked his thumb at Manning. "One, two, three, bang, we're dead." He was silent. Manning knew he was giving it another run-through. "I still think it smells."

"But you'll do it. For me."

"No. For the million."

So that's what they did. Took a room at a Motel Six in Garden City in Nassau County. No car, not even a rental. Everything by taxi or the Long Island Rail Road. All calls on the new cell phones. Adam kept an all-night clerk otherwise occupied at a Kinko's in Queens while Manning pasted up new IDs for them both. At the end of the week they were almost ready. They had dinner at a fish place in Minneola. "That's it, we're all set." Adam said. "All we have to do is walk in, pick up the money, walk out, get shot." Adam had finished a bottle of white wine all by himself. Manning didn't like it. Adam never drank.

"We don't even know if anybody knows the money's there," Manning said.

"We don't know they don't." Adam toyed with his swordfish. "We don't know anything."

"We know they don't know about you," said Manning. "You pick it up. You'll have a notarized letter from me authorizing you."

"Great," Adam groused. "We can have Howard Sergeant notarize it." He looked over. "I'm the bank manager, I'm not gonna hand over that three million to anybody but Henry Toledo."

"That's where I come in," said Manning.

"This is irregular," said Edward Bachman. He was branch manager for Citibank in Cleveland Heights, outside of metropolitan Cleveland.

"Irregular is not the same as impossible," said Manning. He was sitting at Bachman's desk in one of Henry Toledo's most sincere suits. He put on an impatient, imperious face. "Do I need to go over this again?"

"I guess you do, Mr. Toledo. Please."

"All right." Audible sigh. "One more time. You are satisfied that I am Henry Toledo?"

"Yes, sir." A driver's license, passport, and Citibank credit card in Toledo's name were lined up on Bachman's desk in front of him.

"Okay. Here I am in Cleveland. A deal is going down in Manhattan. A deal. You understand?"

"Yes, sir." Bachman had no idea what a "deal" might be.

Manning spoke slowly, wearily. He was dealing with children. "I need three million to clinch the deal. Cash that I have carefully compiled in your Manhattan branch. I'm here. It's there. My associate will pick it up in an hour." Manning made a show of glancing impatiently at his watch. "Half an hour, now. You have my notarized letter authorizing him to pick it up. The money. My money. Signed here in your bank, in front of your notary, right?" Manning stifled a yawn. He had flown to Cleveland on the first flight that morning.

"Yes, sir." Bachman was running out of reasons to stall. Everything seemed in order. Still. . . "I don't have the authority to release your money."

Manning leaned over the desk, speaking slowly and softly. "You don't need it. You're not releasing the money. Manhattan is. You're just faxing this authorization letter and phoning to tell him that I'm here, in person, you've checked me out. The rest is up to them."

Bachman relaxed. Mr. Toledo was right. He wasn't authorizing anything. "What was that number in Manhattan?" he asked with a smile.

Adam sat in the office of the Manhattan Citibank's general manager, while the manager and an area vice-president looked at the same line-up of identification cards that had faced Mr. Bachman. Adam was, for the occasion, Morgan Kennedy, Jr. He and Manning had decided that Kennedy was a green-light name in New York.

The vice president and manager talked together inaudibly. Adam sat perfectly still. His palms and underarms were wet. How did he get talked into this? The money wasn't worth it. He looked out the window for flashing lights on the tops of police cars.

The vice president was smiling at him with old, yellow teeth. He was at least 75. "This all seems in order."

"There is some time sensitivity," Adam barked. Easy does it.

"Of course." The vice president watched as the bank manager counted out 32 money packets into Adam's leather snap-up brief case. Each packet held $100,000. The three men had spent 20 minutes verifying that. Adam didn't care. Three million, two million, who cares? Snatch the money and run. He looked at the wall clock. He had been in the bank over an hour. Interminable.

Then. . . the case was in his hand. Adam signed a receipt and release form with his right hand while his left hand held the briefcase in a death grip. "I'll need a Xerox of these forms," he said. It seemed like the right thing to say. The vice president nodded and the bank manager scurried off to find a copier.

Then. . . he was outside in brilliant sunshine with three million dollars in his hand. He waved at curbside, and a Yellow Cab from the taxi stand on the corner rolled up.

"Hyatt on Park," he told the driver. Adam couldn't hide a smile. He would be early for his confirmation call to Manning. A piece of cake, his brother would say.

"Right away, sir," said the cabby. The high-pitched voice meant nothing to Adam. Nor did the watery blue eyes behind the thick glasses. Manning hadn't had a photo of Howard Sergeant and hadn't taken the trouble to describe him to his brother.

Manning sat on the bed at his motel in Cleveland and watched the six o'clock news and tried not to stare at his cell phone. Adam's call was three hours late. Something was wrong. Manning had phoned a teller at Citibank Manhattan. The three million was gone, withdrawn today. Finally, he phoned Adam's cellular number.

"Hello?" The voice was not Adam's.

"Hello. May I speak to Morgan Kennedy please?"

"Who is this?"

"I'm a relative. Who is this?"

"This is the 12th Precinct, NYPD. Who am I speaking to, please?"

Manning made up a name, stomach clenched. "I'm Morgan's brother. What's happened?"

The cop's voice became softer, slower. "Mr. Kennedy, your brother has had an. . ." There was a long silence. The cop cleared his throat. Manning's heart had turned to stone.

"Mr. Kennedy, your brother has been shot. Killed."

Manning nodded at the phone and closed his eyes and saw a ten-year-old boy with dreamy blue eyes and a head full of tight blond curls looking up with a shy smile. Adam, hoping his big brother would play with him.

The cop talked on. "Shot, sir. Found in a public parking garage. Wallet was empty of cash and credit cards. Address didn't check out. I just left his cellular on, hoping for a call."

"He's recently moved," Manning said. "Who's. . . do you have any clues?" Manning knew the answer.

"Nothing. It was clean. . . I'm sorry. I mean whoever did it didn't leave anything. Mr. Kennedy, can you come in? Identify your brother. We'd like to take a statement."

"Of course," said Manning, knowing he wouldn't. Couldn't. He stood with the phone in his ear for a long moment, not wanting to end the call, knowing that when he did Adam would really be dead.

After a while he could hear clicking on the other end. The cop said, "This phone is low on battery. I'll phone you back on another one. Give me your number." Manning gave him a made up telephone number and hung up. He wanted a drink. He wanted a cigarette, the first cigarette in five years. He wanted to get out of the room, go anywhere. Adam, his little brother. It wasn't the money. Adam had wanted to please his older brother. Manning had talked him dead.

Manning paced the room, wall to wall. He opened the curtain and peered into the busy street. He ran water in the sink, splashed his face, stared at the man in the mirror. Finally he opened his wallet and unfolded a slip of paper with a number on it. He picked up his cell phone and dialed the number.

"Mr. Talmud, this is Henry Toledo. I need your help. I'm willing to give you everything I know."

chapter 12

"Y No Lo Creo."

The good people at St. George's Mews were buzzing. The Mews was a blue-collar cul de sac near Heathrow Airport on the outskirts of London. Its residents called to each other across the fences of their tiny backyards and on the phone. Where were the black limousines coming from? Five within the hour and but one poor man in each, walking up the rain-slick red bricks to George Hargreaves' place. And here comes another! Is it a wake, then? Is old George Hargreaves done in? Is it Maude, his wife? Calls to George fetched only his voice mail. George and Maude were, in fact, on holiday in Cornwall spending some of the thousand quid that Isaac Talmud had paid for the use of their home for the evening.

Isaac had come in the first limousine. He greeted each of his guests as they arrived. The greetings were muted. The smiles and backslapping of Easter Sunday on Paco's yacht in Monaco were missing. The men had flown in on short notice. That meant all-night flights and long layovers—tough travel even in first class.

Only six of the nine men answered the summons. Two were just too committed. One was in Hong Kong and too far away. But six were a quorum.

"There have been developments," Isaac said without preamble. "Enrique's imposter is on the loose, and dangerous. We should rethink our strategy."

All eyes except Isaac's went to Hermano Tomaso, who said, "Our strategy is sound. The man has not said anything to anyone. He won't. Nor will the IRS investigator. We sent a team in. The attempt failed. We shall try again. This time we shall succeed."

"The imposter phoned me," Isaac said. He pushed a small cart with Maude's pewter tea service among his friends. "He told me of three attempts on his life. All failed. The last was Andres. Andres failed, Andres is currently the best there is, as we all know."

"Andres will try again," Hermano Tomaso insisted.

"He will not," Isaac said sharply. The men shifted in their seats. Isaac went on, "He will send word that he declines the contract." A sharp glance toward Tomaso. "You didn't know that? Odd, wouldn't you agree? The imposter told me why. Andres is being blackmailed."

The men stirred again. Isaac continued, "This man posing as Enrique has proven. . . resourceful. He eluded Andres. More than that, he prevailed. He has taken Andres's photo and fingerprints. His DNA."

"This is a formidable man," said Esteban, rubbing his bald head. "Or perhaps Andres has lost a step or two."

Isaac nodded. "That may be, but it doesn't matter if Andres won't try again. This new friend of ours promises to make the information he has on Andres available to the authorities if anything unfortunate happens to him."

The six men looked in a circle at each other. "Have we

ever had so much trouble neutralizing one man?" asked Martinez.

"Not in a very long time," answered Paco.

"Then what is our problem? There are professionals for hire other than Andres," Pablo Cisneros said. "Is it money? Spend the money."

But Isaac waggled a finger at him. "Think, my friend. This man has access to all of Enrique's papers. Enrique kept careless records. How can we be sure that another package filled with information compromising all that we have kept hidden for so long doesn't rest next to Andres' envelope? We must assume that it does. No, there are other ways."

"What ways?" asked Martinez.

"This man has asked for my help," said Isaac. "Someone close to him has been killed. His brother." Isaac's eyes flicked once more toward Hermano Tomaso, then away. "The man is filled with anger. He wants only to discover who is doing this, to repay him. He is that much more dangerous to us. I have invited him to meet with me near my estate in Hawaii. I should work with him."

"That plan comes with its own risks," complained Hermano Tomaso. He turned in his chair to speak to the others. "The simplest and surest way out of our situation is to allow the man to meet Isaac at his home, and then kill him."

That brought Isaac's head around. "I have invited him to a meeting. I promised him safe passage. . ."

"You made a promise to a thief who's stolen Enrique's identity, his fortune, his life. Probably he took Enrique's life as well." Tomaso flashed his ivory smile again. "An eye for an eye, as your prophets have written."

Talmud swung his head in a wide negative arc. "My prophets, and most of yours, write more convincingly about mercy than justice."

"What does it matter?" Tomaso muttered. "I propose a simple solution for this."

"You have the same simple solution for everything," Isaac said. "The situation is stable. The man will do nothing. He may be useful. We have time to think, to plan."

"The situation is far from stable," snapped Tomaso. "It unravels by the minute. What leverage do you have over the man? Nothing. What is he doing at this moment? To whom is he talking?" Tomaso's voice became conciliatory. "Isaac, you have done well. We know much more now. We know we are in danger. Finish him, or I will come with you and do it."

Isaac shrugged. "Perhaps." He bent over George Hargreaves' coal hearth, warming his hands. "Perhaps not. We have been successful through the years by playing the waiting game, withholding our hand. Time is always on our side."

"This time we have only one thing on our side," Tomaso said. "We need to act, now. You will have the man alone. Finish it." Tomaso raised his arms to the other men in the room. "Am I right?"

The four other men looked at each other. Heads began to nod. Tomaso knew better than to say more. He knew how Los Viejos would vote. So did Isaac.

"As you wish," Isaac said. He rubbed his hands over

the coal hearth as in an imaginary basin. Pontius Pilate.

Tomaso remained after the other four had hurried to their limousines in the cold rain. "The woman IRS agent is still loose," he said to Isaac in a quiet voice.

"She is on a cruise ship. The man told me."

"Ah," Tomaso said.

Isaac looked out of the open door into the darkness. "There was an attempt on this imposter's life after Andres, old friend. The man's brother was shot. Killed. What game are you playing, Tomaso?"

Tomaso shook his head. He held up his hands to show Isaac empty palms. "The man's brother. . . this is none of my doing. You have my word, hermano."

"Ah," said Isaac. "Your word. Such a comfort." He walked Tomaso to the door. "Buenos noches."

Isaac closed the door. "No lo creo," he whispered to himself. "I don't believe it. Y no soy tu hermano." He set about cleaning the room and wiping fingerprint sites with a cloth.

chapter 13

Alice And The White Rabbit

Sylvia Trent sat floating on a rising tide of dark rum at a seaside cabana in Ka'anapali, a tourist beach on the Hawaiian Island of Maui. The specialty of the house sat in front of her in a half coconut shell—a mai tai. The hotels usually watered and sugared them shamelessly for the tourists, but the Filipino bartender had made this the right way, with 151 proof rum. It was half gone. A sunset, tinting the cumulus clouds at sea with pinks and golds, was also half-gone. Sylvia had toasted a lot of sunsets in the past few weeks. This was her second straight cruise. Six Caribbean islands and Miami. This was her third Hawaiian island. This was her third mai tai.

A young blond with a smile as wide as his shoulders sat down at the bar. "Where'd you get those big eyes?"

Sylvia stirred her drink with the little Japanese parasol that came with it. The rum warmed her stomach and numbed her cheeks.

She had once, in a previous incarnation, been Audrey Cobb. Presently, as Sylvia, she sailed the Seven Seas endlessly, a mystery lady playing to an audience of young and not-so-young men looking for shipboard romance. It had been, mostly, fun and flattering and a world away from

IRS auditing and Winston Churchill. She had discovered that life was full of things she never knew she needed. Food, drink, day-tours, clothes—she simply signed Sylvia's name. At the end of the cruise there was a cashier's check from Henry to pay the bills. But tonight reality was catching up with her. Tonight, like many nights, usually just before dawn, she worried about her mother and wondered whether Andres or someone like him was circling out there in the darkness.

The young man moved one chair closer. "So, where you from, blue eyes?"

"Lately, all over," Audrey answered truthfully. She was making a mistake answering and she knew it. Probably the rum talking.

Sure enough: "I'm from the Bay Area. Been here a week."

"What bay would that be?" Shut up, she told herself.

"What bay do you think?" Wide, crooked smile. Straight teeth.

"Let me guess. Bay of Pigs?"

The smile wavered. Audrey opened her mouth to nail him again, when someone tapped her on the shoulder. She turned on her barstool. Henry Toledo.

"Sylvia, please come home. You've got to come home. The children cry for you. Give up this empty life. You can't keep running."

The blond man watched with wide eyes. Audrey hid her grin behind her little Japanese parasol. "Joseph, go away. I need space. I'm finding myself. Find a sitter for the little rascals. Get your mother."

"Mother's dead. Her funeral is next Wednesday. You must attend." Manning seemed to notice the young man for the first time. "Sylvia and Mother were very close," he said to him. To Audrey he said, "Is this someone I should know?"

The blond got off his bar stool, making a big show of taking his jacket off, all shoulders and biceps. Manning lounged on the bar, facing Audrey and the young man. His raw silk jacket hung open, the dark metallic butt of a Glock peeking out. The automatic they'd taken from Andres, Audrey realized. She wondered how he managed to smuggle it into and out of airports.

The young man put his drink and a twenty on the bar and wandered away. Actually, he wandered very fast.

Manning and Audrey smiled at each other. "You again," Audrey said. "About time. Where in hell have you been?" She shook blond hair out of her eyes with a quick gesture that Manning liked.

"You look nice in a tan," Manning said with a smile

"Nice? 'Nice' is for your grandmother's hairdo."

"I mean. . . beautiful." Manning hoisted himself onto a wobbly stool next to her.

Audrey nodded, pleased. "What are you doing here? Are you on this cruise?"

"No, no, I'm not." Manning shook his head, no longer smiling. "Neither are you. You're jumping ship. Where are your things?"

"On the ship, of course. We've got three more days." Suddenly Audrey wanted very badly to finish the cruise. With Henry on board, it would be fun.

"A lot has happened," said Manning, thinking of Adam. "You'll have to get them. Your clothes. Where is the ship?"

"Anchored, offshore. Near a town not far from here."

"Is there a boat to the ship?"

"Every hour," said Audrey. His tone sobered her. "Where are we going?"

Manning took a deep breath. "Remember that 'perfectly reasonable explanation' I promised you about my birth dates? Here it comes. He held up her drink. Can I freshen this? You'll probably need it."

Audrey opened her mouth to speak. Closed it. Opened it again. Finally, "I don't believe it!"

"I suppose it's difficult to imagine all at once," Manning said. His words sounded familiar. Where had he heard them? He remembered: Isaac Talmud had said almost the same thing to his at his club, the Stuyvesant Club.

Audrey kicked seawater with her bare feet. They had their shoes off and were walking along the wide sandy beach in front of the hotel. They had it to themselves in the dark. Manning had been talking for an hour.

She gave him a long look. "What a wild story."

"No kidding. I have trouble believing it myself."

"Why, Henry. . . Manning? You're impersonating a dead man. . . you've stolen his estate. Lied to the IRS. . . to me. Illegal, immoral acts." She dropped her eyes. "Why?"

Manning couldn't look at her either. "Why? Why does a man leap from the Brooklyn Bridge? Last month a Wall

Street stockbroker held up a bank two blocks from his office. Cops had him before he got to his car. Know what he said? 'I don't care.' That's me. Manning Crenshaw, Eagle Scout, working hard, thinking hard for thirty-nine years. Dressing for success. Result? No wife, no job, no money, no prospects. Then, here's a winning lottery ticket, just lying there. I pick it up. Why? Why not? Toledo wasn't using his life any more, and I had used up Manning Crenshaw's. I wasn't thinking illegal or immoral. I wasn't thinking at all."

"But later? All those attempts on your life. . ."

"Later, when reality started crowding me, I could have run. Just cut and run, left it all behind, should have. But, God help me, I was hooked. I had cheated death three times. I had handled Andres. . ."

"We did."

"We did. I was fireproof. Toledo had all that money lying around, why not stay just long enough to scoop it up? So I endangered you, killed Adam. . ."

"Now? How about now?"

Manning looked out at the dark water. "Now I'll find the men who killed Adam and kill them. All of 'em. I want to run the table."

They walked on. White sand crabs skittered across their path into sand castle mounds next to borrows in the sand. Normally they would have given Audrey the creeps; tonight they seemed part of the scene. "Manning Crenshaw," she said. What kind of a name is that?"

"Family name," said Manning. "Manning was Grandma's maiden name. Dad got it too. I'm a Junior."

"So do I call you Manning or Henry?"

"Anything but Manny. Henry, I guess. It's who I am, now."

Audrey wrinkled her nose. "You can go to jail being Henry."

"I can get killed being Henry. I finally got that through my thick noodle when my brother got killed. . ." Manning found he couldn't speak.

Audrey stopped walking and faced him, looking up with those big eyes. "Henry. . . Manning, look. I'm so sorry about Allen."

"Allen?"

"Your brother." She took both his hands.

"Adam. Thanks." But he could tell she meant it.

They held hands for a long minute. Neither wanted to let go. Finally they did, with sidelong glances at each other.

"Are you still fireproof?"

Manning smiled and shook his head. "I can't even work the safety latch on a handgun. No, I'm working with someone. Maybe I won't have to get anywhere near Adam's killers. If they get what's coming to them, that's enough."

"And me?"

Manning looked at her, small and vulnerable in the moonlight. "That's why I'm here, to pull you out, get you someplace safe. This is too dangerous for you."

"Too dangerous? No one looks at cruise ships, you said so yourself."

Manning waved his hands. "That's no good any more. They'll be looking. I screwed up." He glanced over. "You're too vulnerable, too beautiful to . . ." He stopped.

Say some more, Audrey thought. Impulsively she asked, "Beautiful?" She stopped walking, amazed at herself. Was the rum still talking?

Manning stopped as well, facing her. "Are you kidding? Yes, you're beautiful. I'm no good with good looking women."

Audrey cocked her head. "You? All that money? All that charm?"

"Haven't you been listening? That's another guy named Toledo. I'm just walking around with his American Express card for a while."

Audrey took his hand again, and his pulse picked up speed. "It's you I'm talkin' about, Manning Crenshaw. I'm not talking about convertibles and penthouses. I'm looking at a man who smacks down assassins and leaps clear of racing motorcars."

"You're looking at a fraud, someone playing 'Who am I?' For money. Who stole a dead man's life. Who talked his little brother dead for more sacks of money."

"You're too tough on yourself."

"Ellen didn't think so." It was the first time Manning had mentioned his wife.

"Why did your wife walk out?" Audrey asked like she really wanted to know.

Manning looked up and down the beach as if he expected to find Ellen in the shadows. "She and I just stopped talking. Whose fault was that? Mine, I guess. Too much career, too much TV, even too much in-laws." He looked around again. "On the other hand, she didn't just jump into my BMW with our next door neighbor. She went looking for him, or someone like him. She could have come to me, talked about it, suggested counseling."

"Would you have gone?"

"I don't think so. There were reasons, good ones, why she drove off to Florida. I was self-absorbed, indifferent." Manning couldn't look at her. "Look, I'm no saint. I've made my bed. I'll lie in it. You need to think about your own life. . . getting back. I'll get you there. It's what you want."

Audrey pictured her IRS cubicle with Post-It notes stuck to her desktop computer. "I don't know what I want. I'm in a dream. I'm a tax auditor. I get off on balance sheets. Audrey the Perfectionist. I live a cubicle existence. I work in a cubicle, sleep in a cubicle; even my Toyota looks like a cubicle. My big scene is a musical at the Kennedy Center. Here I am on a beach in Hawaii with a tough guy with two names."

She focused on the quiet man in front of her. "I'm Alice, you know? And you're the white rabbit. You keep taking my hand and leading me somewhere way, way away from my little cubicles. You're rich, you're a hundred, you drive a Mercedes. We're being hunted down by we don't know who, they want to kill us, we don't know why. This is not me. I've got a tidy little job, a 401K, car payments. The white rabbit takes my hand, I go into a samba step, I dance away from all that. I phone my boss, tell him to keep a package for me so we can blackmail a killer. Tell him, don't phone the police. Did he phone the police? Is the FBI looking for me? Is my face on milk cartons? Is my mother worried about me? No, 'course not, she's a hostage herself!"

Manning took her hand again. "I don't think she's in danger. I think I can get her out. You don't have to be Alice. You can be Audrey again. I'm taking you to Honolulu, to a safe place. A hotel. Then I'm going to see a guy. . . Isaac Talmud. He's involved with your mother's disappearance, with this whole mess, in some way. James Greenway, they're associates. Now wait. . ." Audrey had spun on him angrily. "Just wait. Okay, they frightened you to death. Talmud's got something to hide, I don't know what. I've talked to him. On the phone, after Adam died. He thinks we'll work together, but I've got other ideas. I'm gonna find out what he knows—about Adam's killers and about your mom. She's safe, I think."

"You think."

"Yes. He says so. I'll see him day after tomorrow. He'll give your mother back."

"Give Mama back? What is she, a videocassette? He's giving back what he had no business taking. Henry. . . Manning, I don't want you to see Greenway. . . damn it, Talmud! Everyone has two names. Even me!"

She held her head in both hands. "This is not fun. It's a series of near-death experiences. This guy Talmud isn't on your side. He's evil. You told me before you don't trust him."

Manning was composing his words while she talked. "I don't. I called him, talked to him on the phone, to find out where he is. He's here."

Audrey looked around in the dark. "Here? On Maui?"

"No, Honolulu. We're meeting day after tomorrow at a private club, golf club or something. I'll figure out how to get the jump on him, force him to tell me. . ."

Audrey snorted. "Here's a guy, hires platoons of killers to put us down. He's not gonna be anywhere near that meeting. You'll wind up toast, Manning."

Audrey, he's all I got. I'm going to force him to talk to me. I'm betting he can lead me to my brother's killers. To your mother."

"How do you know he isn't behind Adam's death?"

"Maybe. I don't know. If he is, I'll get it out of him."

"You'll get it out of him? These guys are killers. His buddy Greenway squashed me like a cockroach."

"Okay, it's a long shot. Nothing is perfect. I'm not. I got my brother killed. This guy knows things. He can lead me to the killers. You get your mother back. Maybe I pull this off, maybe I don't. Maybe I die trying."

Another shake of her head. "What do I do, wait outside in the getaway car?"

"You're nowhere near. You're somewhere safe, starting tonight."

"I am safe. I'm on a cruise."

Manning stooped and scooped some sand, threw it into the sea. "When I was talking to him, your name came up. Talmud asked where you were. I screwed up. . . without thinking, I said that you were on a cruise ship."

It was Audrey's turn to stop walking. "See what I mean? You're gonna out-maneuver, out-think this guy, and you blurt out something like that?" Shaking her head. "Anyway, who's to say I'm in any more danger than before?

There are hundreds of cruise ships."

"These guys are good," Manning said. "When you went on board, they took your photo, right? If they've got access to that file, they've got you." He took her arm. "Audrey, I could put the screws to you to make you come. You have no money. I'm not forcing you. I'm asking."

They reached a pile of black lava rocks at the end of the beach. Audrey bent to touch them. Long seaweed strayed from the lava like green hair in the sea foam. She had had a cellophane hula skirt the color of the seaweed in a play in third grade. She had been a hula girl. She remembered looking in the mirror in the dressing room at school and wondering if she would ever go to Hawaii. When she became a teenager she still wondered if she would get there, only then she wondered about romance, about a man. Someone with gray hair and a long nose, she wondered now. Who owned a red convertible and a Portuguese mandolin. Who couldn't work the safety on a handgun.

"I'll come," she said.

But first she had to pack. Her ship was anchored off of the little seaport town of Lahaina. Manning walked her to the waterfront where she caught a water taxi. "Check out of the cruise," he told her on the way. "Something came up. Somebody's sick. Do that before you pack. When you come back down your bill will be ready." They reached the small boat landing. "Pay cash," Manning said. He handed her a wad. Audrey took the money and gave him a kiss. An elderly couple in the boat looked on disapprovingly. A kiss after an exchange of cash—that did look bad, Manning thought. He gave them a wink, watching Audrey climb on board with her blond hair bobbing. The boat took off. Manning touched his fingers to his lips.

An hour later she was back with a roll-on bag and a big straw handbag that said "St. Thomas, Virgin Islands." She was flushed, smiling. Manning thought she looked spectacular.

They looked around for a cab. Three taxis were parked at the end of a long pier-side building 50 yards away. "Stay with the bags," Manning said. "I'll bring the cab." He walked down the empty street, his mind full of his meeting with Talmud. How could he get the drop on him? They were to meet in Honolulu, in the lobby of some hotel. Mona? Mauna? Maybe if he came early—cased the situation, could figure out a way to steer Talmud away, into a private room. . . Glancing back, he saw Audrey talking to two men, one tall, thin, distinguished looking, the other much younger, blond hair. He walked on, irritated. He's paying for one cruise after another, and Audrey can't wait to get cozy with the passenger list. That good-looking guy at the outside bar made a cameo appearance in his mind. Manning shook his head and smiled. I'm pretty far gone if I'm gonna get green-eyed every time Audrey talks to a man.

He stuck his head into the first cab he came to. "Can you take my wife and me to the airport?"

"Sure thing." The driver was Asian, maybe Chinese

or Malay.

Manning opened the passenger door, looking back down the street. The blond kid had Audrey by the arm now, with the tall man on her other side. They were walking away from the pier, Audrey pulling back. Manning realized that she was resisting. The two men were dragging her!

Manning jumped into the taxi. "Get down there, fast," he yelled at the driver. "Those guys are taking my. . . my wife!"

The cabbie looked over his shoulder with wide eyes. "I cannot get involved, sir."

Cursing, Manning flung himself from the cab, door swinging. He sprinted down the road. The two men had the rear door of a dark SUV open, were pushing Audrey inside.

Manning ran all-out, gulping for air. Tourists on the pier turned to watch him. "Stop them!" Pointing. "They're taking my wife!"

Audrey looked his way. The blond shoved her inside the car, slamming the door.

Manning had his Glock out now, still sprinting. The blond man climbed into the passenger side, and the SUV started rolling. Manning pointed the gun at the car, which made a sweeping U-turn and sped away. Couldn't shoot, might hit Audrey. Hell, he might hit anyone—he couldn't shoot. He watched the van drive down the pier.

He looked around. Everyone on the pier was looking at the Glock. "Police," he said.

A fat man showed him a cell phone. "Want to call for

backup?"

"I'll phone from my patrol car," Manning said. He watched the SUV slow, make a wide turn, and head back up the pier toward him. What was going on? The car got closer. He could make out the passenger pointing—at him.

They'd recognized him. They were after him, too!

Panicked, Manning looked around. Nowhere to run. He started a sprint down the street, away from the vehicle. When he looked around, lungs bursting, the SUV was getting really, really close. Oh, God! He sprinted right, into a crowded space between two tourist stores, now closed for the night.

He could hear the SUV's tires squeak as it turned down an alley between stores. When he reached the open lane on the far side of the buildings, the black van was already turning into him. He spun on his heel and ran back between the buildings again. He ran on, eyes closed, praying. When he opened his eyes again, he couldn't believe what he saw. He was back pier-side again, and a cop car cruised slowly toward him. The real police had arrived.

Quickly he put his gun in the waistband at the small of his back and slowed to a walk. He waved at the police car, then walked up to the window. The policeman rolled his window down. He was a big native guy: Hawaiian or maybe Samoan.

"Officer, can you help me? I need a cab."

The cop's eyes narrowed. "Why you running, mister?"

Manning thought fast. "My wife. . . she's sick. I've got

to get her to a hospital."

"Where is she."

"Back there." Manning gestured vaguely toward the boat landing. "She's really sick." He realized that he was looking directly at the SUV. He straightened and pointed directly at the car. Let them chew on that.

The cop looked concerned. "Bring her in. I'll take you folks to the hospital."

Now what? "She's. . . bleeding. I don't want to get your car bloody. Can you just drive me to a taxi?"

The cop nodded, clearly not anxious to get blood on his seats either. "Cabs up the road, there. Get in." Manning climbed in, and the cop backed down the street toward the cabstand.

Manning thanked the policeman and got into a cab. He looked out the taxi window. The SUV was nowhere in sight.

Manning locked the door to his hotel room, an el-cheapo four or five blocks back from the airport. He poured himself a straight vodka in the bathroom's plastic cup. Then he took out the Glock that he had taken from Andres Chamineaux. It was gun-metal gray, compact, sleek. It looked expensive, and it looked like it would kill people efficiently. The barrel was threaded to receive its silencer, but Manning had lost the silencer somewhere.

He sat on the edge of his hotel room bed holding the gun in both hands, turning it over and over. He wasn't sure that he wanted anything to do with it. He sipped vodka.

In the end he took a soft rag and light machine oil that he had purchased from a sewing machine retail store two days earlier and cleaned the weapon. Then he carefully took it apart, cleaning the interior with a Q-tip from the bathroom. He didn't have a bore brush, so he pushed his oiled rag through the barrel with a ballpoint pen the hotel provided. He fiddled with it until he understood how to load and eject the clip and how to jack a shell into the chamber. Oh, yes, and how to work the safety. Thinking all the time: cleaning this damned thing ain't the same as firing it at someone.

He phoned Aloha Airlines to check the time of his flight to Honolulu—two hours away—and to cancel Audrey's seat. He packed his suitcase, folding the Glock into one of the hotel's bath towels. Before he left the room he splashed water on his face in the bath to clear the vodka.

He looked carefully at his face in the mirror. He was becoming a third person.

chapter 14

"I'll Tell You A Story. Shall I?"

Downtown Honolulu was different from most cities. Greener, colorful, with palm trees and bright sunshine under a China-blue sky. Colorful people too, in reds and blues, warm-weather clothes, who walked with a bounce. They smiled a lot. I'd smile too if I lived here, Manning thought.

He found what he was looking for. The Public Reference Room rested comfortably in Room 123 of the Department of Land and Natural Resources' Bureau of Conveyances section of the modern concrete Kalani Moku building. "Kalani Moku, island of heaven," said the building's custodian, who looked old enough and Hawaiian enough to have greeted Captain Cook in 1778.

Room 123 housed a half-dozen desktops and large ledgers that lined the walls. File cabinets promised to give up lots more ledgers. Three other patrons who looked like realtors or mortgage agents doing their property-owner homework worked a line of computers. Manning found a little gray Japanese-American lady holding down a steel desk in the center of the room.

"I'm researching a property here on Oahu," he told her. "Is there a charge?"

“No charge.” The woman smiled. “Pick a computer. You can search by name of registered property owner.”

Fine. “Search by name” was what he wanted. Manning sat at a vacant desktop.

He searched the index for Isaac Talmud with no success. Tried Talmud only—still no hits. Not on the computer, not in the dusty books. Manning scanned a tax record at random, flipping pages. It was like reading the phone book. After two hours he knew nothing more than when he started.

Nuts. This is nuts. He found a coffee machine down the hall and paid a buck for a warm, bitter liquid that was either sour coffee or sweetened motor oil . He drank it anyway, staring at the computer. “Surname,” the entry field asked. Manning went back in his mind to the afternoon in Manhattan when a TransAm had almost made a grease-spot of him on Fifth Avenue. Four girls, jumping rope, chanting a little-girl song:

Surname, dear sir
Have I none,
Use my first name
I’ve got one.

Talmud had told him, in the apartment in Westwood, “My real name is Isaac. Call me that.”

Manning typed Isaac into the given name field and hit enter.

Three hits:

Isaac Kealoha Kawahakui
Isaac Benjamin Trust
Isaac and Maria Joseph

Manning dismissed Mr. Kawahakui as too Hawaiian to be of interest. He opened Isaac and Maria Joseph and read about a married couple who purchased a leasehold condo in Honolulu in 1987 and sold out three years later.

The Isaac Benjamin Trust was more promising. It was listed in tax records as owner of record of a plot of land on Kawailoa Beach on the North Shore of Oahu. Current appraised value: eight-point-seven million. Manning scrolled backwards. The Benjamin Trust was still listed as property owner at the beginning of computer records in 1976.

He wrote the street address and tax key in his notebook and walked to his friend the file clerk. He showed her the tax key number. "Can you help me find earlier records on this property?"

The woman studied the numbers through high-powered spectacles for a long time. "The hard-copy records are sometimes by tax key, sometimes by name of grantor or grantee of property transfer," she said. She waved her arm at the bank of ledgers lining the walls. "Try look."

Manning "tried look." After an hour he gave up. Small needle, very big haystack. He wandered around the room, searching for the oldest record available. In the upper left of the back wall he found a clothbound volume labeled "Lessor, Oahu, 1845. He opened it at random.

Manning found the Japanese lady again and pointed

to an entry. "This transfer of property on December 29, 1857. Grantor is "Bishop, B. Pauahi and hus. What can you tell me about that?"

The woman looked at the ledger entry. "Bernice Pauahi Bishop was the last of the royal line of Hawaiian kings. Her "hus," husband was Charles Bishop. Pauahi inherited the royal lands of the kingdom—thousands of acres. In fact, Bishop Estate, now called Kamehameha Schools Trust, is still the largest landowner in the state." The woman pointed to the entry line. "This transaction transferred two acres of land from Pauahi to the gentleman in question. In 1857. Long time ago."

"Long time ago," Manning agreed, looking at the name of the grantee: Isaac Benjamin.

Asleep, he looked young, no more than 30. Manning wondered how old he really was.

Isaac Talmud stirred, turned his head on his pillow. He opened one eye, focused, blinked both eyes awake. Manning saw how he transitioned immediately from deep sleep to full awareness like a cat. Like a big cat; like a panther.

Pono Wong, his bodyguard, all 300 pounds of him, stood over him in the darkened room, wearing an anguished expression on his wide, flat face. The cause of Pono's angst was Manning Crenshaw, who stood by the bed as well, the dark metal Glock dangling from his right hand.

"Sorry, boss," Pono whispered in a soft rumble. "He just came up from the beach. Nothing I could do."

"S' all right." Talmud sat up in bed, black pajama bottoms and a tanned chest. "I was dreaming," he said to Pono. "Of my wife. A happy dream." To Manning he said, "Weren't we to meet tomorrow?"

"I like to be early."

"Clearly." Isaac padded to the window and pulled the long curtains open to a brilliant blue sky. "May my man leave now?"

"How do I know he won't come back with the rest of the offensive line?"

"I'll tell him not to." Isaac gestured to Pono, who nodded.

"And if he does anyway?"

"You can shoot me with your shiny gun. Isn't that your intent anyway?"

"Maybe." Manning looked down at the pistol in his hand. "Depends on what you have to tell me."

"Go downstairs, Pono," Isaac told his servant. "Have Rosella bring some coffee and juice to the lanai."

Pono looked at Manning, who didn't say anything. The big man left, still looking unhappy.

"Did you have trouble breaking and entering?" Isaac asked.

"None. I walked up from the beach. Your man-mountain. . ."

"Pono. Pono Wong."

". . . Pono was adjusting lawn sprinklers." Manning shook his head. "I saw a standard security system—video cameras. Is that it?"

"I did away with heroic measures to preserve my life

long ago," Isaac said. "I no longer care." He shrugged into a cotton shirt and crossed the room.

"What kind of name is Pono Wong," Manning asked.

"Part Hawaiian—Pono. Part Chinese—Wong." Isaac opened a French door to an outside balcony.

"He looks mostly muscle mass." Manning followed Isaac outside with the Glock still in his hand. The balcony overlooked an impossibly lovely Pacific Ocean in dark and light blues. Isaac's estate was on a peninsula composed of green grass and coconut palms above flat, black lava rock. Isaac sat at a glass coffee table and Manning sat across.

"Why did you come early?" Isaac asked.

"If I had come on time, you would have killed me."

"That was not my intent."

"Your intent? You've tried to kill me three times. You killed my brother. Now you kidnap Audrey Cobb." Manning watched Talmud's eyes widen. Was he acting? "I phoned you, remember? Asked for your help. 'I'll do what I can,' you said. I was coming empty-handed, without this gun. Two goons took Audrey, Talmud. Snatched her at her cruise ship. Who knew she was on a cruise? Only three people. Audrey, me. . . and you, you weasel."

"And one other," Talmud said, more to himself.

Manning stuck his pistol into Talmud's face. "I want her back. Now!"

Isaac took the measure of the man sitting across from him. This wasn't the same man he had ragged at the Stuyvesant Club. That man was unsure, probing for answers. This one had quiet moves and hard eyes. Isaac shrugged. "My friend, I know nothing about this. Believe it or not."

Manning smiled, but with just one side of his mouth. "I'll take the 'not' option." He waved his automatic at Isaac. "I feel. . . I don't know how I feel. You're one of those who killed my brother. Maybe just you. Maybe not with a gun, probably not. Maybe with a phone call, which is worse." Manning looked out to the sea. "I can hardly bear to look at you, you scum!" He turned again toward Talmud, pointing. "You stand here with your Hawaiian tan, on your estate, with your servants, with your private club. . ."

Movement behind him. Manning turned, raising the Glock. A young Filipina stood with a tray carrying a silver coffee pot and pitcher of orange juice, with breakfast rolls, looking terrified.

"It's all right, Rosella," Isaac said. "Leave the tray. Go on." The girl set up cups and glasses on a bamboo table and left, her eyes fixed on Manning's gun.

Isaac sat down. "Coffee? It will do you good."

"I don't want your goddamned coffee. This isn't a morning drop-by. I'm here to kill you!"

"So you keep saying. I don't feel threatened, except for the danger that your pistola, there, will get away from you and murder me by accident. You don't look like a man who has done much shooting."

Manning said nothing. He had never fired a gun in his life.

Talmud poured a cup for himself. He looked up. "I first learned of the death of your brother from you, when you phoned."

"No."

"It's true. And I know nothing of an abduction of Miss Cobb, also true."

"What's true is that you have tried over and over to kill me, kill Audrey Cobb. You took her mother. . ."

Shaking his head, Isaac said, "I tried to reach an agreement with you at dinner. At the Stuyvesant Club. I told you then, work with me or take your chances. You refused."

"I refuse, you kill me? That how it goes?" Manning's voice rose. He looked out from the lanai banister again. The sea had turned from deep blue to green. Five white boats dotted the horizon. Weekend fishermen. Manning remembered that it was Sunday. Several dozen young men and boys danced an elegant dance on head-high waves.

"These are the best surfers in the world," Isaac said unnecessarily. A black bird hung high in the air, with bent wings like a pterodactyl, to seaward. Isaac noticed Manning watching. "It's a frigate bird. The Hawaiians call it an iwa. . . 'ee-vah.'"

"I'm not here for a lesson in Hawaiiana," Manning said. "What do you want?"

"Want? You phoned me. I didn't phone you."

Manning pointed with his gun. "You set me up. I was gonna show up tomorrow at some hotel in Honolulu, and who knows who would meet me? Someone hired to kill me. Again."

"We don't want to kill you. We want your silence," Isaac answered. He smiled and opened his palms. Such a small thing to ask.

"What's your game?" Manning asked.

"Game?"

"Did you kill my brother?"

"I don't know myself how he died," Isaac said. "Adam? Is that his name?"

"That was his name."

"I'm sorry." Isaac rubbed his eyes with his thumb and index finger. "I'm so sorry. And, I'm sorry to say I do know about the other attempts on your lives. What I know, I'll tell you. You have my word."

"Your word. I had that before. Your word as a gentleman, right? Some gentleman killed Adam. Some gentleman took the three million he was carrying."

Isaac blinked his eyes. "Three million?" He drank more coffee and set his cup down, then steepled his hands together, almost in prayer, and touched them to his lips. "It doesn't have to be like this," he said. "We can work this out. Together."

"Together." Manning repeated the word. "Let me get this straight. After weeks of trying to murder me. . . us. . . now you're on my side?"

"More or less, yes."

"And this isn't just a trick to get out from under this cannon?" Manning waved his gun around a little, maybe to remind both of them that it was still there. "All right, explain that one."

Isaac poured orange juice for them both. Manning shook his head. A fat cinnamon cat with one bent ear wandered out from the bedroom and stood hopefully with front paws on a chair seat, begging food. Isaac ignored him, but the cat was patient. His plump haunches testified to his skill as a mendicant.

Isaac said, "It's not so easy. To explain, I'll have to tell you a story. It's a long story, I'm afraid. And an old one. All the best stories are old ones."

Manning shook his head again. All this talk. He was losing the anger, the resolve that he had when he entered Isaac's bedroom. He leveled the gun. "It was you, and maybe others too, but I won't find their names from you. I'll find them another way, long after you have cooled and stiffened."

Isaac looked up, unafraid, it seemed. "Don't do something you will regret."

"I already regret it."

Isaac looked his visitor up and down. "I've become, over a long time, very good at reading people. You're a brave man, Manning Crenshaw. Resourceful. You're not a killer."

Manning blinked at the mention of his name. "How about you. Are you a killer?"

Isaac considered the question. "I suppose I am. Odd. I never considered myself one." He relented and broke a croissant for the cat, then put both hands flat on the table and looked up. "I'm not sure it makes a difference."

"The difference is, I want to kill you," Manning said.

Isaac waved his orange juice glass in a circle. He wore a tired smile. "You're in good company. You are not the first to want that. Maybe not even number one-hundred."

Manning pointed his gun. "Maybe the last."

Isaac kept his worn-out smile. "Maybe, yes. You'd be

surprised to learn how little that matters to me." He set his juice glass down. "Now then. You have a choice, Mr. Crenshaw. Shoot me now, or listen to my story, and then shoot me. Or not." He rose without waiting for a reply. "Come. I'll show you some things, and then tell my tale."

Isaac led Manning downstairs into a big room decorated in an Iberian countryside motif, with great stone squares on the floor and white plaster walls under dark wood beams. A sea-turtle shell hung shiny-bright on the wall along with several bright oils by an artist Manning recognized but couldn't name. Sunlight and cool sea air washed in through open windows on two sides. Isaac lifted a bottle of red wine and inserted a corkscrew. "This is better. A little more private. Can I interest you. . ."

Manning eyed the wine. He could use a jolt. But he shook his head. "No wine, no coffee, no social chatter. All that is B.S., just like your invitation here. When you couldn't kill me in New York, you fed me some crap on the phone to get me here so you could finish the job."

Isaac worked the corkscrew. "That's not how it works."

"Oh? How does it work?

"You'll understand better when you hear what I have to say. It's. . . well, it's hard to take."

"Hard to take?"

Isaac popped the cork from the bottle in his hand and set the wine aside. "We'll just let that breath. A bit early anyway." He turned toward Manning. "Some people would find my story hard to believe. Let's say you believe it. Maybe we can work together."

Manning shook his head. "I don't care how good your story is. It's not gonna work. I just don't trust you. Don't know when you'll turn around and kill me."

"If."

"When. You've tried over and over. Now we're gonna work together? Why this change of heart? Why should we?"

"Because you need me. We need each other."

"Why?"

"First the story. You'll see."

"And if I don't? Swallow your story?"

Isaac spread his hands. "Why, then you can kill me." He stood and walked to a dark wooden chest bound by two black iron hoops. Kneeling, he opened it with an old-fashioned metal key that had been hidden behind it. He reached in and pulled out what appeared to be a soldier's helmet from the Middle Ages, tarnished by the centuries. Manning turned it in his hands. The helmet was small, almost too small for someone's head. The metal was hand-hewn, uneven, very thin. Don Quixote could have worn it in Man of La Mancha.

Next, Isaac held up an old sword with a straight, narrow blade and basket hilt. It, too, was dark with age. He swung and thrust it like a fencer. He looked like he knew what he was doing.

"Are these genuine?" asked Manning.

Isaac's eyes gleamed. "They're mine."

"Meaning what? You bought them somewhere? Inherited?"

"Meaning I wore them." Isaac put on the helmet,

which fit despite its small appearance. He struck a pose with the sword in his right hand, pointing down to his bare feet. "You said once that you were open to new concepts. We'll see if that's true. I'll tell you a story."

"Is it a history lesson?" asked Manning. "You look like Vasco de Gama."

"Not bad," grinned Isaac. "Close. Miss Cobb, IRS ferret, was after your scalp in New York. You kept changing your age. Well, she's right. You're older than you look. She was working on a hundred. Try five hundred."

Manning sat in silence. Finally he asked, "Five hundred years?"

Isaac put aside the sword and helmet. He found his bottle of red wine and picked up two glasses.

"Fill your glass," said Isaac, "and I'll tell you a story. Shall I?"

Manning set the wine glass on the table in front of him, empty, and folded his gun in his lap. "Tell me a story," he said.

chapter 15

The Fountain

Our memories are strange things (said Isaac). As I cast back over the years, the centuries, my clearest pictures are of the La Tierra Nova. It was our name for the New World. Much of the rest. . . friends, events, places I've lived. . . even the women, the wives. . . are dim, now. Perhaps God makes our poor brains to hold just so much. Perhaps that's just as well.

The expedition, now, it's like last week. I can see the rain forest. . . tall mangroves with Spanish moss hanging like drapery, our mules, before we ate them, burdened with stores bigger than they were. Paco, our cook, laughing and spitting into the rabbit stew, the campfires at night, the dark swamp that could swallow a man and his horse.

And. . . the heat. I remember that most of all, clinging like a wet nightdress, pressing us into the mud. We knew brutal days in Espana, too, when the sun turned the fields to iron, so that a plow blade could not cut a furrow. But nights in Cadiz brought pure cool air from the sea and a chill toward morning, so that a man could pull a blanket up and fall asleep. But the wet heat of the expedition nagged night and day like a sour wife. Brown mold grew on cook pots and armor. Leather mildewed and stank.

Gunpowder had to be spread to dry in the sun. The soldiers of the column picked leeches from each other each evening like monkeys.

I remember also how young we were. We grumbled, but we also laughed. Paco would call to us over the cook stove, "And why aren't we safe in our beds at home, bellies full of good roast beef? Will someone tell me, please? Why are we marching through this muck? El Jefe promises gold and Indian slaves. How much will we see after His Highness El Rey, may he live forever, and El Jefe, God bless his name, take their rightful share?"

"Gold or slaves, what's the difference?" we would laugh back. "None of us will find either."

We were a hard wrought lot. Conquistadors. . . you need to understand what the term meant in the 16th Century. We came from the lowest, most unfortunate caste of Spain. Illiterate, illegitimate, ill conceived. No money, no professions, no prospects. We hovered over the taverns and brothels of Cadiz like fruit flies, poking into the refuse heaps, sleeping in alleyways, and feeding off of our neighbors and each other.

The stories of La Tierra Nova and of Cristobal Colon came to us like a fresh sea breeze. Tales of a new land full of oro and plata and pearls to be picked from the ground like berries. Young girls who laughed and sang freely, not like the cloistered and guarded women of Spain.

Then one day a caballero, a knight, stood in leather and iron in the town square. There were strands of gray in the black tapestry of his beard, and his face was tanned like a burro's from a thousand suns, but he had a man's bearing. Don Juan Ponce, the whispers said. A warrior who had fought against the Moors and a conquistador from the new world. Juan Ponce, from the city of Leon. . . Ponce de Leon.

He spoke with the lisp of Castile but his story was simple and direct. Our king had commissioned him as governor of a new island across the sea, discovered by him. . . the Island of Bimini. Ponce was raising an expedition to colonize it. He had ships. He had weapons and armor and horses. He lacked only men with stout hearts. Who would go?

We stood spitting into rain puddles and talking among ourselves, but we didn't talk long. Gold, land, but mostly. . . opportunity! We were Spaniards. For all of our diseases, black teeth, body lice, sins and guilt, the blood of Iberia flowed through our veins. To others it was the blood of Visigoths, Jews, and Moors. . . to us it was the pure blood of a people chosen by God. We dreamed of a life befitting that birthright.

What did we have to lose? Laughing, my comrades stood in line to mark an X or a circle on a parchment full of words that meant nothing. The caballero watched as I signed with my name. Isaac, from the Jewish faith of my fathers. Santana, because my father had chosen a Catholic baptism over the gentle mercies of the Inquisition. "Santana" sounded better to my Christian brothers than "Cohen."

"You are educated," accused El Jefe. I confessed my sin and was commissioned a lieutenant of the expedition on the spot.

Once at sea, we learned something of life. Our tiny caravel, Santa Margarita, tossed like a wood chip in the Atlantic swells. We poor landsmen hung like laundry along the life lines, retching our stomach lining out and praying to a merciful God to sink us like stones in a peaceful death in the dark sea.

After a week God heard our prayers. The sea calmed, and we learned to ride the swells as a man rides a stallion. We arose on the seventh day at sea as hungry as black bears and learned something more of life. The ship's sailors explained to us, grinning, that ships only carry so many provisions. And who needed the first meal of stale hard tack and the first ladle of warm, bitter water? The men who trimmed the sails and steered the ship, that's who. We poor soldiers went on half-rations. Five days later water was reduced to one cup per man at noon. The grumbling began.

I sat alone on the ship's stern, two weeks at sea and two hours after the sun had set into a cloudy horizon ahead of the ship's bow. Don Juan squatted next to me. We sat in the dark with our legs dangling over the ship's rudder like schoolboys, rolling with the swells. The only sounds were the infrequent flap of a sail and the gurgle of the sea.

Don Juan broke the silence. "To whom were you talking just now?"

"To God, Jefe. The Lord of the Heavens and I were having a conversation. He was mostly listening."

"Ah," said Don Juan, then, "the Rosary?"

I considered my answer. We were far from the reach of our Mother the Church. "The Rosary is for the true

Catholic," I said. "I am a devout follower of our holy father, of course, but from my birth, and for four thousand years before that, I am a Jew. We Jews speak directly to Jehovah without the need of the litany of the beads."

"A Jew." Don Juan turned and considered me. "I should have known. A nose like that grows only north of the Nile and west of the Jordan. Tell me, what do you say to your Jewish God on the deck of a Spanish ship in the middle of the vast sea?"

"I am starving, thirsty, filthy, and occasionally seasick," I said. "Jewish law forbids me to complain to Jehovah. The correct response, apparently, is praise. But nothing in the Torah prohibits asking Him some pointed questions. I was just asked Him about our bishop who prayed so magnificently at pier-head the day we sailed, for the success of this expedition. Latin prayers in port are fine, I tell Jehovah, but wouldn't a cow out here do our souls more good? Or, may my Hebrew ancestors forgive me, even a roasted pig? This is what God and I talk about."

Don Juan grinned at me in the starlight, then turned serious. "I'll tell you something, Isaac. God speaks to me, too, in dreams, almost every night. He tells me things."

"You have the advantage, Jefe. To me, He mostly listens. What things does he tell you?"

"He tells me that we are on a holy mission, to save the souls of the heathen in this new world. He promises blessings to you, to me. . . all of us."

I sounded a low whistle. "Blessings. I like that. See if you can get him to promise a little more on the plate in the present tense."

"It's dangerous to treat holy things with irreverence," Don Juan said.

"To me, a little humor is not irreverent. We are different, you and I."

"Not so different," said Don Juan. "We are from different worlds, but equally disenfranchised. Perhaps we both need to claim our birthrights." He leaned forward to spit into the water bubbling astern. We sat for a time in silence.

I cleared my throat. "You have spent a great number of years in El Tierra Nova, Don Juan." I wanted to keep him talking. We Jews have made our living for centuries by lifting men's thoughts like a pickpocket.

"Many decades," Ponce agreed. "I sailed with Cristobal Colon on his second voyage. Seventeen ships. Over a thousand men."

"Colon. You were. . . what? A Captain of Troop?"

"Captain? No. I sailed as a foot soldier." Ponce smiled at my surprise. "Ferdinand's war against the Moors in Spain was recently over. Colon had his pick of veteran army officers. I was a knight, a caballero, but only nineteen. Who wants a teenaged officer? I was happy to be chosen even as a common soldier." Ponce blew his cheeks full. "Nineteen. That was twenty-seven years ago."

"And what in that distant land bid you to stay so long?"

"And to return," said Ponce.

"And to return."

"You expect me to say gold. If that were all, I would be growing fat on roasted duck in Castile instead of starving along with you on this endless sea. No, the world you will see soon enough sings a lovelier song—freedom. The New World is just that. . . a new world." He pointed to the ship's wake fading into the darkness. "Back there is the old world, with its old ways. Spain gives us the tools of conquest, nothing more. Tierra Nova frees a man to be what God calls him to be."

Ponce lay down on his back with his face to the stars. "My birthright was denied me in Spain." He turned to look at me. "Your birthright is denied you, too, perhaps. You are a Jew in a Christian land, anything but one of the 'Chosen People.' I don't know how you feel. . ."

"I'll tell you how I feel," I said. "My family was forced to renounce our God, the God of Abraham, Isaac, and Jacob, at the point of a sword. Our choice was simple: conversion or exile."

Ponce nodded. Every Spaniard remembered the Edict of Exile, signed by Ferdinand in 1492, the same year Cristobal Colon was occupied discovering a new passage to China. All "unbaptized" Jews had four months to sell all that they had and leave Espana. My father had made the detestable choice. He, and I, and 50,000 other Jews had accepted a Christian baptism. My older brother and sisters had made their own choice—suicide instead.

I kicked my heels in a drumbeat on the sternpost, looking toward the Spain I was escaping. "'Freedom' is precisely why I shipped with you, Jefe. My prospects in Spain? Poor, or worse. I hope in this new land to breath again."

"Lo mismo," said Ponce. "I am the same, a highborn

bastard, the illegitimate son of Count Juan Ponce de Leon. I used to watch my father ride by, in crimson and silver. Once my mother, the daughter of a share farmer on his estate, lifted me to him, him on his horse, me perhaps six. He held me at arms length in gloved hands, smiled, and winked. That was, in total, my communication with my father, and the sum of my inheritance. You long for your Jewish heritage. I long for my birthright."

"You have had more success with your dreams, it seems to me," I said.

"Perhaps. Certainly God has smiled on me off and on. At thirteen I became the page of Pedro Nunez de Guzman, a friend of my father, learning the art of war and when to use which fork. One spring day my half-brother Rodrigo visited Guzman."

"Half-brother?"

"Same father, but he had the correct mother. No small thing when it comes to opportunity. Rodrigo was on his way to fight the Moors. King Ferdinand had commissioned him a captain of horse. When he discovered a Ponce as Guzman's squire he took me along."

"You won a reputation in that war."

Don Juan nodded. "Rodrigo and I fought side by side for two years. He saved my life, I saved his. Together we saved Ferdinand's kingdom. Rodrigo came away with titles and lands."

"I recall now," I said. "He is the Duke of Cadiz, and Marquis of. . . "

"Marquis of Zahara." Don Juan spat out the title. "And I? I 'won a reputation,' as you put it. The disadvantage of having the incorrect mother. Our sovereign bid us, we two brothers, to appear before him. Rodrigo received his honors and his land. I knelt, and Ferdinand tapped my shoulder with his blade. I arose as Don Juan Ponce de Leon, caballero and bastard. No dukedom, no lands. . . an unemployed knight, to stand and starve in his majesty's service until the next war. Do you wonder why I enlisted with Colon as common soldier?"

"I wonder how that foot soldier has a king's commission to colonize a new land."

Ponce crossed himself. "God Himself smiled on me in the New World. I fought for Ferdinand, 'Christianizing' the natives. They had no experience with war. They fell like wheat. At length I led an expedition to Borinquen—the island to which we now sail. Because of its rich gold mines, some call it Puerto Rico. In gratitude the king made me governor. I married and lived as a governor should live for two years. Then Diego Colon, the Admiral's son, came with a piece of parchment, a decree from Ferdinand. Diego was appointed governor over an island he had never seen, in place of the man who had colonized it for Spain at the risk of his life."

"The inequities of life." I was no stranger to them.

"The reality of politics. Diego's father had discovered an empire for Ferdinand, and had been sent back to Spain in chains for his troubles. His family deserved some justice. I handed over the governorship with good grace. Diego made me 'Captain of the Island.' I had a certain reputation for military success. Diego Colon had never raised a sword except to cut his wedding cake. Then I heard of an island, to the north."

"Bimini?"

"Bimini. The Indians told of it. They told of a land rich with gold and pearls, overflowing with game." Don Juan leaned toward me, his voice a whisper. "And. . . a fountain."

"Fountain?"

"A fountain with wonderful powers. Whoever drank would never grow old."

"I have heard many tales of miracles in the New World," I said carefully. "Pearls as large as apples, called by the friars 'the tears of the Virgin.' Seven golden cities. This fountain has the same wonderful ring to it."

"Isaac, listen to me. I myself heard the Indians tell of it."

"And I myself have heard my Jewish brethren extol the virtues of the Christ-child from the rack and the stocks," I said. "Torture frees the tongue remarkably."

"Ah, but this Fountain is not set in a dream-like fairyland, Isaac. These same Indians told me the way to the Fount, to Bimini. North, north of any known islands. I have been there."

"You have been to the Fountain?"

Don Juan shook his head. "No, to Bimini. I led an expedition there. Two ships were found, and eighty men. In the year of Our Lord 1512 we left Puerto Rico and sailed north.

"Our ships dropped anchor in six fathoms in a sheltered bay on Easter Sunday morning the Second of April. It was Bimini. We landed on a white sand beach beautifully set in the bright colors of hundreds of wild flowers. I called the place Pascua Florida. . . 'Flowery Easter.'

"We took Indians captive who spoke of a fountain in the land of the Calusa, a warrior tribe on the west coast. They told of a Calusa chief, Cacique Carlos, who knew of the fountain."

"Cacique?" I was puzzled by the name.

"'Cacique' is what the Spaniards in the New World call someone high born—a chief. As for 'Carlos,' who knows where he got a Spanish name? We sailed in search of him, and found him on the bank of a great river with fifty canoes filled with warriors. These were not the Indians of Borinquen or Hispaniola. They were Calusa, a fierce race. We returned to Borinquen."

"To sail again for Bimini?"

"No, to sail instead for Spain. I paid in gold for a title, Marquis de Florida, and for a thousand hectares in Padua. I had my title and land at last."

"And yet, here you are."

"And yet, here I am. Because of a vision each night for a month. Of a fountain bubbling clear and cold into a blue-green pool. And of our Lord, saying, 'The man who drinks here will retain his strength and youth. Come and drink.' Do you believe me? My wife didn't. She put her hands over her ears and hid in her closet whenever I spoke of the vision. The new king, Ferdinand's successor, never had the chance. I applied for an Adelantamiento, a commission to conquer and colonize Bimini, listing gold, furs, and slaves as tribute to the crown but omitting anything about a fountain with strange powers. The gold and slaves were enough. I was awarded the commission. I sold my land and manor to pay for this expedition. My wife and children are at her father's house, in Cordova, disgraced." He looked at me almost shyly. "Do you think that I am crazy?"

I looked up at the triangular sails in the moonlight. That intense, brave, moody cavalier could indeed have been crazy. Or, God might have talked to him in the night. I've had time in the past few centuries to consider those two alternatives. I think there's a third explanation. The disappointments of his life—Ferdinand's failure to reward his heroics against the Moors, his replacement as governor by Diego Colon—were a fire in his stomach. He looked to the Fountain for Quixotic redemption. I was to play Sancho to his Don Quixote.

We parted, finally, to find our beds. I awoke refreshed, thinking that Don Juan's sacred mission could be true. And so it seemed. A steady trade wind pushed us westward. And there on the horizon, dead ahead of the bowsprit, was land, just five weeks after we had lost sight of the Spanish coast. We landed in Borinquen the next morning.

We sailed again in February of 1521—two caravels and almost 200 men. Don Juan went straight for the spot on the western coast of Florida where he weighed anchor nine years before.

The Indians who peered at us from the forest were not Calusa. Santiago, an Indian from Hispaniola who followed de Leon, talked to them with grunts and the waving of hands. The natives told us the way to water, smiling and nodding. But the Fount? "No aqui—not here." De Leon opened their backs with the leaded whip and learned that they knew of a Fountain with magical powers further inland. We headed inland.

As we lost sight of the sea the terrain seemed designed more by Satan than by the Holy One. Mud and slime. . . insects and snakes like the plagues of Moses. And always the heat!

By the fourth week seven men had died. Five others rode the mules, too weak to walk. We slogged through marshland watching for deep holes like the one that Juanbaptiste had found the week before, slipping out of sight noiselessly in his armor. The judgment of God de Leon had intoned. Juanbaptiste was a noted blasphemer, with most of his oaths aimed at El Jefe. God's judgment perhaps, but we stepped carefully all the same.

We camped one night with no fire in the pouring rain, cursing de Leon and his visions. But we cursed softly, remembering Juanbaptiste. Around midnight the pickets brought in Sergeant Gomez and his two-man patrol, sent foraging the day before. They had a Morro family with them. "Morro," or "Moor," was our nickname for the natives of Florida. Three of them: a tall male, a much smaller woman, and a boy of about three. We sat them down in the rain while Santiago grunted with the man. Santiago stood and whispered into Gomez's ear.

"Awaken el Jefe," Gomez said.

"He needs his sleep," Captain de la Cruz replied. "He has seen Morros die before."

"This devil is different," said Gomez. "He is a Calusa. He has seen the Fountain."

The circle of soldiers became still. The Indian sat straight and strong. A single black feather parted his hair and drew down the back of his neck toward his shoulder blades.

De Leon, awakened, knelt to stare directly into the Indian's face. Neither turned his eyes. "Ask him where," de Leon said to Santiago. The Indian tossed his head.

"He will not," said Santiago.

De Leon waved his hand. Captain de la Cruz unsheathed his knife and removed a circle of flesh the size of a silver Real from the Indian's chest. The Indian looked into the distance silently.

Don Juan bent the woman's right index finger until it snapped. Still the Indian said nothing. De Leon nodded approvingly at his manhood. He pointed to the boy. De la Cruz lifted the child to his knee and put the point of his dagger under the boy's chin. The Indian spoke in a low voice, so low that Santiago had to bend into the Indian's face to hear.

"He says not a day's journey from here," said Santiago.

"We march, then, at dawn," said de Leon. He turned to where his small tent lay in the wet grass. "Feed them."

We fed them cold beans. The woman cradled her child with her fist over her broken finger, whimpering. The man lay on his back, offering his blood-caked chest to the flies.

We broke camp at dawn, full of excitement, marching in a loose scouting line with the Indian and Santiago in the lead. We marched all day, and walked after dark into a deserted village of thatched huts, muskets at the ready, pikes lowered, swords drawn.

The column stood in a circle in the center of the village, surrounding the still-warm ashes of a communal fire pit. Five minutes passed while we shuffled our feet and creaked our leather jackets. Then our prisoner began to sing in a soft, low voice. He was answered note for note by a male voice from the shadows. The duet continued for some time, echoing eerily from the surrounding cypress forest. We glanced at one another and shifted uneasily.

A man emerged from between the huts, still singing. He could have been the first Indian's twin—just as straight and proud, with black hair that draped his shoulders gleaming in the faint moonlight and with the same black feather pointed down. The two Indians gripped the other's forearm, grinning. The first Indian turned and lifted the boy. The other took the child and held him to his chest. Santiago spoke to our prisoner.

"He is presenting his son to be acknowledged," Santiago told de Leon.

"What are they?" asked de Leon. "Brothers?"

Santiago scuttled forward to ask. He cocked his head at the Indian's reply. Santiago seemed to ask again. The Indian spoke briefly. After a moment's hesitation Santiago returned to de Leon. "They are. . . relatives," he said.

"Are they brothers?"

Santiago looked down at his widespread toes. "The boy's father, the one we took prisoner, he says that the other one is a chief. His name is Cacique Carlos. He says that this man Cacique Carlos is his grandfather's grandfather."

De Leon took a step backward. Santiago's words seemed to stagger him. "Madre de Dios! Gacias a mi Dios! The Fount! The Fount!"

Ponce de Leon's manner changed as quickly as the weather changed in that land. He started a long palaver with Cacique Carlos through Santiago. Don Juan spoke low, so that we couldn't hear, and we knew nothing of the Indian grunts. Finally Carlos spoke what seemed like a full sentence. . . a long speech for him. "He wants to see the gold," translated Santiago.

Don Juan pointed to a leather bound chest among the pack mules, green with moss. Two men pulled it down. Don Juan opened it with a key kept around his neck. It was full of doubloons. We looked at each other. None of us had known. Just as well.

The two Calusa led us along a faint path leading from the village. It soon ended at a point of land that projected into a bayou. Cacique Carlos stopped. . . his face like iron and his arms folded across his chest. He spoke to Santiago.

"He says the water is here."

"Where?" asked de Leon.

The Indian walked to a flat rock perhaps ten meters across, gleaming a dull pink in the moonlight. A curved outcropping arched like a palm tree from the rock face to hang over the water. Carlos stood looking down. De Leon and Captain de la Cruz joined him and knelt with their hands on the rock edge. We crowded behind them. A trickle of water ran into the swamp.

"Hardly a Fountain," said Sebastian Garcia bitterly.

But de Leon stood and addressed the column in a loud voice. "We will give thanks to Almighty God for leading us at last to this sacred place." We all knelt and crossed ourselves.

The two Calusa exchanged glances. They seemed to be impressed by our reverence. The first Indian spoke to Santiago.

"He asks that his son may drink."

"First el Jefe," said Captain de la Cruz, but de Leon was shaking his head.

"Let the boy drink," he said. "We will watch him."

The two Indians held the boy while he scooped water into his mouth with his hands. The boy stood and wiped his mouth. We all watched the child for signs of distress. "Why not the woman?" asked de Leon of Santiago, referring to the Indian boy's mother.

Santiago grunted at Cacique Carlos. "He says the Fountain is not for women."

De Leon nodded, taking a final look at the boy. "Gentlemen," he said, "We will now by the grace of Almighty God receive His blessing." He motioned to Hermano Tomaso, our Franciscan, who took from his monk's robes the silver chalice that we used in the Sacrament of the Mass. Don Juan knelt and filled the chalice, then drank. "Good," he pronounced. He nodded to de la Cruz.

We passed the chalice among us. I remember waiting for some sign as I drank, a feeling of holiness or revitalization. I felt only relief from the thirst we all felt in that heat.

Finally Pablito, the youngest, drank. We stood looking at each other. De Leon, clearly overcome, led us in prayer. We crossed ourselves again, and camped for the night.

The next morning de Leon assembled the column for mass. He spoke of a dream God had given to him in the night. "The Fount is a singular gift from the Almighty, given to us for His good pleasure. He has forbidden us to speak of it to anyone, on pain of His certain displeasure."

We took an oath on this with our bread and wine, remembering again Juanbaptiste. Then Don Juan spoke again.

"Form for battle. We came to colonize these people, to claim this land for our king. We will begin here."

I stood, full of anger. "Jefe, what are you doing? You gave your word to these people. . ."

Don Juan shrugged. "They are not people. They are heathen, spurned of God. Can you remember how Jehovah instructed Joshua concerning the heathen of Canaan? They were to be killed, along with their women and children."

"This is not Canaan, Don Juan," I said, sick to my stomach. "You are not Joshua. The Calusa are not Philistines."

"They are to me," Don Juan said. He turned away to form a battle line. And I? To my everlasting shame, I took my place in line of battle. De Leon led us on a mission of murder as evil as the murder of my people in Spain. But I hadn't the courage to turn my back on my comrades.

We took the village unaware, firing into the huts and setting them aflame. Men, women, and children fell before our muskets and crossbow. But the Calusa were not the Indians of the Caribbean. They recovered more quickly than I imagined. Soon we heard their keening song and saw gray shapes in the trees. Our soldiers faced a storm of arrows from the rain forest.

We fought, too, like Spaniards. We formed a square of cross-bowmen and musketeers, firing at flitting shadows in the surrounding forest. Sometimes a scream or grunt told us of our good aim or an Indian's carelessness. But Carlos led his warriors with skill and patience. We stood looking at an empty forest and listening to nothing while the arrows came. Some were no more than sharpened sticks, some were the fine-feathered shafts from our crossbows, returned to us. Some found their way between helmet and armor and a man would go down, cursing.

So matters stood until noon, when the arrows stopped. We reloaded with dry powder, cranked our crossbows tight, and waited. Some men dozed at their places in our square. The wounded in our center moaned and cried out to the Virgin.

Then a single Indian stood like a monument in a clearing near the forest, naked except for a loincloth, fine muscled and gleaming with sweat or oil. His right hand held a spear that stood a meter taller than he was. Cacique Carlos. He shouted to us—one word over and over. "Ponce."

Don Juan drew his sword with a clang of steel. His eyes flashed and his teeth gleamed white in his black beard. "Goliath! There he stands, the uncircumcised heathen blasphemer! By the power of the living God I will kill him and win this day!"

The soldiers in line of battle looked at him and at each other. Finally, I cleared my throat. Carlos was no Goliath, and Don Juan was no David, and so far as I knew everyone present was uncircumcised except me.

"Don Juan, listen," I said. "There is no better swordsman in all Christendom than you. But this heathen means to fight with other weapons. He challenges you alone, but look. See how near to the forest he stands? I have a certain proficiency with crossbow and musket. One or the other will bring Carlos down before I am within arrow range of those trees. I will go."

But Don Juan was already striding through our ranks onto the sun-speckled clearing, as we all knew he would. The moment fit his caballero spirit like the soft leather gloves he wore fit his fingers. "Ponce he calls for, Ponce he will have," he shouted over his shoulder. "Pray for me. God is with us."

Maybe. I prayed to Jehovah just in case, crossing myself if Our Lady was watching.

We stood silently in line of battle and watched a ballet. The Spaniard in boots and armor circled his enemy with quick stutter steps, sword blade flashing in the sunlight. The Indian, shining with sweat, turned to meet him, keeping the sword point at bay with darting spear thrusts. Don Juan parried the spear, charged in, leaped back. Carlos wore a red stripe on his shoulder—first blood. The Indian passed his hand over the wound and glanced at his crimson fingers, then smeared a wide red stripe across the bridge of his nose. War paint. He swung his spear like an axe and drove Ponce back ten steps. Ponce's boot caught in the tangled grass and he went to one knee, then rolled to his right as the spearhead buried itself in his previous spot.

Then Ponce was up and the two warriors stood silently, facing each other. Both men were panting in the heat. Carlos crouched with his spear across his body and sang again the keening song we had heard the night before in the Indian village. He cut the melody off after a few seconds, and in the sudden stillness a dozen arrows flashed from the trees, and then Carlos was gone, and Ponce sat in the mud pulling weakly at a pair of shafts sticking straight up, one in each thigh.

We charged the clearing with a yell and carried him back to our lines. It was our last attack. The heart had gone from us when Ponce went down. Captain de la Cruz formed a column, and we turned seaward. I organized a rear guard of twenty men without orders. Almost at once arrows flew from the trees. Two men went down. My men fired shots at the empty rain forest until I stopped them.

We carried the wounded on our backs until more men took arrows. Then we left the wounded.

We fought our way to our ships all afternoon, fighting shadows and phantoms. Just before sunset we could smell the sea. At last we were out of the trees and onto white sand, and there were our long boats with the sun dipping into the ocean behind them. I formed and held one last skirmish line, while the soldiers carried Ponce to a boat and tumbled in after him. The boats pulled from the shore, and my skirmish line and I threw our weapons down and splashed after them, hauled aboard like mackerel, while the Calusa launched a final arrow volley. Finally we were beyond their range and safe. We had landed in Florida with almost two hundred men. We left with one hundred twenty.

chapter 16

The Bimini Boys

Isaac stirred in his chair, his story told. Manning came back to the 21st Century. Isaac rotated his glass in a circle, watching the red wine swirl. "One hundred twenty of us walked out of that jungle," he said, "out of perhaps one hundred and ninety men who drank from the Fount.

"We anchored in five fathoms in Havana Harbor in Cuba two weeks later. The only Spanish doctor on the island attended Don Juan at once, but it was too late. The arrows had been poisoned, or the wounds had infected, who knows? The result was the same. His legs swelled like sausages, and his blind eyes wept yellow mucus. He mumbled and whispered himself in and out of a coma. The doctor bled his patient, then as a last resort took off his legs. At the end he called Brother Thomas for last rites.

"We soldiers prayed at mass and drank native rum, while we waited for de Leon to die, and finally he did. He looked and stank so bad that Captain de la Cruz gave him over to the Indian who ran the waterfront inn. He hammered him into a casket, and we dug him into a grave on the hill overlooking the harbor. A few prayers and some shovels full of dirt and the adventure was over."

Manning kept his gun steady. "I suppose this is where I say, 'Gee, I never imagined. Now Adam's death and Audrey's kidnapping make perfect sense.'"

Isaac made a complicated face, with what looked like disappointment mixed in. "There's more to the story."

"Save your breath," Manning said. "The fountain of youth is a fable. It's a fairy tale."

"The Fountain is a story passed down over five centuries," Isaac replied. "There's a difference. Even a fable has some basis in reality. Some old stories have a lot more."

"Like for example?"

Isaac smiled. "All right. Old Norse stories told of Leif Erikson's discovery of the new world, 'Vineland,' west of Greenland, five hundred years before Columbus. They have trickled into Europe from Scandinavia for centuries. In 1960, archeologists found old Norse turf-and-timber wintering quarters, and Viking artifacts, on the northern tip of Newfoundland, carbon-dated to about AD 1000."

"Not the same," Manning said.

"Not the same." Isaac kept his quiet smile. "All right. The Bible tells us of the first woman, Eve. Is that a fable? DNA mapping has proved pretty conclusively that all of mankind is descended from one woman. The Bible also tells us that God spoke the universe into existence. For three or four millennia Christians and Jews have taken that one on faith. Now, in the last fifty years, astronomers tell us that the universe was created from nothing in an instant."

"Big bang."

"Big bang," Isaac agreed. "It happened once, fifteen

billion years ago. Never repeated. 'In the beginning. . .' Leif Erikson, Eve, God. Why not Ponce de Leon?"

"It's still a fable," Manning said stubbornly. "There's nothing in my physics or chemistry book about any water, or anything you could add to water, that will preserve youth for five centuries."

Isaac rocked his head from side to side like a rabbi. "There was nothing in my 16th Century physics book, either, about magnetic lines of flux, or radio waves, or nuclear fission. Doesn't mean all that wasn't going on in the 16th Century. We just weren't aware of it. Can't we just as easily be unaware of life-preserving water?" He walked to a table lamp. "I don't think much about electron flow through a filament," he said. "I just turn the switch." The light went on.

Manning was silent. Then he said, "Where's the Fountain now?"

"I don't know," Isaac said with a smile. "I'm here. Look at me if you want evidence."

"I see a man, that's all," said Manning. "A man with a fable."

"I have proof," Isaac answered.

"What, that the helmet fits?" asked Manning.

Isaac laughed and removed a book bound in cracked and aged leather from the library shelves lining the wall of the room, opened it, and handed it to Manning, pointing to a passage.

> I was called to the country home of the Earl of Knightsbridge outside of London to the west, down

> the Thames. The vile plague that has already claimed over 60,000 lives this year had visited his house and estate with virulent ferocity. Only two house girls greeted me, the rest having died or been sent home with symptoms of the disease. The Earl had seen to the death of his own wife and two daughters, the plague seemingly striking women preferentially, as noted previously.
>
> I examined all in the great house. None exhibited signs of distress. The Earl himself was a remarkable specimen. I personally had known him to be in residence some 50 years. Yet this septuagenarian gave all appearance and medical evidence pointing to an age of thirty-odd, the only oddities of his own physique being a great curved nose and a remarkable sixth toe on each foot.

Manning turned to the book's flyleaf. It was an account of the Bubonic Plague, the Black Death that had ravaged London from 1664 to early 1666. The original publishing date was 1667, authored by Doctor Charles Peppys of the Royal Medical Academy.

"I have an original first edition in London," said Isaac. "Everyone mentions my nose."

But Manning was staring at Isaac's bare feet. An extra small toe lay alongside its brothers on each foot. Isaac bent over and rubbed his toes, starting with the tiny sixth one. "Grandmother had the same toe set," he said. "She always told me that we were extra lucky because of them."

"You're presenting an interesting case," said Manning. "Not a conclusive one."

"Nothing is conclusive to some people," Isaac said. "Most people believe it when they see it. You're the kind who will see it when you believe it."

"Have you got something more? Real proof?"

Isaac shrugged. "I have spent my life destroying evidence of my existence, not saving it." He pointed to the old chest in the corner. "That box contains essentially everything that I have saved over five centuries. We can go through it, but I don't think you'll be any more convinced."

He spun his hand in a circle to include his estate. "I have wealth, stature—more than I need. Why would I tell a story like this? Ask yourself, did I just spend two hours spinning a lie? Did I present all of this proof on a whim?"

Manning thought about that for a while. "It might be true," Manning said at last, to Isaac and to himself. "You really might be five hundred years old."

Isaac filled their wine glasses without asking. "Maybe you believe me, maybe you don't. It's enough that you allow the possibility." The two men stood facing each other in Isaac's big room, while Manning thought about that. Finally Isaac said, "So you're gonna keep that gun on me until you pass out?"

Manning smiled in spite of himself. He had been thinking the same thing. "Or until I kill you."

"Nonsense!" Isaac pointed his wine glass at Manning. "You need me alive if you have any hope of finding Adam's murderers."

"And you?" Manning asked. "Why do you need me

alive, after trying so hard to kill me?"

"Because I've changed, these past few days. Past few months, actually. Turns out, my value set was exactly backwards." He smiled, sipped. "You have nothing to fear from me."

"A change of heart. How convenient." Manning leaned forward. "How come?"

"To know how I've changed, first you need to know what I was before," Isaac replied. "I need to complete my story."

"Your story runs 500 years," Manning said. "Can you just give me the headlines?"

Isaac laughed again. "I'll try to keep it short. I was saying that we soldiers, the soldiers of the Bimini expedition, were at loose ends after de Leon's death in Havana. What to do? We had tentatively decided to stay together, to hire ourselves out as mercenaries to whoever offered the most money for a band of professionals, when to our surprise, to our astonishment, we discovered that the waters of the Fountain were miraculous after all.

"The first sign was a cure, a healing of the men with the French disease. That was our name for syphilis. We had carried it to the New World and presented it as a gift to the women there. The women gave it back, so that the old campaigners of our expedition carried the pain and the seepage of it. Poof! It was gone.

"We found that the other curses of the age passed us by, too: the pox, the Black Death. The Fountain restores the body and resists disease. However it has no power over poisoned arrow tips. . . or bullets, or knives, or any of the ways men have found to kill each other." He held up an index finger. "That's the first lesson that the Fount taught us. God gives life, but man can still find ways to take it.

"So we buried Ponce de Leon and then scattered to begin lives free from death."

"Lives free from death," Manning repeated, "What was it like, that moment when you first knew you would stay young?"

Isaac shifted his gaze to stare out of his window at the bright daylight. His face softened and brightened. "What was it like? How do you think you would feel if the weight of years, of illness, of death, were all lifted from your back? Looking back now, the feeling reminds me of a moment in the nineteen-forties, when I first sat through a Technicolor movie after years of black and white, you know? I awoke each day to a bright new day. . . to endless days that seemed to stretch on forever."

Manning nodded. He had felt the same during his first days as Henry Toledo, when he realized that a new, prosperous life was in his hands. How long ago that seemed now.

"We all felt the same," Isaac continued. "We split up and left Cuba to live lives of adventure and fame. . . the songs that men sing to each other in each generation as they march to battle. We were, after all, conquistadors.

"I myself campaigned with Desoto, who was a good general and a better explorer, and with Pizarro, who was a horse's ass. I marched up and down Central America chasing after tales of gold, and by God I found it. Not the mountains of it that the natives screamed at us from the torture pits, but enough for me. I sailed home to Spain on a treasure galleon with a fifth of her cargo of gold and silver plate belonging to me. I bought an estate and a grandee's title in Valencia, the city of my birth. And I fell in love.

"One Sunday a teen-aged maiden came to mass at the cathedral. A hundred candles lighted her face, it seemed, as in a Rembrandt. Each Sunday I sat across from this vision, entranced. The Mass, which had always dragged, now seemed too short.

"I made inquiries. Maria Magdalena was the only daughter of the mayor. . . guarded like a citadel by an army of duenas. Her father loved the hunt and red wine, however, and yellow gold even more. A few days on horseback after the stags on my estate, a few nights spent sipping the fruit of my vineyards, and some words concerning a dowry given by the bridegroom instead of the bride, and we had struck a bargain."

Isaac leaned back, hands behind his head, eyes somewhere else. "Maria was. . . perfect. As graceful and lovely as a rainbow. I never touched her until she took my hand during our marriage ceremony. We didn't kiss until two days later, when the marriage fiesta ended. God Himself chose her to warm my heart. Her goodness blunted the hard edge I had sharpened in Tierra Nova, and her mercy blessed the families of our estate. She bore me seven sons, and all but two grew to manhood. Five sons and four beautiful girls. 'Te presento tu hijo,' she said to me with each boy. 'I present to you your son,' with Maria more beautiful each time she came down our long staircase to greet the family with a newborn in her arms.

"In time the countryside around our estate was filled with men and boys who carried the long curved nose of Zion and with maidens with the long black lashes and dark curls of Valencia." Isaac's smile softened, remembering. "Forty grandchildren. Who knows how many great-grandchildren? We were married for fifty years, the happiest years of my life. Maria lit a room like a thousand candles with her beauty. So in my arrogance I arranged settings to display her beauty. . . dinners, banquets. I 'wore' her like a diamond ring.

"But God watched too. He prepared a lesson for me to cure me of my hubris, the second lesson of the Fount. . . the lesson of time." Isaac closed his eyes. "Time, the great equalizer. Maria grew old. Our friends and children watched with wonder as her hair turned snow white while my beard stayed shiny black. My sons became my brothers, then my elders, graying while my hair remained shiny black under a white wig I dared not remove. I affected a limp when I walked, taking care to sit and raise myself slowly, complaining of aches I didn't feel.

"The day finally came when Maria could no longer leave her bed. A 'wasting disease' took her. . . cancer, perhaps, or tuberculosis. She smiled and sang to me from her bedroom for a long summer. Then she was gone." He shook his head. "I would have given anything to save her." A shadow crossed his face. "Almost anything.

"I dug her grave with my own hands. Then I gathered money and jewels into a carpetbag, left a suicide note for my sons promising a watery death, and laid my conquistador's uniform on the sands of the Mediterranean. I rode to

France and into the life of Le Comte du Toulon. I married again. Why not? A Parisian, as supple as a sapling. Ah, but she was not Maria.

"And the day came again when we were no longer husband and wife but mother and son, and I had to escape rumors of the unholy count up on the hill who never aged. This time I was abducted by highwaymen, complete with ransom note and severed ears. Another generation, another country, England, and another beautiful woman."

Isaac pointed to the old leather-bound book. "You've already read that the Earl of Knightsbridge's wife and family were done in by the plague. It was time to move again. I married again. And again." He shook his head, smiling with closed eyes. He opened them finally to look at his guest. "The Fountain's second lesson. We outlive our relationships." He pointed his wine glass at Manning. "Take you. Here you are, holding a gun on me, ready to kill me and my dearest friends. Yet, we could become friends. You have the cojones I had as a young man. We still should work together. . . must work together. But I don't want to be your friend, because sooner or later I'll have to tell you goodbye."

"So you've renounced relationships? No more family, no more wives?"

Isaac smiled his secret smile. "Exactly. How often can a man watch them whither and die? How many children, grandchildren, great-grandchildren. . . great-great-great. . . can an ancestor track? I confess to you that I can't remember the names of some of my children." Isaac held up two fingers. "That's the Fount's second lesson, and the third lesson is similar."

Manning rubbed his face with his left, his non-gun hand. It had been a long day. He peeked at Isaac through his fingers. "Your third lesson. Let me guess. . . it's how to compound interest over five hundred years? In all that time you must have made millions. What do you do with all that power? Which are you, robber-baron or philosopher-king?"

Isaac smiled his little smile again. "Perhaps both." He waved his hand again to include his lodge. "I'm not so much rich as indifferent to wealth. I give a new meaning to the term 'old money.' Money, money, money, and all that it brings with it, and no one to show it to." Isaac's glance moved across the room, stopping at Manning. "Find someone to show it to."

He folded his hands in front of him and studied his thumbs. "No, the third lesson of the Fount is that given enough time, everything. . . I mean everything. . . grows tiresome. I don't know if you envy my life or not, but I envy yours. You're like a child. The world is new to you every day. Me. . . this is where I came in. As the centuries pass, what adventure, what amusement, what possession doesn't grow old? It's the same with the endeavors, the goals of life. People grow up, they try to get better, they wind up making the same mistakes over and over. Societies too, governments. We of the expedition too. We go on and on like redwoods. Like vampires, who don't need blood, who don't sleep days."

"Could we come back to the point here," Manning said. "Someone's trying to kill me, remember?" He pointed to one of Isaac's large picture windows. "He could be peering at us with a telescopic sight right now. Does his contract have your signature on it?"

Isaac held up his hand to keep Manning quiet. "Stick with me, I'm almost there. You be me. You're three hundred years old and you look thirty. Sick of life, thinking of dying, no one to talk to. Whom do you turn to?"

"Someone who understands, I suppose."

"Right. Who's that?"

"The boys in the band," said Manning. "The Bimini boys."

Isaac's head bobbed up and down. "Exactly. The soldiers of the expedition. They know how to keep secrets; they've learned the same lessons of the Fount. They've also abandoned family and friends." He looked out of his window, and the late morning sun reflected off of the planes of his face. "Loners. We're all loners.

"By the late 18th Century we began to search each other out. We met in the spring of 1792 in a castle in Portugal, forty of us. It was Easter Sunday, the anniversary of the day Don Juan first landed in Pascua Florida, and also the anniversary of the day we all drank from the Fount."

Isaac closed his eyes, smiling. "That first Easter was wonderful, full of stories of the old days and the lies men tell each other when they think they won't be found out. We raised our glasses, then our swords, and swore to defend with our lives the secret of the Fount, and to meet each year to celebrate the Easter of the Fount. And we do, somewhere in the world. The meetings are secret, like our lives. 'Los Caballeros,' we called each other at first, arrogantly, 'The Knights.'"

"What do you do, these days, at your dinners?" Manning asked.

"These days we are not so romantic. We have taken to calling ourselves, instead of 'Los Caballeros,' 'Los Viejos.' The Old Men. We celebrate. . . ourselves. Good food and rich wine from our own vineyards. It's always comforting to see one other again, to find each other alive."

"How many of the Bimini Boys are alive?"

"Ten," said Isaac. His smile turned wry. "Nine, with Enrique gone."

"You were very interested in how Toledo died," Manning said. "So was my Aunt Dot, one of your hired assassins. Why?"

Isaac sat down again and lifted his feet onto a bamboo stool. "Fifty years ago seventy of us gathered for Easter. Today—nine. Something is happening."

"What?"

"I don't know." Isaac folded his hands and rested his chin on them. "We ask after those who. . . haven't come. . . and we take the action necessary to protect our secret, the secret of the Fount, the secret we swore to God and to each other to protect. We make sure no one is sniffing around. If anyone is, we. . . neutralize him." Isaac swept his wineglass to include Manning. "Like you."

"You're killers then," Manning said evenly.

Isaac turned his chair to look out of his window. "I tried to convince you, reason with you, when we first met at the Stuyvesant Club. We could have worked together. You refused. You didn't know a thing, but you refused anyway. You were a danger to us."

"Like I said. You're killers."

Isaac took his time answering. "There is one of us," he said finally. He blew out his cheeks. "You know of him: 'Hermano Tomaso' we call him. 'Brother Thomas.'"

"The Franciscan, the monk on the expedition,"

Isaac nodded again. "Afterwards. . . well, he renounced his order and his faith. I think he became a priest in the first place out of fear. . . fear of death and an eternity in Hell. When he drank from the Fount and death receded, fear receded. Tomaso has become very evil. He does the dirty work for Los Viejos, to keep our secret. People simply disappear. We don't know the details. . . don't want to know them."

His eyes returned to Manning. "When we first discovered that you had stepped into Enrique's shoes, and we learned of Miss Cobb's IRS investigation, Los Viejos gave both of you to Tomaso."

"To murder us," Manning said.

Isaac stared into his wine glass. "I call myself a Christian. God forgive me, I handed you, and many others before you, over to Tomaso, to protect our secret, out of loyalty to my comrades." He covered his face with his hands. "God forgive me." His hands fell away, and he looked at Manning. "No more. I have decided to work with you."

"Work? What does that mean?"

"I don't know. Whatever works."

"And if it doesn't work?" Manning asked.

"However it turns out, I am through with killing."

"Are you? Maybe you killed Adam too."

"Think I did?"

"I don't know. Would you? Did you have a brother, Isaac? Who murdered your brother?"

"I had a brother," Isaac said, so softly Manning had to bend close to hear. "And two sisters. All killed, forced into suicide, for being Jewish. By the inquisitors of the Catholic Church and the Spanish crown. The church I joined and the crown I swore to serve." He raised his eyebrows to Manning. "You carry your brother's death around with you. So do I. Jesus didn't tell us to carry His cross. He says to carry our own. We each have our own."

"And now?"

"Now? Now, if I call myself Christian, I'll act like one. I've kept quiet too long while my comrades and I murdered to protect our secret, starting with the Calusa in Florida. Now Tomaso is out of control. He killed your brother without telling any of us. He probably kept this three million you just told me of. He's kidnapped your lady friend. I've got to act to prevent any more killing."

"You think Tomaso took Audrey?" Manning asked.

Isaac bit his upper lip while he thought that over. "I think so."

"Why?"

"Why? He wants you. He'll use her to get to you."

Manning sipped some wine at last. He dipped his finger into it and rubbed the rim of his glass, getting a musical tone. "Why me?"

"I don't know. I do know that I need you, too. I can trust you."

"Trust? Me? Why?"

"Because I looked you up, Manning Crenshaw—identified you from a fingerprint you left on a water glass at my club. You're an interesting case. Forty years of careful living, and you jump right out of your life and into Enrique's shoes. You've escaped several attempts on your life, including prevailing over Andres. Here you are with a gun to my head, ready to kill me. You'd make a good Spaniard. A better Jew. You want Tomaso. I want Tomaso. You want Audrey Cobb back. . ."

"And her mother."

". . . And her mother. Our goals are similar. We can work together. We don't have to like each other. It's enough that we trust each other."

"Trust." Manning looked at his hands. "Adam trusted me. So did Audrey. Trust is overrated."

"No. It's underrated. Like love."

"Love," Manning muttered. "What is love? Isn't that what Pontius Pilate asked your friend Jesus?"

"Pilate asked about truth. It's the same thing."

"Is it? Don't tell me Pilate was a friend of yours too?"

"Sometimes it seems like it," Isaac said. He took another little trip to somewhere else, then shook himself back into the room.

"Why should I sign on?" Manning asked.

"You?" Isaac grinned and shook his head. "You have no other choice. Still want to find Tomaso? Miss Cobb? Without me. . . not a chance."

"Is that how it is?"

"No. This is how it is. I can use your help, but I'm good without it. You, on the other hand, can go nowhere without me." Long pause, and Isaac smiled his quiet smile. "But, I owe you, my friend. Because you're right: I did try to kill you. Didn't stop Tomaso, anyway. So I'll help you."

"That's the deal?"

"That's it. Or you can crawl into a hole somewhere. How will you sleep nights, waiting for Tomaso or someone like him?"

"And how do you sleep, Talmud? No blood on your hands, right? Tomaso takes care of business, while the Bimini Boys look the other way. Maybe you can reconcile your Christian principles with kidnapping and murder to protect a musty secret. I can't. Whose side are you on?"

Isaac pointed an index finger. "I just told you, I'm through with all of that. I'm on your side. Don't be so self-righteous. If you hadn't been greedy and unwilling to work with me to begin with, your brother would be alive." He nodded at Manning's gun. "You can't shoot me for killing your brother. I didn't. Didn't know of the plan to kill him, or you, that time. Or the three million."

"You tried to kill me before."

"True, but I—we—didn't, did we? Isaac stood up and walked toward Manning. Manning pointed his Glock. "Are you gonna shoot me for trying?" Isaac asked. He put his fingers to the gun barrel and slowly moved it to one side.

Manning shook his head. He took a deep breath, put his pistol on the lanai table. "Until I don't trust you any more. Or vice versa."

Isaac nodded. "We're not far from there already. Okay. Get your head back in the game. We have things to do."

"Like get Audrey back."

"Don't let it get personal."

"It is personal."

Isaac shrugged. "She's a woman. No more, no less."

"You can afford that attitude. You've had lots of women. I've had one."

"How did she work out?"

Manning bit his lip, thinking of Ellen. "Not so hot."

"Exactly, my friend. Why do it all over again?" Isaac sounded angry, and his eyes burned straight ahead. Manning reckoned that he was remembering Maria Magdalena. "We have work to do. There are still pieces of this thing that make no sense. Do you have enough gas left in your tank to work some more tonight?"

Manning nodded. "I'll tell you all I know. Whatever it takes."

Isaac turned his wine bottle upside down into a wet bar. "Enough wine, then. I'll make some coffee. Tell me about the attempts on your life." He pointed the empty bottle at Manning. "Everything."

It took two full pots of coffee. Finally Manning rubbed his eyes. "Let's put a sock on it, Isaac, get some sleep. Hit it again in the morning." He stood up.

"Sit down. There's always something," Isaac said. "Tell me about the will again. The one Andres made you sign.

Manning slumped back into his chair. He stared into his coffee cup like something important was written in the lip. "What else can I say? We've been through so many wash and rinse cycles on that damned will. It looked like a standard legal document. Lots of 'whereas's and 'wherefore's'. All of my. . . Toledo's. . . money went to some trust."

Isaac was making notes. "We have three different trusts. We funnel money through them to distribute to Los Viejos.

"Tannerberg. No, Tannenbaum, like the Christmas tree."

Isaac stopped writing. "Tannenbaum? What about Tannenbaum?"

"That was the name of the trust. Like the song, the German Christmas song."

Isaac sat with his hands cupped over his chin and nose. "That's not one of our trusts. Never heard of it. What game is Tomaso playing?" He looked at Manning. "Was there anything more? An address? The name of a trustee?"

Manning swirled lukewarm coffee in his cup. "No." He was tired of talking.

Isaac shook his head. "We have to sniff that out. Later. For now we should pursue other leads."

"What other leads?" Manning asked.

Isaac shrugged. "I don't know, exactly. We haven't got much except Tomaso." He asked a question of his own. "Can you access your voice mail in Manhattan remotely? Let's see if Tomaso has tried to contact you. He may play the Audrey Cobb card."

Manning nodded. He used his new cell phone to dial the number to his condo. "Wait," Isaac said. He plugged a thin black wire into Manning's phone and led it to a sound system. "We can both listen."

Manning dialed again. He punched the numbers that let him listen to his answering machine. The first two callers were nothing. The third was more interesting.

"Mr. Toledo, this is Andrew Trotter. We haven't met. I need to speak with you when you have time, please. It concerns the difficulties you are having with the IRS." Trotter left a phone number.

Manning and Isaac looked at each other. "What do you make of that?" asked Manning.

"Can't tell how much he knows. He could be dangerous. You'll have to deal with him."

"Me? Your five-hundred-year-old friend is out there somewhere gunning for me."

Isaac nodded. "Precisely. We must deal with Tomaso. First we need to understand the game he's playing. So I'll pursue this Tannenbaum Trust. I also want to find the true story on the murder of your brother. That calls for a separate agenda, an agenda of my own. You'll have to do business with our new friend, Mr. Trotter. Find out what he knows. Meet with him if you have to. Then we'll decide."

Manning shook his head. "This guy Trotter wants Toledo. He doesn't want Manning Crenshaw. I'm just in the way. Well, I'm getting out of the way. I can access Henry's bank account, some of his securities. Goodbye, Mr. Trotter, goodbye IRS. Goodbye, Isaac Talmud. You handle Mr. Trotter."

Isaac looked almost painfully at Manning. "As I said before, I may grow to like you, Manning. You're smart. You're audacious. I'm risking a lot by working with you. If you take Enrique's money and run, well. . ." Isaac shook his head, ". . . you become a threat to us. . . to me. You can be exposed, accused of murdering Enrique, stripped of your wealth. . . or worse."

"A threat?"

"Let's call them possible scenarios, shall we? Similar scenarios apply to Miss Cobb. You're forgetting about her. The best scenario of all is the one we're working now. You have a secret, I have a secret, and we're cooperating to keep our secrets safe. Do you agree?"

Manning shook his head. He was pinned. "I'll stay. One reason. Adam. No, Adam and Audrey."

"Okay, " said Isaac, "you want to get Tomaso. So do I. I'll be running him down starting tomorrow, God willing. You should pursue this phone call from Mr. Trotter. Will you call him?"

Manning looked at his watch. Four A.M. He got up. "I'll call in the morning. It's too early in LA now. He looked out at the blackness. They had talked all day and most of the night. "I'm tired."

Isaac stood too. "I'll show you to your room. We'll pick this up again in the morning." The two men shook hands without smiling. Manning followed his host, wondering: Why didn't I just shoot him in his bedroom?

chapter 17

Henry Aaron And Mr. Maxwell

The phone jangled Andres awake. He didn't mind. He was a light sleeper, which was an asset in his profession. Besides, most of his business calls came in before dawn when he was sure to be in. He didn't use telephone voice-mail. Sooner or later someone else would listen to his messages.

"Mr. Adams, my name is McFarland. I understand you deal in baseball cards."

"I do." The names were meaningless. Andres waited for the code word. It didn't take long.

"I'm looking for some specials. Ty Cobb, Hank Aaron, Tris Speaker."

"I have them, and others too," said Andres. "We should meet."

"Yes, fine. How about Oswaldo's in Washington Square? Ten o'clock? We can have breakfast."

Andres agreed and hung up. The café, Oswaldo's, was also meaningless. There was to be no meeting. The address in Washington Square was the key. Andres kept a post office box at a Mail Boxes near Washington Square, one of several he had throughout the city. A package would be waiting after ten.

Andres got up and brewed some coffee. Alarm bells were going off in his head. The call was routine, the code word, "Hank Aaron," was all right, and the caller had identified a correct mailbox. The problem was the caller. Always before it had been a woman. The same woman. This time a man.

Andres sat at his kitchen counter and sipped thick dark coffee. This required thought. Usually he dropped a job flat at the first whiff of danger. But the Hank Aaron connection was old and true. He had worked it for 15 years. And, he had already turned this client down once—the Henry Toledo contract. Andres made a face. Never before had he been so careless, and now this man Toledo had his photo, his DNA. . .

He should retire, Andres knew. He had money enough. And Felicia was in Athens, waiting. She would not wait forever. But the truth was, Andres enjoyed his work. He was the best there was, and he knew it, and those he worked for knew it. Life was a corrida, a bullfight. He was a torero, working a few inches from the horns and that much more alive because of the danger.

Andres shrugged. A few more jobs. A few more months. This job had a tincture of danger. The horns were a little closer.

He went at noon and opened the box at Washington Square.

The envelope contained a further problem. There was no usual target name, no background information, and no instructions for disposal. A single white sheet said, in block letters:

JFK AIRPORT
AMERICAN AIRLINES
ADMIRAL'S CLUB 2 PM ASK FOR
MR. MAXWELL

Andres smiled. A game. He liked games. He tore the edges off of the sheet and ate the printed words in the center, chewing thoughtfully.

At 2 p.m. Andres rode the elevator to the second floor of the JFK Admiral's Club. The lady at the counter smiled glossily. "Mr. Maxwell, yes. He said he would have a guest. He'll be here shortly."

Andres found a seat at a table near the bar and sat down gingerly. That woman's—Audrey Cobb's—bullet hole still hurt at unexpected times. He ordered an Amstel, paying cash. A mix of business travelers, young and old, men and women, sat around with cell phones in their ears, peering at Palm Pilots or laptops. Andres wondered how his life would have unfolded had he not chosen to be a murderer.

A man with a young face but old eyes sat down across from him. "Hello, Andres." Really big curved nose.

Andres leaned back in his leather chair in the Admiral's Club and sipped his beer. He felt at peace. He knew his abilities. He also had an eight-inch stiletto holstered along his right calf. He would have preferred a pistol but airport security discouraged that, especially since the

World Trade Center attack. Security was tight. Andres had even had to purchase a commuter ticket to Boston to get past passenger check-in and into the club. Perhaps that was why Maxwell chose the Admiral's Club. However the stiletto was Kevlar, so it passed through the security cameras.

Andres smiled. Maxwell smiled back. "The man to my left. Next table. No hair. See him?" Andres looked over. A square bald man smiled at him. Everyone was smiling. The bald man opened his suit jacket to show Andres a pistol butt in a belt clip.

"Yes, I see it," Andres said. They were good. "What do you want?"

Maxwell passed an envelope over. "Information."

Andres looked inside. One-hundred-dollar bills. He put the money out of sight in his lap and riffled through it like a bank teller, counting with his eyes. Ten thousand. "What can I tell you?" It would be all right. If they were killing him they wouldn't be paying him.

Maxwell laced his fingers together behind his head and bowed his back, stretching his muscles. "You accepted a contract for a man named Henry Toledo."

Andres shrugged. "I. . . reconsidered."

Maxwell widened his eyes. "You turned an assignment down? After accepting? Why?"

"I. . . I have my reasons. The situation seemed—sub optimum."

"Toledo tells it differently. He says he learned enough about you to blackmail you into backing off."

Another shrug. "And if I did? Perhaps something better came up."

"Perhaps it came up last week. A man was shot in the city. The bullet entered the back of the base of the skull and exited at the top of the head. We thought of you."

Andres nodded again. It was his M.O. A single bullet severed the spine that way, and traveled all the way through the brain. It was always fatal. This one knew a lot. Too much.

"The man was Henry Toledo's brother," Maxwell said. His young mouth was smiling but his ancient eyes weren't. "You gave your word."

"It wasn't me."

"Who?"

"I don't know."

Maxwell stopped smiling. "Your photo, your prints, your DNA, remember? Do you want them on file? FBI? Interpol? You could make People Magazine."

Did these people know everything? "I have an associate. He has seen me work. Sometimes he contracts separately. I don't mind." Andres gave him up with little regret. The idiot had also given his word on Toledo. If he broke his word he deserved what he got.

"His name?"

"Howard Sergeant."

chapter 18

"There's Always An Alternative To Evil."

Manning met Andrew Trotter the next morning at the Marriott at Los Angeles International Airport. Trotter had said he would be in a white polo shirt and there he was, also in dark pleated slacks with topsiders on his feet, no socks. The little Ralph Lauren guy rode his polo pony on the shirt. Very LA

"Mr. Toledo. A pleasure." Trotter was beaming. Lots of teeth. Here was a guy at the top of his game at eight in the morning. Manning felt lousy. Isaac had already left—flown to New York—when Manning awoke at his estate in Hawaii. He had left instructions: phone Trotter, set up a meeting soonest.

Manning had set up something for the next day, had flown all day and half the night on a bumpy flight from Honolulu into San Francisco, long layover, then down the coast on a commuter. Isaac had made him dog-leg like that because he didn't want anyone to be able to trace Manning directly back to Hawaii, and that was cool, but it didn't make Manning feel any less crummy. He wasn't ready to cross swords with some Southern California swifty.

They walked to some tables in the hotel lobby. Manning sat down, but Trotter kept standing. "You don't mind if I frisk you for a recorder?"

Manning stood back up. He minded very much. He was wearing a wire. A receiver-transmitter in his suitcase sitting at the bell desk 50 feet away received the signal, pumped it up, and was sending it to Isaac in New York.

Manning and Isaac had talked by phone about a response to a body search. Manning said, "Mr. Trotter, you asked for this meeting, not me. I came here of my own free will." He pasted a thin veneer of irritation on his face. "We are off to a bad start." He walked away.

Trotter caught up with him, smiling. "Come on, I'm sorry. It doesn't matter." Manning allowed himself to be led back to the table. This time Trotter sat down too. "I represent certain parties who are prepared to offer you a handsome deal."

Manning just looked at him. Time ticked away. Finally Trotter continued talking. "You have a. . . secret. We know that. We are prepared to pay a substantial amount." He waited hopefully. Manning continued to stare. Just don't respond, Isaac had said. Let him talk. He'll say more than he intended to.

"Very substantial sum," Trotter mumbled.

"What secret?" asked Manning.

"We know that you have found a way to. . . reverse the aging process. My associates are very interested in that information."

"Your associates are in good company," said Manning. "Everyone on the planet would be interested, including me. There is no elixir of youth. What have you heard?"

"I'm not at liberty to say," said Trotter. Manning went

back to his silent routine. After a while Trotter said, “Mr. Toledo, we have incontrovertible proof that your age is at least one hundred and seventy.” He took a deep breath. “We are prepared to make you a very rich man. You can specify any safeguards you wish. . .”

“What proof?” asked Manning.

Trotter’s eyes darted in all directions. “We have. . . DNA evidence dating from the last century. Written records, signatures. Mr. Toledo, don’t force us to make this evidence public.”

Manning was silent again. When Trotter didn’t offer anything else Manning stood up. “There is a perfectly reasonable explanation for your evidence,” he said. “I’ll phone you.” He walked off. This time Trotter stayed put.

Manning checked into a different hotel and phoned Isaac on his cell phone. “What’s the ‘perfectly reasonable explanation’?” Isaac asked.

“How the hell do I know? What do we do now?”

“I know what Tomaso would say,” answered Isaac. “Play along until we know the names and addresses of everyone who knows anything about this, and then kill them. As this thing unravels I’m afraid Los Viejos will agree.”

Manning chewed on that. “Is there an alternative?”

“There’s always an alternative to evil.”

“I’m listening.”

Isaac was quiet, thinking. “We still need to know the other team’s lineup. Tell him you’re willing to talk, but only to his principal. All of them, tell him. Next meeting, try to set it up that way. Phone him. A meeting with his principals. Get their names over the phone, maybe.”

"Okay, then what?"

"Then we see how their backfield lines up and call an audible at the line of scrimmage."

Manning smiled. "I'll phone Trotter and get back to you."

"That's out of the question," Trotter said when Manning put it to him.

"You called me, I didn't call you." said Manning. "I just said I was willing to negotiate. That's the condition. It's the only one. Talk to your people. Yes or no." He hung up.

Trotter phoned back in ten minutes. "You win. I didn't think they'd buy it but they will. Same place, tomorrow, at two."

"What are their names? How many?"

"You'll find out tomorrow." This time Trotter hung up.

"Testy," said Isaac when Manning told him about the call. "He doesn't like to be trumped. Remember that."

"What's next?" Manning asked.

"Time to go to ground. Call Trotter tomorrow and tell him you'll be gone for a while. Give them a couple of days to get nervous."

"What do I do, go to Disneyland?"

"No. You're coming here, to New York. I've talked to Andres. He knows who killed you brother."

"Who?" Manning realized that he was holding his breath.

"Howard Sergeant, his name is."

"I know him." Manning pictured that day at his condo when he had let Sergeant go free over Audrey's objections. Would Adam be alive if Manning had killed him? How could he kill someone in cold blood?

"You'll have an electronic ticket at LAX on tomorrow's noon United flight. I'll meet you."

"You've got the private jet, you come here. I'm fed up with packing my bags every time you snap your fingers. What am I, pizza delivery?"

"You're in this to find your brother's killers, right? Make the flight."

Manning hung up, feeling depressed. He started to repack.

The next morning all the plans got changed. Manning called Trotter from his hotel. Isaac listened in silently on a three-way call. "I tried your hotel," Trotter said. "You're checked out." He sounded suspicious.

"Room service had no pizza," Manning said. "I'm somewhere else."

"We're ready to meet," said Trotter.

"No card tricks."

Trotter sounded smug. "We know about your friends. Your old, old friends. We know about your little fountain. We can spread that around. Or we can keep your secret between us. We just want access to the fountain. We'll pay fifty million, any form of payment you want, anywhere you say. Swiss account, anything. If it checks out."

Manning's cell phone was chiming the tune that

meant Isaac was calling. "Just a minute," he told Trotter, and picked up.

"I'm out of ideas," Isaac said to Manning on the new connection. "You're on your own."

Manning spoke into the hotel phone. "You pick the place," he said to Trotter, with phones in both ears. "Whenever you say. Be ready to wire the money to an account and location that I'll specify when we meet. When I know that the money's safe I'll give you what you want."

"No card tricks, to use your words."

"You hold the cards. You don't like the setup; you walk away with your money. Bring your boss."

"I told you, it's a consortium. They won't come."

"That's what's so great about this country," said Manning, "Everything's negotiable. I think it's one man. Bring him and we do business. But with the Man. Only the Man."

After a couple of beats Trotter said, "Pacific Palisades, in Santa Monica, the grassy park along the cliffs looking at the ocean. End of Main Street. Know it?"

"I know it," Isaac said into Manning's other ear.

"I know it," Manning said to Trotter.

"Tomorrow, eight A.M."

"That's pretty fast."

"Be there." Trotter hung up.

"What now?" Manning asked Isaac.

"What now is I'm flying to LA. Write down this address. Meet me there tomorrow."

"No, no! Wait a minute! We're after Howard Sergeant, remember? My brother's killer? Trotter can wait."

"Trotter can't wait," Isaac said. "He knows too much. We have to resolve that before our secret is exposed."

"Your secret!" Manning exploded. "All you old farts can think of is a five-hundred-year-old fountain, location unknown, probably dried up by now. Let's go see Sergeant!"

"Calm down. I'll take care of Sergeant. Don't worry, he'll keep. See me tomorrow." Isaac hung up. Manning slammed the phone onto its hook. Talmud said jump, he jumped. He was becoming Talmud's gopher.

Howard Sergeant's secretary buzzed. "Gentleman to see you. Needs a signature notarized."

"Send him in." Howard still ran his CPA and notary public service on Long Island, but only four days a week. Assassination had become his profession of choice. Soon he would close the office down completely and work like Andres, on call. Meanwhile it was good cover.

A man entered his office, closing the door behind him. He was young, younger than Howard. Something about his eyes, though.

Howard put on his workaday smile. "What can I do for you, Mr. . ."?

"Maxwell," Isaac said. He put down his briefcase and extracted a Smith and Wesson 32 caliber automatic with attached silencer. He leveled it at Howard and sat down. "Please keep your hands on your desk. Buzz your girl. You won't need her for the rest of the day. She can go early. She's earned it."

Howard did as he was told.

Both men heard the outer office door slam shut. Isaac got up and walked to the inner office door. He opened it and looked out. Then he closed and locked it. When he turned back Howard had a small caliber automatic pointed at him.

Isaac sighed. He didn't bother to raise the pistol in his hand. "Howard, this isn't you. We both know that you're only good at shooting people who can't shoot back. Put the gun down."

Howard dropped his gun like it was electrified.

"Better." Isaac picked up Howard's weapon. "You killed a man last week." It wasn't a question.

"Look. . ." Howard began. Isaac shut him up with a look. It was just as well. Howard had nothing to say.

Isaac came over to sit on Howard's desk. "The man you killed was Henry Toledo's brother. You remember Henry Toledo. He let you live. You and Andres talked about him. You agreed to lay off."

"I didn't know that was Toledo's brother."

This time Isaac shut him up with a sweeping slap to the soft part of his nose with the pistol he was holding. "You were gunning for Toledo, Howard. When his brother came to the bank to pick up the money you shifted targets. Someone inside tipped you. Andres warned you off Toledo, Howard. You took a contract anyway."

Howard had his handkerchief out, full of blood from his nose. Blood covered his hands and the top of his desk. "I'm sorry. I'm so sorry." He was blubbering.

"You're sorry, all right. Toledo wanted to come. I'm

here instead. Toledo's here, you're dead."

"What do you want?"

"We want the name of your client."

Howard found a roll of paper toweling in a desk drawer. He blotted his face, hands, and desk, until the paper was bright red. He was also composing himself. His thick glasses had been knocked off. He put them back on. "I don't know their names."

Isaac nodded. "That's possible. Better be true. It's not true I'll be back, and you'll be dead, and you'll never know I came. What can you tell me about them?"

Howard spread his hands. Blood still clung to his fingers. "Look, Mr. Maxwell, I never met them." He tried a sincere look that wasn't working. "I get a phone call, some voice sets up a pigeon, a price. That's how it's done. What can I tell you?"

"You can tell me about the money."

"What money?"

Isaac pulled his arm back again. Howard covered his head with his elbows. Isaac stuck the gun back in his face. "Adam Crenshaw was carrying three million. That money."

Howard tried his sincere face again. "Honest to God. I don't know nothing about no three million."

Isaac walked backwards to the office door. He opened it and cocked his pistol with his gun pointed at Howard's forehead. "Goodbye, Mr. Sergeant."

"Wait. Wait, wait, wait." Howard kept his eyes on the pistol and silencer. "I don't have the money. You think I had three million, I'd be notarizing signatures? My clients, they warned me. I touch that money, they come after me. They came and took it themselves."

"Before or after?" asked Isaac.

"Before what?" Howard saw the look on Isaac's face. "Before. I'm driving a hack, see? Yellow Cab. These guys, they get in, take the money, get out."

"Let's back up, Howard," Isaac said. "You're losing me. You're driving a cab, you pick up Mr. Crenshaw. Then what?"

Howard leaned forward, the earnest helper. "Here's the picture. My clients, they set me up in a taxi. I pick up the. . . subject. He tells me an address on the East Side, I pull out, two blocks later I pull over, two of 'em get in. Guns out, one on each side of the pidg. . . of my passenger. He doesn't have a chance. We drive to Brooklyn, under the Williamsburg Bridge. There's a quiet place I know. These guys, they take the money, it's in a suitcase. They take the passenger. They pay me, they leave."

"How much?"

"Fifty bills." Howard watched Isaac's gun hand carefully.

"During the drive, do they say anything to Mr. Crenshaw?"

"No. They're not talking, he's not talking. They don't say nothing to me neither."

"Interesting," said Isaac. "A triple negative. All right, now Howard. I want you to describe these two men. Everything. You understand?"

"Young." Howard took a breath. "Thirties. Neat. Expensive clothes. Casual, but expensive. Banlon shirts, slacks, light jackets."

"Tall, short, fat, thin?"

"Small. Short and lean. They looked athletic. Fit. Good looking. They looked Latin, maybe. Hispanic. Middle Eastern, but I don't think so. Dark skin and hair."

"Both the same? Brothers, maybe?"

"Maybe."

"Moustaches, beards?"

"No. That's why I'm not thinking Arabs. Arabs, they're born with a moustache. These two, almost no facial hair. Lots on top, though." Howard ran his hand through his own thinning blond hair.

"And you don't know about accents?"

"Nope. They don't say anything."

"How did they set up the contract?"

"Usual way."

"Which was?"

"Phone call. They use Henry Aaron, I respond. They tell me which mail drop, there's a package."

Isaac asked, "One of these two, did he have an unusually broad brow, wide spaced eyes, flat nose?"

Howard shook his head. "I would remember that. Small heads."

"Tell us, what was in the package at the mail drop?"

"Well, this one was a little different. Usually, it's a photo of the mark, maybe a bio, lets me know where he lives, his habits, where he eats, ID on his car. Stuff I can use to set him up. This time it's just three sheets of paper, telling me where to pick up the taxi, where the cab stand is to wait, and they'll call me with final instructions."

"Which were?"

"There's a cell phone in the cab. They'll call me at the cab stand, tell me which guy to pick up as he comes out of the bank."

"How do you make sure another cab isn't in line in front of you to pick up your target?"

"I pay the other cabbies twenty bucks to let me in when I say."

"Slick. And if Henry Toledo walks out of the bank, and the phone rings, do you set him up?"

"Not him, no," Howard said quickly. "We had a deal."

"Howard, for fifty thousand you'd set up Mother Teresa. How do they know he's gonna take a taxi?"

"Search me. He don't want a cab, I'm supposed to get out, show my gun, put him in the cab, he drives."

"So why did you pick up Adam Crenshaw?"

"Cell phone rings while I'm at the taxi stand, voice describes Mr. Crenshaw. Very tall."

"Let's talk about something else," said Isaac. "You're gonna tell us all about Tannenbaum Trust."

"Tannenbaum?" said Sergeant. He blotted his nose again, looked at the blood. "Oh, the designee on that will Andres wanted Toledo to sign. Listen, all I know, he tells me to put Tannenbaum Trust on the document." He spread his hands again. "I'm sorry."

"Yes, you're still sorry," said Isaac. He hefted Sergeant's chrome automatic. "Think I'll use this one. It'll look like a suicide."

"Okay, okay," Sergeant said. "Here's what I know.

Tannenbaum is a blind trust. You understand? It's just a dodge, a delivery vehicle for something else."

Isaac was thinking. "Someone wants to send Toledo's estate somewhere and he doesn't want it traced. Fine, Howard. You're doing fine. Now tell us where the money really goes."

"Pardon?" Sergeant looked confused.

It didn't work. Isaac was shaking his head. "Howard, you were doing so well. You had almost saved your skin. The money. Where does Tannenbaum send the money?"

"Suppose I tell you," Sergeant said. "What happens?"

"To you? You get to live. You get to retire as marginal gunman and resume your original career as CPA. I walk out of that door and you never see me again. Unless, of course, you decide not to stop killing people. Then I put the law on you and you go away and are never heard from again. The money. Where does it go?"

Sergeant was quiet for a while, but both men knew what was coming. Finally he opened his mouth, head down. "There's an address. In Berlin." He opened his desk drawer and pulled out an envelope. Isaac opened it and read the single sheet inside, a legal document appointing Howard Sergeant as agent in the United States of America for Tannenbaum Trust, with authority to collect monies, etc. The signature at the bottom was identified as

Hermann Gruber, Principal Partner
Estates Management
Kriegsbank
Berlin, FRG

Isaac put the paper in his jacket pocket. "Okay, Howard, that's all." He lifted some of the toweling that Howard had used to mop up his blood, and held it in front of his face. "You're out of business, Howard. Andres too, except he doesn't know it yet. Your DNA is on this paper. Maybe your prints, too. I have your gun. Who knows, maybe you're stupid enough to have kept it after you used it." He nodded as Howard's eyes shifted. "You stay in business and the police get all of this. Go back to notarizing signatures, Howard."

Isaac walked out. Howard sat rubbing the dried blood off of his hands with his fingers.

Winston Churchill came to work drunk the next morning in Washington. He spent his commute on the Metro Blue Line watching the other passengers and wondering what they did for a living. Everyone was so glum. Did he look that crummy every morning? Yep.

By the time Winston got to his little glass office the alcohol was wearing off. Miss Crawford, his newest temp hire, looked at him. "Who slugged you?" she asked.

"Johnnie Walker. Coffee. Black." Winston shut his office door and looked at himself in the full-length mirror he kept hidden on the door's opposite side. No wonder Miss Crawford had stared. Pink shirt, cream tie. He looked like Colonel Sanders. He ran his hand over his face. He had forgotten to shave.

Audrey was driving him nuts, that was it. She had left three voicemails on his machine at home in the past three weeks, recorded in the middle of the day, when she knew he was at work, like she didn't want to talk. "Hi, it's me. Listen, I'm fine, things are fine, I can't talk about it. Give me a little more time, will you? I've got plenty of vacation time, okay? Just a little more time. Square it with HR and Stinky, will you, dear? Love you, bye." All the calls ran something like that. HR was Human Resources, who kept book on everybody. Stinky was Albert Simmons, Winston's boss. "Dear" and "love you" were poor compensation.

Winston's phone had Caller ID. He looked up the area and country codes of her calls. First call: St. Thomas, Virgin Islands. Second: Athens.

The third call came yesterday after a 12-hour zoo at work. Winston stood, exhausted, listening to Audrey's voice. Caller ID listed the area code: 808. Hawaii. St. Thomas, Athens, Hawaii. Winston went to his wall safe and took out the envelope Audrey had mailed to him for safekeeping. Inside was another envelope in Audrey's handwriting: "To be opened in the event of my death or the death of Mr. Henry Toledo."

Winston had poured the first of many scotches. In the event of her death? Henry Toledo? Audrey was supposed to be investigating Henry Toledo, not dying with him. His girl was globetrotting with a tax felon while Winston was covering for her at work, like a jerk. Winston gulped his drink with his eyes closed and poured another. Secretly, he hated scotch. Tasted like varnish. It just sounded so cool to order.

Winston spent the first half of the night sipping Johnnie Walker Red in an almost pitch-black club on Capitol

Hill full of anxious female office workers and pompous male staffers. Show her, he mumbled to himself, hoping one of the girls would talk to him. None did. Winston knew why. He was a loser in a seven-hundred-dollar suit. He spent the second half of the night curled around another bottle watching a TV infomercial about a magical workbench that built incredible abdominal muscles. At 5 A.M. he dialed the 800 number and used his credit card to order it. It was a bargain at $29.95. Now as he sat nursing his coffee in his glass office it dawned on him that the bench was $29.95 a month for six months.

Winston glanced out his window. The outer office was humming with IRS employees busily fleecing the public. To work. Winston listened to his phone messages.

"Winnie, Albert here. Meeting at nine sharp, on that workman's comp grievance. See you."

Albert was 'Stinky,' Winston's boss. Nine A.M. Did he have time to shave? No need. The quartz clock on the wall read 10:30. So soon? Winston realized he had come to work three hours late.

His voice mail bleeped along. "Winnie, it's Jack McIntosh, Accounting. One of your girls owes me a travel claim. Audrey Cobb. Trip to New York, two weeks ago. I don't have it yet. Can you send it down? Thanks."

Winston drank more coffee. The scotch buzz was on its way out and a dull hangover was on its way in. Audrey. His voice mail droned on. Winston pressed the 'Erase' button on his phone. After several seconds the phone's computer-female voice told him, "All unheard messages have been erased."

All? Hmmmm. Didn't mean to do that. Must have held the button too long. Still. . . Winston felt strangely relieved. He selected "Saved Messages." The digital number 27 came up. Winston pressed "Erase" again. "All saved messages have been erased," the voice said.

Well, that's a good day's work. Winston walked out to Miss Crawford's desk. "I'll be leaving now," he told her.

When he got to his too-cramped, too-noisy, too-expensive flat in Georgetown another message from Audrey was waiting. It was the same one, essentially, with a couple of kickers: "Listen, could you go over to my place? Water those ivy plants on my window? And the keys to my Toyota are in the desk drawer. Just take it somewhere, will you? Keep the battery up. You're a dear." Same 808 area code.

Audrey Cobb, jet setter. Winston Churchill, stooge. He's tending her plants and automobile now. What does he get for it? "You're a dear." Winston took the envelope "to be opened only in the event of my death" out of his wall safe and opened it. He looked at Andres photo, fingerprints, and resume. The accompanying letter politely requested that the information be passed to the NYPD and FBI.

Winston read it all again. This guy was a world-class killer. ". . . In the event of my death." The hangover that had been hovering in the wings of his head settled behind Winston's eyes. He went to his bathroom and opened the medicine cabinet. Three toothbrushes were lined up on a shelf—two were dry. He took two aspirin. Then two more. Then he thought. Then he walked down to Eagle Firearms on M Street. "I need a big handgun that shoots big bullets," he told the clerk.

"You bet." The clerk handed over a .357 Magnum.

Winston looked at the carved wooden handle. He looked at the oiled steel. He hefted it in his hand. The gun was enormous. He pointed it at himself. The round hole in the barrel looked like a railroad tunnel. So did the round holes in the cylinder. Winston looked at the clerk. "This thing is dangerous. I could murder someone with this."

The clerk smiled through a toothpick. "That's the design concept, killer."

Isaac wore a white apron and chef's hat, whipping up a soufflé in the chrome-and-marble kitchen in a West LA condo that looked and felt about 15 minutes old, that overlooked the green trees and brown hills above UCLA's Westwood campus.

Manning watched him squeeze garlic into a saucepan. Manning had arrived at the condo two hours ahead of Isaac, met by a spectacular female property manager who gave him a key, explained how the security system and entertainment center worked. She smiled like she meant it, and left Manning wondering how many places Isaac Talmud called home.

Manning was not enjoying himself. "People we don't even know are threatening to spill your secret and maybe mine," he told Isaac. "We're meeting them with no plan, no leverage. You're playing Martha Stewart."

Isaac grinned. "Will Durant wrote, 'Each society begins stoic and ends epicure.' I've had lots of time to become slightly epicure. Take this soufflé. Got the recipe from a

Frenchman in Paris. Richelieu's chef."

"Richelieu. The Cardinal?"

"The Cardinal. Hell of a politician. Never much for praying. But Lordy, how that man could eat."

"Name dropper." Manning pinched some soufflé with his fingers and tried it. It was good.

Isaac nodded comfortably. "Told you. Talmud's taste treats."

"Talmud," Manning repeated. "Not the name you were born with, right?"

"Right."

"So where'd you get it?"

Isaac winked. "Let me ask you instead, what's the first step to getting a passport or an identity card?"

"I don't know. Social Security Card, I guess."

"Nope. Birth certificate. You need that to get a Social Security Card to begin with. And how hard is it to get a birth certificate? It's easy. In California, it costs twelve dollars. You can mail a check to Sacramento. All they ask is, 'Give as much information as possible.' Really, all you need is a name and a date of birth. So you read the obituary page of a newspaper, here's Joe Schmo, the age you want, right skin color, no real connections that you can see, right? The obit lists his date of birth, birthplace, you're in business. With the birth certificate you can get a social security number, driver's license, passport, then apply for a credit card, open a bank account. It's why I am a California resident. Isaac Talmud was born in Van Nuys, California, in 1960. He died young, in 1989. I found his obituary in the LA Times."

"So what do I call you?" asked Manning. "What's your real name?"

"My real name is Isaac," he smiled. "Call me that."

Manning looked at his wrist. Midnight. "Not trying to step on your fun, Talmud, but we've got a problem to solve in here somewhere."

"Working on that," said Isaac, stirring egg batter into a large skillet.

"Very comforting," said Manning.

Isaac flipped the soufflé in its skillet like a short-order chef flipping pancakes. His face was unconcerned. Manning was worried by his flippant attitude.

Isaac saw Manning's look. "Okay," he said. "They know about the Fountain. Can we preserve the secret any way other than playing ball with them? No. So we give them a little something."

"'We' sounds like too many people," said Manning. "I'm not a contestant. You care about keeping the Fountain quiet, not me. I can exit any time, leaving you and the Bimini Boys with this problem. You fix this one, Superman."

Isaac cocked his head. "We've been through this before, haven't we? Mr. Trotter and his friends have only one lead. You. You go away, they go away. Can you see how fragile your future becomes?" He looked into his skillet. "One must always wait for the soufflé. Well, our wait is over." He dished the meal onto two plates.

They sat down at a table by a picture window. Isaac closed his eyes. He's praying, Manning thought. Manning closed his eyes too, asking anyone who might be listening for help. Is God listening all the time? And if he is, then he's probably watching all the time, too. Manning hoped not. He didn't want his track record for the last few weeks written in some celestial book somewhere.

He picked up his fork and said, "Let me ask the same question Ponce de Leon asked you in that little story of yours. Do you pray to a Christian or Jewish God?"

Isaac looked up from his meal. "I had to make a much more fundamental choice, my friend. I had to decide if I wanted to pray to a God at all. All of Los Viejos made the same choice sooner or later. But first we all had to learn the Fountain's third lesson. Remember?"

"I remember you said that life got pretty tired after a while."

"It's in the Bible... Ecclesiastes: '... all is vanity... uselessness... a chasing after the wind.' I could have written that myself. All the wealth, the houses—castles—horses, cars, the women... after enough years, enough centuries, it all grows old."

"What doesn't grow old?"

"Peace." Isaac closed his eyes. "Our word, the Hebrew word, Shalom, means contentment, prosperity, health. Maybe the best English word is 'happiness.' It's what the world turns on. People just want to be happy, although they call it success, or money, or 'to make a difference.' Hitler did all his monstrous things simply to be happy. The same with Attila the Hun, and Charles Manson, and Muhammad, and Francis of Assisi. Happiness is one of the Devil's great lies."

"What's the Devil got to do with anything," said Manning.

Isaac smiled his secret smile again. "Satan's an interesting guy. I know him well. I followed him and his pan flute down a primrose path a lot longer than most men. His shopping cart is full of goodies, all as phony as the Wizard of Oz. 'The father of lies,' Jesus called him. I should know. Like Solomon, I found out it's all phony—like the western town on MGM's back lot. It looks real, but you walk through the saloon's swinging door and you're on the back lot again.

They both worked on the soufflé for a while. "You became a cynic," said Manning, finally.

"No, I bought the Devil's line." Isaac reached over to a fruit bowl at the end of the table and held out a mango, gleaming plump and rosy. "The Devil, or the world, if you prefer, holds his promises out like this. Round, juicy, perfect. But take a bite, and it turns to ashes in your mouth. Eve found that out." He found Manning's eyes. "You found that out, Manning. You looked at what Enrique had and you wanted it. To be happy. But when you bit into the mango it was a little sour, eh? It could bite back. It bit your brother."

Manning looked away.

"Each of us comes in his own time and place to a fork in the road, " Isaac continued. "Some of us go left, some go right. One day in the 18th Century I stood, figuratively, at that fork. To the left was the path I was already on. . . the primrose path, the way of the world. To the right, a different way.

"So I stood one morning in front of a heavy wooden door at a Benedictine abbey in the hills of Alsace and knocked. I had set everything aside to get to that door, and it wasn't easy. A count's title and a king's ransom. I left it all on that doorstep in Alsace and entered the abbey as a novice. I took vows of silence and poverty and slept on a pile of straw for forty-five years.

"For five years I cleaned fireplaces and chamber pots. When the Father Superior judged that my humility was real he set me to translating the Holy Bible into Spanish. A formidable job, don't you think? But I had four decades to do it. Now I read the modern translations and shake my head over my poor job. But it taught me classical Hebrew and Greek. And it taught me the Scriptures."

"The Jew became a Christian."

"The Jew became a Christian. A real one this time, not spray-painted to escape the Inquisition. Understand, it wasn't the Benedictine order, or vows of silence or poverty, or cleaning chamber pots that made me a Christian. It happened in here." Isaac tapped his chest.

"You don't look like a Benedictine," said Manning. "Have you renounced your vows?"

Isaac smiled at the ceiling. "Yes. . . and no. The Fount drove me out of the abbey. Over the decades my brother monks grew old and died. Fathers Superior came and went. The monks began to whisper about Brother Isaac, who had not aged a week in forty-five years. A miracle. He is touched by God. Their attention was drawn off of our Lord to me. So I came out into the world again, but inside I'm still a Benedictine. No. Not a Benedictine and not a Catholic. A Christian."

"Have you ever regretted it?"

"Regretted turning to God? What decisions don't you question at some time or other? I did lots of that in the next three hundred years. But I always come back. Peter said to Jesus, 'Where else can we go? You alone have the words of life.'"

The two men ate quietly. "How's dinner?" asked Isaac finally.

"Wonderful." Manning was too worried to taste anything. He picked up a forkful of soufflé and looked at it, then put it down. "Tell me, Saint Benedict, does it say somewhere in your Bible that it's okay to step into the shoes of a dead man from the LA Times obits? Or to kidnap and kill to keep a musty secret safe?"

Isaac stopped eating too. "I turned my head when Tomaso killed to protect our secret. I did what I could to stop it, I told myself. But I was trying to wipe my hands clean with a bloody cloth." He pointed his fork at Manning. "I'm no saint. Or maybe I'm like all saints. . . a sinner too."

The two men ate in silence. Manning finished first and put his napkin on his plate. "Look, I'm sorry. You can be a Christian or Benedictine or Hindu for all I care. I mean, I respect your religion. I just want to get this Andrew Trotter stuff behind us and go get Howard Sergeant. And Tomaso. And Audrey."

Isaac put down his fork. "Relax. If you think bad things are gonna happen they will. We'll meet Trotter and go from there."

"That's your plan?"

"If you've got a better one I'm open."

"They're gonna discover my wire sooner or later," said Manning.

"No wire. I'm going with you."

chapter 19

"No One Looks At A Beggar."

Manning and Isaac showed up 20 minutes late for the meeting in Santa Monica. Trotter was pacing up and down. He was alone. "Where's your principal?" Manning asked.

"In time, in time. Who's this?"

"My name is Isaac Talmud," Isaac said. Manning looked at him, surprised that he used his real name. Who said it was his real name?

"So why are you here, Mr. Talmud?"

"You want to know the secret of long life. I know more about it than my friend here."

Trotter nodded toward the Pacific glinting gunmetal gray a hundred feet below the cliffs. "Enjoy the view. I got to make a call." He moved out of earshot and punched some numbers into a cell phone. He talked a long time, glancing at Manning and Isaac now and then. Isaac stood relaxed with his hands in his pockets. Manning watched Trotter talking on the phone and puffing on a cigarette, wishing now that he hadn't given up smoking.

Trotter came back. "He says he'll see you," he said, sounding surprised. "We're going for a drive. Follow me." He pointed with pride to his Porsche.

Manning and Isaac followed Trotter east. They wound up Sunset Boulevard to the estate in the hills. Manning watched the Great Man's iron gate swing open. "Is this a trap?" he asked Isaac.

"We have information they want. We hold some cards," Isaac said. He was calm and in control. The conquistador.

They climbed the hill and parked in front of the rambling California style house under its red tile roof. Trotter led them into the great front room with its wall-to-wall Los Angeles views. "I'll tell him we're here," he said, leaving the room.

Manning was struck by the view. Beverly Hills spread out below them in greens and browns, and then West LA and Santa Monica marched down to the dark Pacific. He could see Catalina Island lumped on the horizon. Isaac was looking at something in the center of the room. He walked to a dark Mediterranean-style table and lifted an old silver chalice from it. Manning joined him. Isaac was turning it over in his hands. It was paper thin and gleamed faintly through centuries of oxidation.

"It looks like the Holy Grail," said Manning, but Isaac was silent.

"It's Spanish, 16th or 17th Century," said a deep voice behind them. The Great Man had come into the room. He was in dark green sweat pants and a white tank top and he looked pretty good. Maybe ten pounds overweight, with some sag in his chest and stomach, but his shoulders and arms were all right. "I'm Anthony Webb." He came over and shook hands. "Call me Tony, please." This was his house and his world, and he knew it.

He led Manning and Isaac out to the pool deck. It was bathed in the soft warm sunlight of a spring day in LA. Manning could smell the sharp dry desert scents of the Hollywood Hills. "Who do you work for?" Isaac asked.

The Great Man raised his brow and cocked his head. "You have something that extends life. Maybe it extends youth. I'm getting older, I can use a few more years of productive life," he said, answering a different question. "We're willing to pay well, a great deal."

"I'll tell you how for free," Isaac said. "No fat, no sugar, no smokes, and ten miles a week as fast as those fat thighs can take you."

The Great Man stiffened. Trotter held up his hand, smiling with all his teeth. "Thank you for the wonderful advice, Mr. Talmud. We're all grownups here. Let's talk about what you've got to offer and what we're willing to pay."

"Let's talk about who you two work for, like I asked a second ago when no one was listening," Isaac said to Tony Webb. "Mr. Trotter here has told Henry Toledo more about himself than his Mammy knows. You guys have that kind of line on us, you can't tell us who calls the shots."

Webb looked up the hillside over his shoulder. For the first time Manning saw a house up there. It was built into the hill and camouflaged by palm and olive trees. A wall of darkened glass looked down on them.

Webb started over. "You have it. We know you do. I'm interested for business as well as personal reasons. You can pretty well name your price."

"Who are you representing?" Isaac asked again. Manning looked at him. Where was he getting this? But the Great Man's cell phone was ringing. He answered, then nodded and walked to the edge of the pool deck to some wooden steps that led uphill. He started up without a word. Manning and Isaac followed. The steps led to the house on the hillside. They entered without knocking.

The house was really just one room. A bed stood in one corner and Manning could see a small bathroom behind an open door. The wall facing downhill was all glass with the same panoramic view that the Great Man enjoyed. The wall next to it was colorful in a different way. Four large video screens took up each quadrant. Two showed muted TV channels: a tennis match and CNN news. The third displayed an e-mail in-box. A spreadsheet flickered on the last screen—something about cash flow. An aging man sat in the center of the room looking at them.

He had dark hair going gray and a neatly trimmed gray beard around a thin face. He didn't get up. Manning saw why. He sat in a motorized wheelchair. A blanket covered his lap. It draped over emptiness below his thighs. No legs. The man's hands gripped the chair's arms tightly. His right eye was bright and alive. The other looked out uselessly. He nodded to the Great Man, who left the room without a word.

No one spoke for a long moment. Finally the man in the wheelchair said, "You must be Isaac Talmud. And Henry Toledo. I knew a Henry Toledo," he said, almost to himself. "He was. . . older."

Manning was tired of the verbal dancing. "We're here

to negotiate. Are you the decision maker on this deal or not?"

He could have been talking to the furniture. The two men in front of him stared at each other. Isaac took a halting step, then another, toward the man in the chair. He reached out his right hand. The other man took it in his own. Each man covered the handshake with his other hand.

Isaac looked down. "The cup. In the other house. It's our cup, isn't it?"

The man in the chair nodded. "Yes, my friend. Yes, it is."

"Is someone going to tell me what's happening?" asked Manning.

Isaac Talmud, always so put together, looked at Manning, thunderstruck. "You said you'd believe my story of the Fountain if I produced some 'real proof.' Here's your chance."

"Proof?"

"Here is Don Juan Ponce de Leon, back from his grave in Havana."

Manning gaped. The cripple smiled and bowed his head. "Exactly three men in the world know that," he said. "We three." He turned to Isaac. "I watched you down at the pool. You look good. You haven't had cosmetic surgery on that beak."

A slow smile spread over Isaac's face. "I've grown to like it."

De Leon turned serious. "Your secret. . . our secret, is safe. Tony Webb and his man Trotter both work for me.

They know nothing of value. Forgive me for worrying you. I wanted to flush you out of the underbrush, Isaac. I need to talk to you."

The two men still held their handshake. Isaac stared at de Leon. "I saw you dead and buried in Havana."

"You saw an empty coffin lowered into the dirt."

"And you let us think that you were in it."

"I did nothing," said de Leon. He released his grip on Isaac's hands and arched his back in his chair. "You saw me in Havana, Isaac. I remember you carrying me ashore. What did you see?"

"A man as bloated as a dead pig and twice as foul."

"Exactly. I remember nothing of those last days until I awoke like Lazarus on a stable floor behind the inn run by Jose Blanco. Do you remember him?" When Isaac shook his head de Leon said, "Jose was a native Cubano. You gave me to him to prepare for interment. Jose had laid me out and was tearing strips of muslin to wrap me when, as he told me later, the hair on his arms stood up. My chest rose and fell. He put his head to my lips and heard the rattle of my breath. He had a live man on his hands.

"Jose sat and watched me for an hour, while he consulted the Virgin in prayer. The Virgin spoke back. Jose was to care for me in secret until I recovered."

"Why?" asked Isaac. "Why not simply notify us, your soldiers, to come for you?"

"I asked Jose the same thing. He replied that when Our Lady spoke he obeyed. I watched his eyes and asked again. The real reason was that he was afraid of you and the others. He had seen his Indian countrymen beaten and killed for reasons that seemed more innocent than the discovery of a corpse that still breathed.

"Anyway, for whatever reason, Jose and his wife cared for me, and there could not have been more caring nurses in all the Caribbean. They cleaned me, turned me, and dripped water into my mouth for a month. The Fountain was at work, you see. It needed time to heal my body."

De Leon glanced at the blanket on his lap. "It would probably have cleared up my legs as well, if the idiot doctor had not been so eager with his saw. At any rate, they fed and bathed me until my strength began to return.

"I say began to return. Believe me, Isaac, I was still a mess. My legs were gone and my left eye was blind." De Leon touched it with a finger. "When Jose's wife held a mirror to my face I remember thanking God that they had nursed me in secret, far away from all of you. And in secret I stayed, in their barn, for a year. In that year Jose and his wife never stopped caring for and feeding me, even when the corn meal that I ate meant that they and their five children went hungry. They taught me what Christ meant, when he told us to love our enemies. I had many opportunities that year to reflect on the loving mercy of a God who sent two Indians to save the life of a man who had murdered so many of their people."

De Leon shook himself. "Anyway I had no choice but to accept their charity and put myself in God's hands. Don Juan Ponce de Leon, ambitious self-serving opportunist, became Juan, a half-blind cripple. After that year, I ventured outside. I sat on the cathedral steps in Havana wrapped in rags, with a coconut beggar's bowl in my hands, from first mass until the church emptied at sunset. Then I dragged myself to Jose's barn, where I slept with the rats.

"The life of Job," said Isaac.

"The life of the prodigal son. As I sat on the cathedral steps in the rain and the hot sun, I came to my senses like the prodigal did. I sat there for three years gathering silver coins bit by bit." De Leon looked up at Isaac. "One of those silver coins was yours, Isaac. Do you remember?"

Isaac didn't return the look. "I don't, no."

De Leon smiled to put his friend at ease. "No one looks at a beggar. I blessed you and prayed that you wouldn't see Don Juan Ponce in that miserable bundle. You didn't. None of my old soldiers recognized me, and I saw many. I could live as a crippled beggar. I couldn't bear to re-emerge as what was left of Don Juan.

"At the end of three years I had saved three gold coins. One I put into the cathedral's poor box. The second I gave to Jose and his wife." De Leon laughed in a strong baritone. "I had to tell them what it was. They had never before seen a gold coin. I took the third coin to a moneychanger in the city and struck a bargain. He would lend the money, and we would divide the profit. I returned after four weeks for my share. The scoundrel called the soldiers of the Crown down on a poor cripple who was telling lies about him."

De Leon shrugged. "It taught me a lesson I carried with me over the centuries. You learned it too, Isaac, or you wouldn't be here. The moors in Espana had a saying: 'Trust in Allah but tie your own camels.' After two more years I had three more gold coins. This time I loaned them out myself."

De Leon watched the smile spread across Isaac's face. "I know what you're thinking. Who would repay a moneylender with no legs? Well, some didn't, but some did. At the end of the sixth year I had a little more. Only a little, but I had lots of time. Money that grows slowly becomes formidable over time, doesn't it, Isaac? 'Gather your increase little by little,' Proverbs teaches us, 'and it will grow.' I gathered it, and I gathered wisdom too, little by little over the years. A man can learn a lot about his fellow man by begging up at him from the dirt and by calling in a loan. I begged, I loaned, and I kept the increase safe.

"I made enough finally to take leave, thankfully, of my seat on the cathedral steps. I bought Jose's inn from his landlord and gave it to him. He and Maria were overjoyed, but it was nothing to the debt I owed them. Do you know, Isaac, there are three direct descendents of Jose and Maria who still receive a gift of money each Christmas from a mysterious benefactor? They have no idea who." De Leon smiled a contented smile. "I like that. It suits my style."

"Your style seems to favor the shadows, old friend," said Isaac. "Why do you stay out of sight? My God, five hundred years! You knew how to find us. We would have been overjoyed to have you join us. Was it. . ?"

De Leon looked down to his lap again. "Was it my legs? A little, I suppose. But I'm over that. I would have relished your friendship, too. But I serve better from the shadows."

"Why?"

De Leon pointed to Manning. "Enrique, here, our ersatz friend. You're a recent player in all this. What's your story?"

Manning told his story, with some help from Isaac. He finished with, "Isaac and I are working together. . ."

"Somewhat reluctantly," Isaac added.

"Yeah, but we both have an interest in finding Tomaso. He killed my brother."

De Leon shook his head from side to side. "I have watched Tomaso, too, very closely. Yes, he is clever and evil enough to murder in cold blood. However, he's not in it alone. . . it isn't just him."

"Then who?" Manning said quickly. "I'm tired of this ballroom dancing. Who is trying to kill me, and who killed my brother?"

De Leon held up a hand. "In time, in time. First I will tell a story." He winked at Isaac. "We Spaniards love to tell stories."

"Let's just get Tomaso," Manning said. "I don't want to hear another story."

Ponce looked up almost gently from his chair. "This story isn't for you, Mr. Crenshaw. It's for Isaac."

That took a moment to sink in. When it did Manning looked from one Spaniard to the other, furious. "You're not gonna, are you? Adam's dead, Audrey's a hostage, and you two are gonna whisper to each other like spinsters while I. . . Mr. Irrelevant. . . can just wait in the car."

"Manning. . ." Isaac began. He started again. "Manning, Don Juan has good reasons to do this his way. I frankly don't know why. I just know him." He put his hands on Manning's shoulders. "We've come a long way, my friend. Come with me just a little farther."

Manning looked at him with a crooked smile on his face. He felt like a flunky. "What choice do I have? You two drive the bus. I just sit in the back." He crossed the room. "I'll check into a hotel somewhere and wait for instructions." He left without looking back.

Isaac smiled and shook his head at Ponce. "Was that necessary?"

Ponce smiled back. "Let me tell my story, then you decide." He took a deep breath. "How do we die, Isaac?"

"Some get killed. Some kill themselves. Some. . . I don't know."

"Enrique Toledo?"

"I don't know."

"Then I'll tell you a story."

Isaac settled into an armchair facing his old friend. "Tell your story."

"In 1762 I found myself on the island of Martinique," Ponce began. "In the capital city of Fort-de-France. The French and the English fleets sailed in on alternate Wednesdays, it seemed, to knock some more masonry with their cannon from the old Spanish fort that guarded the harbor and raise their flag from the governor's house for a while. I had gathered enough money by then to bankroll voyages for the alcoholic sea captains who sailed from the island with copra and molasses and who returned with European finery or black slaves from the Ivory Coast. I had enough left over for a big house on a hill high enough to catch the cool sea breeze and an office on the waterfront and a chair with wheels on it with a black slave boy to push me around and fetch lemonade. There were enough diamonds in the bag around my neck to buy a voyage back to Spain. I was contemplating the trip when I heard the words I never wanted to hear.

"'Don Juan? By the love of sweet Jesus. Is it you?'

"It was Leonardo Souza, the one we called 'Portagee,' remember, Isaac? Chest like a cooper's keg and a head as thick as a mainmast. There he stood in the doorway looking like he had seen a ghost, and he had. 'Capitano! Is it you? How can it be? I myself lowered you into the dirt of Havana!'

"I looked around. The room was empty except from my black boy. I gave him a coin and sent him skipping and grinning to buy pork and rice for lunch in the slave quarter. 'Close the door, Leonardo.'

"Souza had a simple tale to tell. He had ricocheted from port to Caribbean port in a variety of professions on and off the sea, outliving his various wives and enemies. But poor Portagee hadn't the mother wit to keep any of the money he had made in all those decades. He told me of his life between gulps of dark rum, all the while looking at me goggle-eyed. When he was drunk enough I told him my story and made him my man. Souza became my first agent. . . a front man who swiveled and bobbed in public while I pulled the strings from the shadows."

De Leon wheeled himself to his cliff-like windows and pointed to the Great Man on the terrace below, talking soundlessly into a cell phone while a young maid in starched white and black followed him with coffee. "Souza was the first, and this one down there is the most recent. This one is the smartest, and the world sees him as a primo-power broker. But it's my money he plays with. When he moves his lips my words come out.

"Portagee was the same. He cheerfully did as he was told and kept his mouth shut about my secret as well as his own. He grew rich and I grew richer. Ours was a partnership for the ages."

"So where is he?" Isaac asked. "Why isn't Leonardo down there by the pool with a phone in his ear?"

"Why indeed? The arrangement between us sailed on as smoothly as a three-masted schooner for eighty years. We became 'El Banco de Plata,' the 'Bank of Silver,' named after the river, not the precious metal. Then one morning Souza's upstairs maid opened the door to his bedchamber to find him staring serenely up at his rafters with ten centimeters of stiletto peeking out between his third and fourth ribs. His most recent wife's personal servant girl, it seemed, had confessed to her mistress, in tears, that she was carrying the master's child. The matter quickly went to court and quickly exited. Portagee's wife was excused for justifiable outrage. The servant girl was judged as innocently seduced. Justice was served.

"I started with the magistrate. He had just paid, in gold, for a large hacienda on the Town Square. A remarkable purchase, even for a judge who received a tidy stipend from the slave trade. Two dangerous looking men in my employ called on him one evening. After a brief inspection of the knives they carried, he was happy to tell them that a purse full of gold had come anonymously to him with instructions for a quick and just disposal of the Souza case. My same two employees intercepted the servant girl just as she boarded an inter-island schooner bound for Panama. She, too, had her bag of gold. She was neither seduced nor pregnant, only greedy. I sent her on her way.

"Mrs. Souza had been a more reluctant convert to the conspiracy. She had truly loved her husband. Three 'dark men' had come in the night, she told my agents, and had showed her the stiletto. Did she want to have it stuck into her or into Souza? Terrified, she agreed to the story of a love-triangle. Not too terrified, however, to turn down her own bag of gold.

"So, here was a puzzle to solve. Leonardo had been neatly dispatched at significant cost, after careful planning. Who were the murderers and what was their motive? His business, his fortune, his wife? All were untouched. Revenge? Perhaps, but for what? Portagee was too stupid to do anyone real harm."

"So, what was the answer?" Isaac was intrigued by the mystery.

De Leon tossed his hands up. "My friend, there was no answer. There the matter stood for fifty years, while I found and groomed other agents to manage the bank. The mystery gnawed at me like a tapeworm for those five decades, and finally I had a thought.

"I called in my agent. . . my third by this time, and told him that I was very interested in any information he could dig up on ways to increase one's life span, or to preserve youth. Information came in almost immediately. Herbs, spells, incantations, Indian witch doctors. But with all this chaff came wheat, too. Little by little I learned of men who seemed to have truly discovered the secret of eternal life. Men who stayed the same while the world grew old around them. I sent agents, the best men I could find, to find them and study them. Some, of course, were bogus. Others were genuine."

"Los Viejos," said Isaac.

"Los Viejos, your term for our old comrades," de Leon agreed. "I set about unearthing my soldiers from Pascua Florida the way an archaeologist works a dig. One by one I found you all. In a way I embarked on a second expedition. I lined you up like lead soldiers in ranks, and set you marching. I tracked you across continents. I watched you make and lose fortunes and families, and I watched you die."

"Die," Isaac repeated thoughtfully.

"Yes, die. That was the interesting part. Let me ask you again, how do we die, Isaac?"

"Well," said Isaac, "we are violent men, so we die violent deaths. We fight until someone kills us, or we lose hope and kill ourselves."

De Leon cocked his head to look up at his friend with his one bright eye, like a parrot. "I thought so too. I sent out investigators. At one time I had fifteen teams out. Can you imagine? I had them sift and search each of our comrades' death. I kept book on all of you, if you like. I wanted to see if others had died the way Souza did."

He sat back in his wheelchair, straightening the blanket on his lap. "I found that almost half of the deaths told me nothing. No witnesses, no clues. Half of the rest seemed from the evidence to be as advertised. Jesus Maria Alvarado, remember him? He was indeed killed in a duel just outside of Paris in 1680, and Manuel de Soto actually did mix enough poison into his brandy to overcome the curative powers of the Fount. That sort of thing."

De Leon paused and contemplated the view from his picture window. "Ah, but the rest—the other twenty-five per cent! They were all set up to look like something they were not. Just like Souza. Someone made their deaths look like battle damage or suicide, and they were not."

"Who?" Isaac was up and pacing.

De Leon watched him stride back and forth. "You know. I can see it in your face."

Isaac nodded with eyes as bright and hard as marbles. "Si, por su peusto. I know."

Ponce nodded with a grin. "Now it's your turn. Tell me what I need to know."

Isaac sat back down. "I'll tell you a story about a trust named Tannenbaum and about a doctor in Vienna."

chapter 20

"Meet At The Giraffes."

Manning checked into a room at the Hyatt by noon, tired and cross. He felt like a chess-piece that Isaac and Ponce de Leon were moving around some cosmic board. A pawn. He pulled his laptop out of his briefcase to check his mail, using Henry Toledo's service and e-mail address. There were eight new non-spam messages. None from Audrey, which made him even more irritable. One was from "T. Peterson." Curious, Manning opened it.

> Dear Henry.
> Shall I tell you how you can regain your friend?
> Tomaso (619) 566-1707

Tomaso. He dialed the phone number.

"Hello?"

"This is Toledo."

"Enrique! Wonderful. I didn't recognize your voice. Seems to have changed a bit."

"You have instructions for me?"

Tomaso chuckled. "Right to the point. Good. We will meet at the San Diego Zoo tomorrow at Two P.M. Meet at the giraffes. Understand?"

Manning was silent. Tomaso said, "Do you want to see your lady friend alive again? Do you understand?"

"Understood."

The line went dead.

Manning put the phone down. Now Tomaso had been added to the mounting list of people who told him what to do. He unlocked the small guest refrigerator in the room and took out a beer. He had abandoned Manning Crenshaw's life because he couldn't control it. Now everyone else controlled Henry Toledo. Manning shut his eyes and made a decision. He put down the beer, unopened, repacked his computer, and checked out of the Hyatt. He drove south down the 405 Freeway to a Holiday Inn.

chapter 21

"Freeze, Turkeys."

Audrey Cobb sat with her mother in the sitting-room alcove of a large master bedroom. They were being held captive in a hillside home in the suburb of Los Angeles, north of Malibu.

A tanned young man with long blond hair over dark roots bounced into the bedroom. He looked like an aging surfer. "All right, ladies. Lunch time." He was one of Audrey's two captors.

Audrey helped her mother up. Mama had lapsed into a kind of simple-minded daze that Audrey didn't like one bit. They all went into a sunken dining room that overlooked a dried-up ravine—"Arroyo seco," Audrey remembered from high school Spanish. Two tuna sandwiches waited at the rather formal dinner table. Their second captor waited as well. He had graying, curling hair and was as thin as a soda straw. His frailty was offset by a businesslike shoulder holster that showed the butt of a revolver under his left arm. He was the one who called the shots. He noticed Audrey's sour expression. "Don't look like that, missy. We're only doing a job."

Audrey sat down at the table. "You don't have to look like you're enjoying it."

"Are we having salad with this?" asked her mother, eyeing the sandwiches. "A salad is an important part of every meal." The old woman lifted her sandwich and looked toward the kitchen. She gave a small cry and dropped her food.

Audrey and the two men looked at her, then at the kitchen doorway. Winston Churchill crouched there, feet wide apart, red-faced, pointing his enormous Magnum with both hands. "Freeze, turkeys," he said in a weak voice.

"Just go easy, friend," said the thin man. He had his hands in the air. The surfer looked like he wanted to pass out.

"All right now, let's just take those guns out, slow and easy. Throw them on the floor," Winston said. He was barely audible.

"Oh, Winnie, for heaven's sake! What are you doing?" Audrey was smiling. She got up and went behind the two men, collecting their pistols. The surfer had a tiny 22 caliber stuck into his Levi's in the small of his back. She flicked the safety off with her thumb. I'm developing a certain knack for this small arms stuff, she thought. A month ago she had never held a gun.

"This is none of your business," the thin man said to Winston. "You don't know what you're getting into."

Audrey's mother said, "Dear, isn't this the nice young man from work who's been seeing you?"

Audrey cocked the thin man's gun and pointed it at the two men, too. She felt better. She was afraid that Winston would be provoked into pulling the trigger, and who knows where the bullets would wind up? "Come on," she said to Winston and her mother, "we're getting out of here."

"I haven't finished my lunch," said Mama.

Audrey lifted her to her feet with her free hand, her non-gun hand. "How'd you get here, Winnie?"

Winston smiled a superior smile. He was still dressed for work in pinstripe and flowered tie. "I've got a rental outside. Red Ford Taurus."

Audrey rolled her eyes. "Why don't you give these two the license plate number? We don't want them to have any trouble tracking us down."

Winston produced a set of chrome-plated handcuffs. "These turkeys aren't going anywhere."

"Now you're cooking," said Audrey. "Cuff them together to something so they can't follow us. They can put on their own handcuffs while you cover them. I'll get our stuff. Be right back." She went back to the bedroom and stuffed her and her mother's few things into a handbag. When she returned the thin man and the surfer were handcuffed by their right wrists around the leg of the large dinner table.

"What's to stop them from lifting the table leg?" she asked Winston, who went red in the face. "Unlock them and let's start over," said Audrey.

Winston got even redder. "I don't have the key."

"You don't have the key to the handcuffs?"

"I think it was still in the box they came in. I must have thrown it away."

Audrey sat down in one of the dining chairs. "Winnie, you're a dear. I mean, you came all the way out here to rescue us. But, my God, do you switch off sometimes."

"That's no way to talk to a man," said her mother. "Men have fragile egos. Even if they're so much bigger." She touched Winston on the arm. "She didn't mean that."

Audrey was thinking. She stood and lifted the table leg herself, giving Winston a look. "Come on," she said to her two ex-captors. She stuck one of their pistols in their faces and marched them to the front door. There was an inch clearance under the doorframe. "On your knees," she said to them. She moved the surfer to the living room carpet and put the thin man outside on the porch, with the handcuffs on the door threshold. "Outside," she told Winston and Mama. "Key," she said to the thin man. "Front door key." He hesitated, so Audrey stuck the gun in his nose. He sighed and pulled a key from his pants pocket with his free hand.

Audrey wiggled the door shut over the handcuff chain, shutting it on the surfer, who was still inside. Then she locked the deadbolt. She stood back. The two men were on their knees on either side of the locked door with the handcuffs pinned under it.

"You don't have to do this," said the thin man in an even voice. "We're not coming after you. We're not paid to do that. How do we get out of this?"

"You'll think of something," said Audrey. "You're master criminals." She led Winston and her mother to Winston's Ford parked at the curb. They could hear the surfer cursing from inside the house.

"Someone will come by and let them out," Winston

said.

"Okay, you're a neighbor or a passerby. Here's this guy on his knees, handcuffed to a front door. He's wearing an empty shoulder holster. What's the first thing you do?"

"Call the police?"

"Right." Audrey took the car keys from Winston and they drove off.

"Herr Gruber, your two o'clock is here," said Hermann Gruber's intercom.

"Danken." Hermann Gruber set aside the correspondence he was reading. He looked at his daily calendar. His two o'clock was a Mr. Harold Green-Trenholm from London. Assignment of an estate distribution. That could mean anything. He walked to his outer office. A distinguished Englishman with a thick head of long silver hair stood and smiled. Herr Gruber took to him immediately. Gruber had his own silver mane. Gruber's was a rug. "Mr. Green-Trenholm. What can I do for you?"

The two men shook hands. Gruber's visitor presented his card:

Sir Harold Green-Trenholm KB OBE
Green-Trenholm, Barfield, and Holmes
Solicitors
St. James' Court
London England
Tel 717 114 0000
www.green-trenholmbarfield.com

Gruber knew the address. Law firms from several countries paid heavy coin for offices at St. James' Court and its entry to England's rich and famous. The man in front of him was clearly St. James' Court, with his tailored suit and school tie. Gruber nodded and winked at his wrinkled secretary. The nod meant: bring coffee. The wink meant use the pre-war silver service.

Harold Green-Trenholm leaned back comfortably in Gruber's inner office and sipped his coffee. "I have a very rich client from Herefordshire. Had. Died in her sleep a fortnight ago at ninety-two. Left a sizeable estate to something called the 'Tannenbaum Trust.' Dunno why. Neither do her children and grandchildren. All fit to be tied, want to contest the will, of course. Won't do 'em a bit of good. Will's bulletproof. Wrote it meself. Anyway, I looked Tannenbaum up. Seems you're the trustee?" Green-Trenholm cocked his eyebrows.

Gruber was silent.

The Englishman set his coffee cup down. "Ah, you're a bit suspicious? Perfectly understandable, dear sir. Even commendable."

"My instructions in the case of Tannenbaum are quite clear," Gruber said stiffly. "I'm sorry, Mr. Green. I have nothing further to say."

"Green-Trenholm," Gruber's visitor corrected pleasantly. "Of course, you're only following instructions. Except my need is quite extraordinary, d'you see? The court date for my client's would-be heirs' suit to overturn the will is next week. At that time I mean to tell His Honor, and this pack of money-grubbers, that the estate funds have been delivered to Tannenbaum Trust. I have that power as trustee to the will. At the same moment I must be in a position to describe Tannenbaum in some detail, so as to appear responsible to my dead client. No fair throwing a million at some bogus cat-hospital, d'you see?"

Gruber played with his coffee cup. "How much did you say?"

"Estate rounds out to just over a million." Green-Trenholm flashed his perfectly capped teeth. "Small wonder the children are beside themselves, eh?"

Herr Gruber did a quick mental exercise, multiplying by 15 percent, which was his firm's fee for transactions of this sort: 150,000 Euros. A tidy commission. His take would be half. He cleared his throat. "I am trustee for Tannenbaum, as you supposed. However I am not at liberty to divulge. . ."

Green-Trenholm bent to his briefcase and lifted an olive-green envelope out. "Here is a cashier's check drawn on the Bank of England for one million pounds and change. I am ready to sign it over to you in exchange for details on Tannenbaum Trust, sir."

Gruber sipped some more coffee. Pounds. Of course. English pounds. The number went up by thirty percent. He pretended to consider, but he knew what he would do the moment he saw the envelope. The only question was how much to divulge. "Tannenbaum is a privately held trust for the benefit of a people."

"A people?"

"An ethnic group." Gruber walked to his filing cabinet

and withdrew a file. "They have extensive holdings worldwide, apparently stemming from gold and silver mines in Central America. Tannenbaum was established in 1909 to collect, manage, and distribute assets in Europe on their behalf. Actually, it's a rollover mechanism for a separate trust. . ." Gruber hesitated, ". . . somewhere else."

Green-Trenholm was nodding. "I understand. One trust acts for another. Transfer of assets in absolute privacy."

"You will understand then, I'm sure, that I am not at liberty to say any more about this second trust."

Green-Trenholm was smiling, nodding. "Even its name?"

"Even its name."

More nodding and smiling. "Perfectly understood, sir. If you can just give me the name of the 'people' you refer to. . ."

"I'm sorry. . ."

Green-Trenholm heaved to his feet with a sigh. "S'pose that will have to do." He handed the green envelope to Gruber along with another sheet of paper. "Your signature on this receipt will be adequate, I think." He watched Gruber sign. "I won't take a minute more of your time." He pulled a watch from his waistcoat. "Just make the shuttle to London if I hurry. Good day, Herr Gruber. Awfully good coffee."

"Auf weidersen." Herr Gruber bowed from the waist. He had a tight grip on the envelope.

"Anything yet, Gilbert?" asked Green-Trenholm. He had shed his jacket and waistcoat and stood in starched shirtsleeves looking out of the window of his hotel suite.

"Just logging in, Sir Harry," said Gilbert Belcourt. He sat at the suite's small desk at a laptop computer, pointing and clicking. Gilbert was arguably the best computer hacker in the Commonwealth. He had wormed his way into Kriegsbank's local area net three days earlier. As he watched, a spreadsheet materialized on his screen. "Banco," he said.

Green-Trenholm strolled over to peer over his shoulder. "Splendid. Any transactions?"

Gilbert pointed to the last two entries on the screen. "Here's your deposit, I think. One million, four hundred thousand, seventy-four Euros. Sound right?"

"Right-oh, at today's rates. About what I gave him."

"Last entry is a transfer of a million, four hundred forty." Gilbert looked up at Green-Trenholm, who nodded.

"That's our money again, with Gruber's fee subtracted," Sir Harry said. "All right, here's the million pound question. Where did it go?"

Gilbert was changing fields. "Here's their Internet screen. There goes your money. Today's date. Fifteen minutes ago. Here's the address." He pointed to a coded entry: XXMPF.

"Well, we didn't invest a million for XXMPF." Green-Trenholm spoke lightly. He wasn't worried.

He needn't have been. Gilbert was already clicking away. "It's a well-known international banking code," he said. “Here it is.” His screen read

> Banco do Campos Verdes
> Mexico, Districo Federal

“Splendid, Gilbert.” Green-Trenholm ran his fingers through his thick white hair. “Anything else?”

“Here’s an account number. And a point of contact. Senor Ronaldo Frederico.”

Green-Trenholm turned to the third person in the room. She was a pale blond in a neat business suit sitting quietly in a corner. “Who’ve we got in Mexico City, Penny?”

“Alan Singleton, Sir Harry. You’ve met him. Attorney. American, married to a Mexican.”

“Right. Get him onto this. He’s to find out all he can as fast as he can.”

Penny nodded. “How shall I set his expenses?”

Sir Harry tapped his chin with an index finger. “We’ve already spent a million. Give him a million pesos outright and another million under the table for bribes. Tell him time is of the essence.” He was buttoning up his waistcoat again. “You two stay here for the night. See if you can squeeze anything more from Gilbert’s magic machine. I’ve got a plane to catch.”

“Are you off to London, then?” asked Penny.

“Vienna. Got to see a doctor.”

“Oh. Nothing serious I trust,” said Penny.

“Oh, no, it’s not me,” Sir Harry smiled. “It was serious, though. The patient died.”

Audrey drove furiously down the winding road out of the Malibu hills. After a while she slowed down. Where was she going? Who could she trust? Manning or Henry, or whoever he was, was with Talmud, doing God knew what. She reached Pacific Coast Highway and turned north, toward Ventura.

"Where are we going?" Winston asked, echoing her thoughts. He was a stranger in California. So was Audrey. She pulled over to the left and parked on a stretch of empty beach. The Pacific glinted gunmetal gray 40 feet below the roadway.

"What a nice place to take a walk," Mama said. Audrey got out and opened her door and she wandered away. Winston got out and joined her in the warm sunshine. A cooling breeze blew in from the sea.

Winston still had his magnum tucked into his waistband. "Put that thing in the car," Audrey told him.

"I'm hanging on to it. Did you know it can stop a charging horse?"

"Horses don't charge." Audrey was smiling again. "Winnie, what are you doing here?"

Winston lowered his voice to an action-hero baritone. "Well, Scarlet, dear, I'm rescuing you."

"I mean, how did you find me?"

Winston was smiling now, too. Audrey knew that look. He was proud of himself. "I'm working with Interpol."

"Interpol? The International Police?"

"Yep. I phoned a friend from the FBI. We're in Kiwanis together. He traced the numbers for me of all your voice mail messages. Interpol contacted me through him. They know all about you and your. . . companion, Henry Toledo. They've been on to him for some time. You need to choose your friends more wisely, Audrey."

Audrey was silent. How do I tell him that my 'friend' is impersonating someone over a hundred years old? Finally she said, "What about the office?"

"I took some vacation. I've got the time. Been there twelve years, I think I've taken two weeks in all that time. No sick days."

"It's all that Vitamin C."

Winnie didn't get it. "Victor Rincon called me last week. He's the Interpol guy assigned to the case. From Central America somewhere, very bright young man. We collaborated. Interpol located you in that house in Malibu. I don't know how. Victor phoned me in DC and I flew out. He wanted me to go in to get you." Winnie wore that smug smile again. "So I did."

"Wait a minute. Just a minute. This is Interpol, right? The big international police force? So they use you?"

Winston looked hurt. "Interpol can't intervene in the United States. There's some rule."

"So they use the FBI or the police or the California National Guard for goodness sake. Why are they using a bureaucrat from the IRS with his Wal-Mart cannon?"

Winston's smile vanished. "Victor said they liked the way I operated. Said this operation needed to be covert."

"Covert, so they send in you, against two armed thugs, with our lives on the line." Audrey shook her head. She had been running for a long time, looking over her shoulder. She knew when something smelled bad. This story smelled like an old barn.

They heard the sound of car tires crunching the gravel behind them. Winston looked over his shoulder and his face cleared. "Okay, here's proof. Here's Victor."

A large Chrysler had parked behind them. A short, thin young man with thick black hair combed into a ponytail got out, smiling and walking toward them. Two other men, also small and dark, got out behind him.

"Winston, you did it! Wonderful!" The young man stood in front of Audrey. They were the same height. He had a pleasant open face with a snub nose and coal black eyes. "Miss Cobb, I am Victor Rincon. This has been an ordeal. You're safe now."

Am I? Audrey thought. "How did you find us?"

Victor pointed to Winston's rental car. "We put a locating device under a bumper. We needed to back him up, to make sure he was completely safe. You too, of course."

"Of course. Completely safe. So you send Sam Spade here, he's never even held a gun before, never mind fired one, in to face down two gunmen." Audrey looked at each of the three men in turn. "Who are you, really?"

Victor produced a black leather card case and handed it to Audrey. "Interpol, Miss Cobb. Winston knows us."

Audrey looked at the identity badge in the case. Victor's picture smiled out at her under an official logo and the words:

International Police Agency
Special Operative

A five-digit identification number ran across the bottom of the badge. "What's your ID number?" Audrey asked.

Victor's smile didn't exactly disappear, but it froze a little. "Pardon?"

"Your ID number is on here. What is it?

Victor maintained eye contact. "That's just a serial number for the badge itself. It's administrative, not anything. I don't have it memorized."

"It says ID number." Audrey was still looking at the card. "What's your birth date?"

Victor didn't answer. "Come on, Mr. Rincon, Special Operative. Surely you remember your birthday."

Victor spoke to the two men with him in a guttural language Audrey didn't recognize. They both drew mean looking automatics from their suits. The guns had long snouts on them. Silencers, thought Audrey. Here we go again. "We all need to leave," Victor said.

"Drop 'em or Victor gets it," Winston was shouting. All heads including Audrey's turned toward him. The barrel of his huge Magnum made small circles in the direction of Victor's expensive suit jacket. After a moment Victor spoke again in his unknown language and his henchmen's pistols clattered to the gravel.

Audrey scurried around picking them up. She had seen this video before. Victor looked disgusted. "I'm gonna get Mama," she told Winston. "If they even wiggle, shoot 'em." Winston nodded happily. Maybe his tray table wasn't fully up and locked, Audrey thought, but he was awfully good in the tight spots.

She picked her way down the dunes to the beach. Mama was at the water's edge beaming. "Audrey, look, Dear." She held up two coned seashells. "Turk's heads. Aren't they just lovely."

"Mama, they are!" Audrey said sincerely. Why not enjoy the moment with her? How many girls get to spend time at the seashore with their mothers? How many girls have everyone in the Western Hemisphere trying to kidnap them? She walked back up with her mother, holding hands. She took the keys from the Ford's ignition and took the keys to the Chrysler from Victor. "You can keep this rental and your locating device," she told him. She and Winston and her mother got into the Chrysler and drove off.

"This is a much roomier car, dear," said Mama.

"I'm paying rent on that Ford," Winston said wistfully.

"Report it stolen," said Audrey.

chapter 22

"Remember This. . . He's Afraid To Die."

Manning phoned Isaac on the secure cell phone from his room at the Holiday Inn. "I talked to Tomaso."

"I see." Isaac's voice was quiet, flat.

"Did you know that?"

"Of course not. He is dangerous. . . to us as well as to you. We must deal with him immediately."

"Uh, uh," said Manning. "He wants to meet me. I'm going. Alone."

Isaac took his time replying. "Manning, he will kill you, and then Audrey. Bang, bang."

"Maybe he'll kill Audrey if I don't go. Anyway, I want to meet him. He killed Adam. He owes me."

"You'll never see him. He uses the best in the world. He has no reason to be anywhere near to you."

Manning was shaking his head at the telephone. "No. He'll come. He's a Spaniard. You guys love the mano a mano stuff."

"You're like a small child. 'I'm going to kill someone,' you think. Anyone." Isaac paused. "Long ago I transitioned from a simple Jew to someone who used violence to get what he wanted. I advise you to walk on that path very carefully." He paused again, then said, "But I suppose I'm wasting my time. Here's something that may help, Manning. We tracked down Tannenbaum Trust. Don Juan put a team on the trustee in Munich, a man named Gruber. He traced it through Mexico City."

"Go on."

"That's all I can say right now."

"But you know more."

"If I tell you more it will put you in grave danger."

"Danger? I'm walking into God knows what with this snake Tomaso and you've got something that might help me but you can't because I might be in danger?"

"I'll tell you this," Isaac said after another pause. "Tomaso isn't working alone. Ask him about Chiapas."

"Chiapas?"

"It's a province in Mexico. Ask him."

"I'll do better than that."

"Manning, don't go. Don't meet him until we can find out more about Chiapas."

"Tomaso phoned me, Isaac. He's got Audrey. He killed my brother. He wants to kill me, not you. It's my show."

"Manning, listen."

"No. No, no, no. You listen. This is my movie. I'm starring and directing. I played a bit part in your movie long enough. You and Don Juan Ponce de Leon and the rest of your relics from the Middle Ages can buy a ticket and watch."

There was another long silence on the phone. Then, finally, "All right. Remember this about Tomaso. It may help. He's afraid to die."

"So long, Isaac. Wish me luck. Better yet, you get off on praying, pray for me." Manning hung up. He needed to pack and leave before Isaac could react. He went to the cottage's small bathroom and looked at himself in the mirror. A middle-aged accountant looked back. What in the hell was he doing?

chapter 23

The Hotel Del. . .

That afternoon Manning turned his rental in at the Holiday Inn LAX and bought a commuter ticket to San Diego. He walked to his flight gate wondering what he was going to say to Tomaso. "He will kill you, and then Audrey. Bang, bang," Isaac had said, and he was right.

Manning caught sight of a young woman waiting in line at a departure gate who reminded him of Audrey. Same slim figure, same lithe posture. When will I see her again? Will I ever? The girl turned around. It was Audrey. She saw him at the same moment and put her hand to her mouth, big eyes even bigger.

They met on the crowded concourse, looking at each other. Both said in unison, "What are you doing here?"

Winston appeared from thin air. "You're probably Toledo. I'm Churchill." He sounded grumpy. "Come on, Audrey. We'll miss our flight."

"Winnie, they haven't even made a boarding call yet," Audrey said. The three of them stood awkwardly. "Can you get me a Diet Pepsi?" Audrey asked Winston finally.

"I get it," he said sourly. He walked away, looking over his shoulder.

"What are you doing here?" Manning asked again. It was so good to see her.

"I'm. . . we're on our way back to DC. How did you find me?"

"Didn't. I just happened to see you. I'm flying down to San Diego." He took her hands, "How did you. . . I thought that you had been. . . held hostage. . . your mother. . ."

Audrey pulled her hands free. "I was, you jerk! Winston found out where Mama and I were and came out and rescued me. At gunpoint, Manning. I got tired of waiting for you to do something, so I went with him. Was that too impulsive of me?"

Manning looked into her angry blue eyes. "I didn't know where you were. I thought. . . Hawaii. . ."

"I see. You thought Hawaii." Audrey put her tiny fists on her hips. "So you're taking a plane to San Diego. You and your new friend, Talmud, with all the money in Christendom, can't find me. Winston, alpha geek, figures it out in a day. He springs me, and we're on our way home, while you're still commencing to begin to search for me, maybe."

"I'm sorry." The words sounded so lame. How could he tell her about going to confront Tomaso? It sounded too pat.

Audrey tried a little smile. "No, I'm sorry. Goodbye, White Rabbit. I'm stepping back through the looking glass, back to my beige life. Taking Mama with me."

Audrey looked to her left and Manning saw for the first time the woman who was her mother, sitting in one of the terminal's bucket seats, talking to a white-haired couple in tweeds. "I don't know," the girl in front of him continued, "maybe your life will be simpler if you don't have to deal with Audrey the Hostage."

"I'm just happy you're safe." Manning didn't feel happy. "Tell me what happened."

"I just did. Winston walked in with a horse pistol and got me out of there. In fact, after he rescued me some hoods that looked like Indians tried to kidnap me again, and he drew down on them, too. Twice in one day." She smiled, remembering. "This is a guy, he's so boring he stops clocks, and all of a sudden there he is. Captain Terrific. Someone who cares. Someone interested in me as a wo. . . as a person. Someone who looks his age and often acts it. . . who has only one name."

"Audrey, we haven't finished. . ."

"I know, the IRS investigation. Don't worry. I'll sweep it under some carpet or other. It wasn't a very popular crusade anyway. Tell Talmud and Greenway that, will you? Tell them to call off their hounds."

"You're listed as missing. . ."

Audrey looked at him as if he had horns and a tail. "You mean will the cops treat me like a missing person, come after you? Don't worry, I'll tell 'em something. Winnie and I talked about that. We'll tell 'em I went nuts for a while." She turned her mouth up and down at the same time. "Maybe that I fell for a rich New Yorker, told me a bunch of lies."

Long silence. Manning wanted to tell her how he felt. How did he feel? He wanted to see if she could be part of his life, that's how. What could he offer? Imposter, liar, brother killer. "Audrey, I'm not talking about any IRS investigation. Listen, I'm still in the middle of this. I've got to finish something. Knowing you're okay changes things. I've got to do this. After this is over. . ."

"After this is over we'll all be a hundred years old."

"Can't we meet again? Maybe not right away. . ."

"Sorry, no." Her tiny chin was way up in the air. "I'm tired of acting in a daytime soap. Keep your money and your midtown condo and your mandolin. Probably you're a nice guy, maybe a great guy under all that. I can't tell. Winston is a known quantity." She was trembling. She looked over her shoulder. Winston was shambling over with two soft drinks. "He's waiting. We're flying back. To reality."

"Is he. . . are you. . . serious? About him?"

Audrey laughed a little. "Manning, the look on your face. Am I in love with him, you mean? I don't know. He just saved my life, kind of. I'll give it a shot." She looked toward the gate, where people were queuing up to board. "Dammit, I don't know!" she said loudly. "Goodbye!" She walked to Winston and took his arm. They got in line. Manning turned to find his flight.

The Hotel del Coronado is a magnificent turn-of-the-century pile of white wood and red cupolas on the Coronado Peninsula across the Bay from San Diego. It rises like a vision of yesteryear from the Pacific sand, dominating the skyline to seaward.

Hermano Tomaso stood on the beach in front of the hotel in the early evening darkness and watched the running lights of the ships at sea and the ones entering San Diego bay to the west. He loved this hotel. He preferred old hotels: the Beverly Hills Hotel, the Peninsula in Hong Kong, and the Moana in Waikiki.

He turned and walked across the sand into the beach-front bar. The "Hotel del" had felt better in the old days when it had been down on its heels a bit, and you could get a Mexican beer for two bucks. He slid onto a barstool and ordered a Corona. Five dollars. Progress. He signed it to his room.

It had been a disappointing day. Manning Crenshaw hadn't shown up at the rendezvous at the zoo—an unexpected event. Tomaso didn't like unexpected events. He wasn't too concerned. He had the girl. Crenshaw wouldn't abandon her. He would contact Tomaso soon.

Tomaso sipped his beer for a while and tried to pay attention to a basketball game on the TV over the bar. He watched the tourists watching him until he grew sleepy. He'd sort out his problems in the morning. He took the ancient elevator to his room. He opened and closed the door to his room behind him, then became still. He slipped a small, flat Beretta from its hiding place at the small of his back under his jacket. He could see a figure in the darkness seated on the love seat in the anteroom of his suite.

"I have a gun pointed at your head." Tomaso spoke in a soft, slow voice. He didn't want to spook the intruder into an unwise move. The man was probably pointing his own weapon.

"Please turn on a light," said his guest.

Tomaso flicked a wall switch and a floor lamp lighted the suite. He knew the man. It was Enrique's imposter, Manning Crenshaw, sitting with his hands folded in his lap, looking up. No gun. "Please sit down," Crenshaw said.

Tomaso sat across from him with his Beretta level at a spot on Crenshaw's forehead. "How did you find me?"

"Isaac said you always stay here when you're in San Diego."

Tomaso nodded. It was true. Same hotel, same room. He had become predictable, therefore vulnerable. Was that good or bad? Maybe this meeting would decide. Tomaso sat quietly. The man would say what he wanted to say.

Crenshaw did, immediately. "You killed my brother."

Tomaso nodded. He had the gun, why not? "Your brother stole three million dollars. Actually, you were the thief. I really wanted to kill you."

"You have your chance now."

"I will probably take advantage of it." Tomaso shifted position to lift his feet onto the sofa, and laid his pistol on his lap, pointing it steadily. Crenshaw had not moved a muscle. "You didn't come to meet me simply to be shot. What's on your mind?"

"Adam's murder wasn't in your charter. You've been operating without authority."

Isaac had been whispering to this man. Tomaso inclined his head in the faintest of nods. "You've got it a little mixed up, but that's essentially true."

"Why?"

"Because it suits me. Your death also suits me." Tomaso got up and moved to put his pistol to the base of

Manning's skull.

"You won't kill me," Manning said evenly.

Tomaso took note of the man's calm. "Why not? Because someone will hear the shot? By the time anyone locates this room and brings the authorities I'll be gone."

"You won't do it," Manning said again. He opened the hands on his lap. They held a tan colored hand grenade. Manning kept the triggering lever closed with his left hand. He held up the detached locking pin with his right. "This is U.S. Army surplus. I had a really easy time getting it. Enough money will buy almost anything in Tijuana, apparently."

He held the grenade under Tomaso's nose. "It's got a lethal radius of ten meters. Thirty-three feet. Can you get thirty-three feet away before it goes off? Can you dodge it if I toss it after you? You can shoot me, of course, but you can't stop the explosion. You and me. Chopped hamburger."

"You're forgetting your girl friend. Anything happens to me, and she and her mother die."

"She's not my girl friend and she's not your hostage. She's fine. Call your boys in LA They can tell you, if they still work for you, that is. Given your reputation for mayhem, I'm thinking they're probably in Guatemala by now, learning how to say 'ransom money' in Spanish."

Tomaso was silent. He had phoned the house in Malibu twice with no answer. He eyed the grenade while he reviewed his options. He didn't have any. He bent from the waist and carefully put the pistol onto the carpet in front of him. "What do you want?"

"If I had wanted to kill you I'd have picked you off when you came through the door. Someone is in this with you. I want him too. I want to meet your partner."

Tomaso widened his eyes. He waited a second too long to reply. "I have no partner. I work alone."

"Tannenbaum Trust. We checked it out. Tracked it to Chiapas Province in the south of Mexico. That's the end of the world, Tomaso. Who's in Chiapas, Tomaso? That's where the Zapatista uprising against the Mexican Government is centered. Sub commander Marcos? Is he your partner?"

Tomaso spread his hands, palms up. "Do I look like a revolutionary? I have seen a hundred revolutions blossom and die in my life."

"Maybe your partner is."

"I have no partner." Tomaso pointed to the grenade. "You won't use that."

Manning closed his eyes. "How easy it would be to open my hand and end all this." He opened his eyes to stare at Tomaso. "So many questions. Why do you want to kill me so badly? The three million, where did it go? Who is in this with you?"

Tomaso was still. Manning stood up. "Let's take a trip. Want to?"

"Sounds like fun."

"Okay. Hand me your gun."

Tomaso picked it up and handed it over. Manning handed Tomaso the grenade. Tomaso squeezed the triggering handle tight. "What's this?"

"You can carry that. Keep the actuator closed. Please

notice that I still have the pin." Manning put Tomaso's pistol under a newspaper. "I'll save you some time by explaining your alternatives to you. You can drop the grenade and kill us both. You can throw it away and I'll shoot you and walk away while everyone in the hotel watches the explosion. Or, you can walk with me to your car."

"I'll take Door Number Three," said Tomaso.

"Excellent choice." Manning took Tomaso's elbow with his left hand. They walked out of the hotel room and waited for the elevator. Manning pressed "L."

The elevator stopped on the second floor and an elderly couple got in. She was in a gold jumpsuit. He wore an aloha shirt and white Bermudas over knobby knees. "Is that thing real?" asked the old gent, pointing to the grenade.

"It's a cigarette lighter," Manning said. "We're just bringing it on the market. Like it?"

"I used some just like 'em in Guadalcanal," said the old man, eyes shining. "Japs hated 'em."

"It certainly looks real," his wife said.

"Thank you," said Manning. The elevator let them out in the lobby. Manning put his leather jacket over the grenade. "Keep it that way," he told Tomaso. "Where's your car?

"In self park. Where are we going?"

"Why to your car, of course."

It was a brand-new Jaguar sedan, fully loaded. Silver. Very nice. "Keys?" asked Manning. Tomaso handed them over and Manning opened the trunk. "Get in."

"What's this?"

"Hand me the grenade and get in." The gun was in plain sight now. Tomaso got in. Manning locked the deck lid and spoke through it. "You can bang around in there to attract attention, of course. I'll just have to get out and kill you. Get it? I don't care what happens to me."

Tomaso wiggled onto his side and tried to make himself comfortable. His eyes adjusted to the dim light leaking through various cracks and screw holes. He heard the Jaguar start up and felt it maneuver into the street. After a couple of minutes he felt a smooth acceleration and guessed that they were on the Silver Strand roadway headed south. Then some turns and twists in traffic. Tomaso fell asleep.

After a time Tomaso jerked awake. He was stiff from lying on the hard trunk floor. His wristwatch had a luminous dial—one-thirty. They had been traveling for four hours. He turned on his back to ease the pain in his side. He fell asleep again and then awoke as he felt and heard the car stopping on dirt or gravel. After a minute the deck lid opened. Tomaso looked up into a cloudless sky full of stars. Manning helped him up with one hand. The other held the gun. He handed Tomaso a plastic squeeze bottle of water and a sandwich in a plastic wrap.

Tomaso opened the sandwich. Ham and cheese. "Where are we?"

"Mexico."

Tomaso nodded. "Where are we going?"

"Chiapas."

Tomaso nodded again. Nothing surprised him. "It's a long way. In a car trunk. Long way for you to drive, too. I can help drive. I give you my word, I won't try to escape."

"The word of a Franciscan monk, a Spanish conquistador, or an assassin? Which word?" Manning put him back into the trunk and closed the lid.

chapter 24

Cowboys And Indians

Chiapas is the southernmost province in Mexico and the most threadbare. It sits on the Guatemalan border. It was part of "the Captaincy of Guatemala" in the days when Spain ruled Central America. Mexico annexed it during her 19th Century struggle for independence, when political history was written by whoever had the most pistoleros on site.

The people of Chiapas are a mix of ancient Mayan and Spanish. The short, squat Indian men with mostly Mayan blood either scratch a living from the nitrogen-starved soil of the Lacandon rain forest in the east, or spend long days for poor pay working on the coffee plantations or the cattle ranches west of the rain forest owned by rich families with mostly Spanish blood. The Indian women squat on dirt floors in slat-and-mud huts and watch their children die of tuberculosis or dysentery.

San Cristobal de las Casas is the 16th Century colonial capital. It dresses the part. Red tile roofed adobe buildings cling to the city's hills and cluster around a central cathedral and plaza in soaking rain or warm sun, depending on the season. Manning and Tomaso sat in chilly shadows of early morning at an outside café table on the plaza. They were drinking strong hot espresso to recover from the two-hour night drive from Tuxtla Guiterrez, the provincial capital to the west that everyone calls "Toosla." Manning had driven, terrified, up the vertical, narrow road to San Christobal's 7,200 feet, and Tomaso had almost frozen in the trunk.

"You won't use that here," Tomaso said, talking about the grenade. Manning held it in his left hand out of sight under the table.

"Why not?"

Tomaso tilted his head toward the steady line of Indians ambling by in a variety of grays, hot pinks, and bright blues. "You'll kill them, too."

"Maybe," Manning agreed. "Maybe not. The point is, you can't be sure. The point is, I don't care if I die, and you do. It's what keeps you sitting here."

Tomaso was silent. It was true. He was afraid to die. That terror had kept him docile during the long drive to Chiapas, when Manning had let him out of the Jaguar's trunk to stretch and eat and relieve himself. It had kept him from bolting during the walk from the car to the café, and had made him admit that he did indeed have a partner, and it made him telephone him. "Speak English," Manning had ordered, and Manning had eavesdropped while Tomaso had arranged a meeting at the café.

The two men waited for an hour as the morning brightened and warmed. Then a thin dark man in his thirties joined them. He looked as Indian as the peasants in the plaza, dark hair in a pony tail, but was dressed like a Spaniard in sunglasses and dark silk trousers and a great looking white cotton shirt with no buttons and an open vee all the way down to a string-tie at the waist. He wore gold on his fingers and wrist and around his neck like a toreador. "Tomaso," he smiled as he pulled a chair from the next table without asking and sat down. He looked toward Manning. "?Quien es?"

"English, please," Manning said. "My Spanish is very poor."

The young man's smile only grew broader. He laid his sunglasses on the table and looked lazily over at Tomaso. "?Que tal?"

"This is Henry Toledo," Tomaso said in a tight voice.

"Ah." The man waggled his head from side to side as if that explained everything. "A pleasure, Henry Toledo. Carlito is my name. I have heard of you."

"You tried to kill me, you and Tomaso here. Three times, and you killed my brother. I'm here to repay you."

Carlito opened his eyes wide like a mime. He looked at Tomaso again. "You bring me an assassin?"

"He has a hand grenade under the table," Tomaso said simply.

Carlito handled that one too. He snapped his fingers at a passing waiter. "Un café, por favor." He turned back to Manning with his charming smile. "Do I have time for coffee or do we explode immediately?"

Manning was in no mood for humor. He had been awake for three days, driving the length of Mexico on bad roads, popping Benzedrine. The speed was wearing off, and the coffee wasn't helping, and he was losing his edge. "I want to find out if there are any more of you in this."

"To explode them, too?" The young man's smile flickered and went out. "Mr. Toledo, this affair is much more complex than you imagine. If you will give me some time, I. . ."

Manning wasn't listening. He stared at Carlito's chest. Without warning he reached over and tugged the cotton shirt open. Carlito jerked back, but not before Manning saw an old scar on the man's chest, a black circle the size of a silver dollar. "You are Calusa," he told Carlito. Things were snapping into place.

Carlito's smile flashed back on. "You have a good eye. You remember this cut, don't you?"

Manning pointed to the scar. "De Leon did that, didn't he?" he asked Tomaso. "Out there in Florida. This is the Calusa Indian who led you to the Fountain." He looked at Carlito. You're Cacique Carlos's great-grandson."

"Great-great grandson," said Carlito. He returned his sunglasses to the bridge of his nose. "Let's be accurate. And Carlos was never his name. 'Too-kay' is his name. 'Cacique Calusa,' which is his title, means 'Chief of the Calusa.' You Spaniards corrupted that into 'Cacique Carlos.' Do you know, though, that Too-kay grew fond of the name Carlos? He took it, and I became Carlito. . . 'Little Carlos.' You see?"

Carlito wanted to say more, but the waiter was there with his coffee. He smiled him away and opened a cloth napkin and spread it on his lap. "There is much more to tell, Mr. Toledo. You have things to tell, too. Why are you here?"

Carlito worked like a magician, keeping Manning's

attention with his questions and his eyes, while both of his hands were under the table with the napkin. Suddenly those hands were on Manning's, and on the grenade. They gripped like steel, and in a moment Manning's hand was empty and Carlito had the grenade above the table. He smiled at Manning.

"I have a pistol," said Manning.

"And you can hand it to Tomaso," said Carlito. He took a toothpick from a tin cupful on the table and locked the grenade's actuator lever with it. "I have been a warrior for five centuries. You will have a knife in your chest before you can tug your pistol out from where you are sitting on it." Carlito sipped his coffee while his sunglasses reflected the water of the fountain behind him. "Agreed?"

"Agreed." Manning fumbled the gun from his waistband at the small of his back and handed it carefully to Tomaso. He rubbed his bent fingers. What made him think that he could ride his horse into town like some gunslinger and take on men like these? What made him think that he would ride out alive?

Carlito smiled a celebrity smile. "Now that we understand one another, why don't you tell me why you come hunting us poor redskins. Have you Spanish finally discovered us? There are things I want to know before I kill you, Henry Toledo."

Manning took a deep breath. "I'm not Henry Toledo. Toledo is dead. I assumed his identity several weeks ago. I wanted his money. . . and the rest of his life."

Carlito's eyes seemed to flicker behind the glasses. He looked at Tomaso. "Es verdad—is it true?"

Tomaso nodded, eyes averted.

"One wonders what other surprises you have hidden in that black beard, Spaniard," Carlito said to Tomaso. To Manning he said, "Now you really interest me, Mr. Not-Exactly-Henry-Toledo. What is your name?"

"Manning Crenshaw."

Carlito dipped his head. "Tomaso here has a certain reputation as a tough guy. Somehow, he becomes your prisoner. Somehow you arrive a thousand miles from your country, at a table with me, with a hand grenade. Surely there is an explanation for this?"

"You stole three million from me, and killed my brother doing it. I don't care about the money. I want you to pay for the murder."

"You want us to pay," Tomaso repeated quietly, cracking a grin that a lizard would have worn if lizards smiled. He reached over almost casually and gripped Manning's hair, bouncing his face off the table surface.

Manning rose up and sat back, dazed, eyes full of water. He cupped his nose in his hands and wiggled it. Things that used to be solid in there moved around now and hurt like hell.

He mopped up some blood with his napkin. People at other tables watched him. He waved his free hand, and they looked somewhere else.

"Enough, Tomaso." Carlito toyed with the grenade, spinning it like a hard-boiled egg. None of the other tables seemed to notice.

"It's good to have an enemy," Carlito said to Manning. "A man measures himself against an adversary. But you must take care to win. No excuses." He regarded Tomaso for a long moment. "Everything this one says is news to me. I have this feeling in my toes that these things are not news to you." He stood and put the grenade in his pants pocket. "We are going for a ride, Manning Crenshaw. We will talk on the way."

"This is a bad idea," Tomaso said.

Carlito gave him a withering look. "You don't have a vote, my friend. Remember our agreement."

"I'd be interested in that agreement," said Manning.

"Indeed," said Carlito. "Perhaps we'll come to that."

"Idiot," Tomaso said.

Carlito hardly glanced at him. "I'm an idiot? Am I the one who led a hand grenade to San Christobal?"

They walked to a new red Land Rover parked facing the square. Tomaso pushed Manning into the back, lowering his head under the doorframe like a movie cop.

When they were both in the back Tomaso started in again, with a short chop to the kidneys that wasn't effective in the close quarters, followed by a rabbit punch to the back of Manning's head with his pistol butt. Manning wrapped his arms around his head.

Carlito got behind the wheel. "Enough, enough," he told Tomaso in a mild voice.

"This one almost killed me in my own trunk last night, in the cold," Tomaso hissed. He found an opening and pistol-whipped Manning's head again.

"No more," Carlito said sharply. He pulled out and headed west. "We are going to what you Gringos would call our tribal lands," he told Manning..

The pain in Manning's nose and head triggered a behind-the-eyes headache. "You don't seem. . ." Manning fumbled for the right words.

Carlito helped him out. "I don't seem like an Indian, do I? Smelling like a horse blanket, drunk on firewater, selling turquoise earrings from a cardboard box? You're right. It's because I'm not. We stopped being Indians hundreds of years ago. We noticed that the White Man held all the face cards, so we became White Men."

"We?"

"The tribe. The Calusa." Carlito smiled at his passenger in his rear-view mirror. "You can say we jumped the reservation."

"The trust I followed here, Tannenbaum Trust. Is that the Calusa?"

"Absolutely. We are still a tribe. One of the few tribes without a gambling casino. We live together in estates, on land we bought and paid for, land the size of your Rhode Island. We have invested in gold and silver mines throughout Central America, among other things." Carlito smiled his bright smile into the rearview mirror. "I'm taking you to my great-great-grandfather. He will be interested in you.

"Why do you want to kill me?"

"No one wanted to kill you, at least not anyone named Manning Crenshaw. Our quarrel is with the Spaniards who followed de Leon. Now, it's a different matter. Now you serve us better dead, whether your name is Toledo or Crenshaw. If you step into someone's shoes you must be prepared for them to be too tight."

Manning set the threat aside to worry about later. "Why kill the Spaniards?"

Carlito had cleared the pedestrian traffic in town. He wound the Land Rover up and nodded toward Tomaso. "The Spaniards have written brave tales of adventure and discovery. They brought civilization to us squalid Indians, eh? Savages who needed only Christianity to make them whole. Well, my friend, we're not savages. We are a people, a nation. The Spanish tried to commit genocide. They drove us from our land, far from our Fountain. What would you do?"

"I wouldn't nurse a grudge for five hundred years. The ones who have done that have only paralyzed themselves. The Arabs and the Jews. Northern Ireland. The Balkans. Meanwhile minority immigrants in my own country. . . Asians and Hispanics. . . come, work, and educate themselves into the mainstream."

Carlito raised his hand with two fingers pointed in a "V." "Two things. One, your minorities had the luxury of successive generations. Memories grow old, faint. Scars heal. We are still alive. We still remember that night in Florida vividly."

"Yes, but…"

Carlos held his hand up again. "I said two things. Two, I agree with you. Almost all the Calusa agree. The bitterness has gone on too long. Time to 'bury the hatchet,' if you will excuse a bad pun."

"Then why don't you. . ."

"Almost all. Carlos does not. He lives only for revenge." Carlito lifted his shoulders. "And he is still Cacique."

"You say they drove you from your land?"

Carlito nodded into the mirror again, driving with one hand on the wheel now, relaxed. "The Spaniards drove us from Florida. Carlos led my people in a century-long journey in search of a homeland. We settled for awhile in Louisiana, then Texas, then into Mexico, moving each time to escape society."

"What do you mean 'society'?"

"We wandered like the Jews of the Diaspora. We tried to live apart, to preserve our customs and our language. But sooner or later the good people of wherever we were asked themselves why we thought we were better than they were. We didn't consider ourselves better, just different, but they never bought that. It didn't help that we accumulated more wealth with each passing generation. It's the same all over. Homogenize or move on. We moved on."

"Finally you settled here, in Chiapas."

Carlito nodded. "A century ago."

"Why?"

Carlito held up three fingers this time. "Three reasons. First, most of the residents are too busy scratching out a living to care about us. Second, we feel at home with these people. They are descendents of the Mayan culture. Our ancestry is much the same. We even look like them. Finally, we found our true mission as a people here."

Carlito pointed out the car window to two Indian women squatting along the roadside on dirty blankets, behind cardboard boxes of over-ripe fruit and vegetables. "These people, and Indians like them throughout Latin America, are the victims of the same greed that victimized us when the Spaniards first came. We had outlived it and over time had grown wealthy. We can help."

"How?"

"Do you know anything about the Zapatista movement?"

"An Indian uprising, against the government of Mexico, led by someone called Sub commander Marcos."

"It's an interesting insurrection. It's working. The central government is listening and negotiating. The rebels are getting what they want. But it's what they want that's interesting. Marcos and his forces seized control of the town we just left, and five others, in December 1993. He published the Declaration of the Lacandon Jungle. It addresses the injustice to, and reaches out to, the ethnic poor of all of Mexico. . . really all of Latin America. The Zapatista movement is universal." Carlito turned onto a road that led to foothills in the distance. "We wrote the Declaration of the Lacandon Jungle for Marcos."

"We?"

"The Calusa. Marcos is Mexican, not Calusa. We don't control the Zapatistas, we support them. Our heart is for all native peoples oppressed by intruders, as Spain oppressed us. We have been fighting alongside people like the Zapatistas all over the world for three hundred years. We are not bound by geography. Our lawyers are arguing, right now, seven lawsuits in Brazil and Bolivia on behalf of native tribes under persecution in the Amazon Basin. We have a task force in Australia that seeks autonomy for the Aborigines. We are at work in South Africa, in Indonesia, in the Sudan. . . and every month we find a new cause, it seems."

Manning looked sideways at Tomaso. "All right. Last question. Why haven't you killed this conquistador?"

Carlito looked at Tomaso as well. "We have signed a treaty with this one. He helps us."

"And you help him kidnap Audrey Cobb, right? She said some 'Indians' tried to kidnap her. I know why Tomaso took her. Why did you try?"

Carlito shook his head at the mirror. "She and her employer, Mr. Churchill, knew too much. Sooner or later they would lead someone to us, or to our Fountain. We knew where Tomaso had the women, in California. We posed as Interpol and sent Churchill in to rescue her, certain he would be killed. We were ready to follow up, enter the house in LA, and kill them all. It would look like a botched kidnapping. Churchill surprised us. He actually rescued the girl. Before we could react, they were gone. Then, my men find them on the highway and he rescues her again." Carlito smiled. "It was a mess."

"But Tomaso already had her. Why not simply have his men kill her and her mother?"

Carlito shrugged. "Our idea seemed better. More accidental. We were wrong."

"You might have cut me in on it," Tomaso grumbled.

"Tomaso also helped you try to kill me. Helped you kill my brother." Manning turned sideways toward the dark Spaniard. "Why didn't you tell them I wasn't Toledo?"

It was Tomaso's turn to shrug. "They wanted to kill Toledo. Why not let them kill the only Toledo still standing?"

Manning closed his eyes and shook his head. "You're working both sides of the street. You're killing your countrymen for the Calusa. Judas betrayed Christ for a few silver coins, Tomaso. Why did you sell your friends out?"

Tomaso kept his eyes fixed on the back of Carlito's head. "You're gonna find out in a few minutes."

"Okay, then," Manning said. After a moment, to Carlito's eyes in the mirror, "Why do you need three million? The Spaniards made all the money they'll ever need. Are they smarter than you?"

"No. And yes. I told you why we settled in Chiapas. . . our work for the oppressed native peoples of the Americas. For this we need money. Lots of money."

"You had five-hundred years to get it."

"We had, and we did. Then, twenty years ago, we blundered badly. We were citizens of Mexico, and Mexico was full of promise. Vast oil fields had been found. The country needed venture capital to develop them, and distrusted the Norte Americanos. Everything else. . . agriculture, manufacturing. . . was ready to bloom. All they needed was money. We had money. We collected all of our eggs and put them in one basket."

"The basket had a hole in it."

"Exactly. Everything went south. Government impossibly corrupt, corporations incompetent. The peso lost its value. Foreign capital left Mexico on the next flight home. We were stuck with a worthless stock portfolio and valueless currency. We needed cash, badly. For ten years we sold off everything we had left. . . property, equities, even our wives' jewels." Carlito looked to his right. "Then, we found Tomaso."

"Then, I found you," mumbled Tomaso.

The Land Rover crested a hill and Carlito pulled over to the side of the road. A wide valley lay before them, green with crops and orchards in neat rows. Carlito pointed. "Coffee, sugar cane, and cotton. This is all Calusa land. Can you see the houses?"

"Yes." Large walled country manors spotted the valley.

"Each of our families has an estate," said Carlito. "Each of the warriors from the old days is a patriarch. His extended family lives with him."

"But those families die off," said Manning. "Don't your wives and children wonder that you go on?"

"No, because we tell them the truth. The Spaniards live lives of deceit. Our wives know the true story, and die content. Our children benefit from the truth. We are still one tribe, one people. We live and die together. If someone wants to leave, they leave. We require only that they keep our secret."

"And they do?"

"So far."

Carlito pulled back onto the road. "I live nearby. I'll show you."

He drove for ten more minutes to an enormous house built of yellow stone. A wall of the same stone surrounded it, and a youth in jungle fatigues and an Uzi automatic waved them through. An elegant man of 50 or so, with iron gray hair and moustache, walked from the iron doors to greet them. He shook hands with Tomaso and kissed

Carlito on both cheeks. "My son," said Carlito.

"Does your wife live here as well?"

"I'm not married at the moment." Carlito talked with his son in Spanish, and then said to Manning and Tomaso, "Cacique Carlos has risen from a nap and is in the garden in back. We should see him now, while he is rested." He led the way along a stone walkway under fruit trees.

The "garden" turned out to be a manicured lawn the size of a football field bordered by avocado and papaya trees, with islands of bright flowers. A swimming pool faced a tennis court. In the middle, in a large grassy plain, an old man sat in a bamboo chair watching two small children play with a black and white kitten. The closer Manning got, the older the man looked. As they approached, the man looked up, then got up, pulling himself up onto a metal walker with difficulty. The man was tall, as tall as Carlito and Manning, but now was bent. Ancient skin hung like drapery over high cheekbones and thin white hair stirred with the breeze. The hands that hung onto the walker were bone-thin, with large dark spots of age on them. The hands and head trembled to an involuntary rhythm. Manning was looking at an old Sycamore, still standing but dying from the roots up.

Carlito sang to the old man in a soft, clear voice—only a few notes. The song of the Calusa. The man sang in return, swaying on his walker. Carlito bent close and the two of them touched their cheeks, one side, and then the other. Carlito spoke rapid-fire in a language that Manning guessed was the Calusa tongue.

The old man regarded Manning with eyes dim with film. "I am Cacique Carlos," he said with pride, in a voice like a rusty gate. He called the two children to him and circled them with his arms. "These are my jewels," he said, "Carlito's grandchildren." He sent them running, following them with his eyes.

Manning couldn't take his own eyes from the ancient figure in front of him. Finally he turned to Carlito. "What. . . what's happening?"

"What do you think?"

"I don't know."

"Sure you do. Enrique Toledo, your namesake: how did he die?"

Manning thought about that. "Until an hour ago, I had no idea. When I found Carlito here, a Calusa, still alive, I'm thinking that you killed Toledo, somehow, in that restaurant in Manhattan. But that doesn't make sense either. If you had killed him, why were you gunning for me? He must have been very sick. His medicine cabinet is full of pills. Antibiotics, strong headache medicine..."

"Headaches are one of the first symptoms," said Carlito.

"Of what?"

"Of the end," said Tomaso. "Enrique died of old age. The powers of the Fount are ending. Enrique confided in me. He had no immune system left. He went to Vienna to see a doctor, someone expert in the disease we call 'old age.' Finally his body just shut down." Tomaso shook his head. "We're all next. It's a matter of time. I didn't want to die. I came to the Calusa because..."

"Because we are going back," Carlito interrupted. "We discovered the same thing, that the Fountain's strength is ebbing." He gestured toward Carlos. "You can see that for yourself. We were beginning to die of natural causes: old age. We started a hunt for the Fountain in Florida. A team of geologists, archeologists, and historians searched for clues to its location. From time to time we would 'review' their work, based on what we remembered from the old days. We tried to guide them without revealing what we knew. We are very close. And Tomaso wants go back with us to drink again."

"And Tomaso's part of the bargain was. . ?"

"Tomaso helped to raise money. We needed money; he needed the Fountain. He showed us how to transfer the estates of dead Spaniards to us through Tannenbaum."

"And how were they dying?" Manning asked. He angled a look at Tomaso.

"I killed them," Tomaso said tightly.

"You betrayed your comrades for the sake of a drink from the Fountain?" Tomaso didn't answer.

Carlos coughed an old man's cough, sounding like he wanted in on the action. He looked Manning up and down. "You come seeking payment in blood for your dead brother. We will talk about that." He started what would have been a very long struggle across the lawn on his walker, but Carlito set it aside and carefully took his arm. The two of them made slow progress onto the house's patio.

Carlito spoke to two servant girls in clipped Spanish, and two sweating pitchers of tea and lemonade appeared on the patio table. Carlito saw to the seating of his ancestor and then sat. Tomaso didn't take a seat until Carlito did. Manning sat last.

"You are American," Carlos said without preamble. "You have taken el nombre. . . the name, you understand. . . of one of the Spanish pigs. Why would you do that, senor?"

Manning was asking himself the same question. "It's a long story, sir. My life was at low tide. Henry Toledo died in front of me. He was rich. I thought I could assume his life without being discovered. I was wrong."

Carlos nodded. "And you want to know why your brother died." He spoke to Carlito and Tomaso in Spanish. Both answered in short sentences. Carlos looked at Manning. "I am not familiar with the details of your brother's death. We were after the man you pretended to be. After his money. Apparently your brother got in the way." Carlos inclined his head. "This isn't the way we like to do business. Can you accept my apology?"

Manning looked at the Indian maid serving tea in tall ice-filled glasses. He didn't know if he could or not. He didn't see how it mattered. For all of Carlos' graciousness, Manning promised to be a dead man himself, on his way to a grave on some hillside in Chiapas.

Carlito took note of his confusion. "Our guest has no feeling for the reason for our vendetta against the Spanish, Cacique."

Carlos waved his hand above his head as if to clear the air. "I led de Leon to the Fountain for the sake of the lives of my family. For my life too, and a chest full of gold, if you like. I kept my word, you see, and he didn't." His milky eyes flashed fire. "I gave him life and youth, a gift worth more than a thousand chests of gold, worth more than all the treasure the world has seen. He gave my people betrayal and death.

"They were all smiles, de Leon and his bandits, after they sipped from the Fount. We exchanged gifts, food. De Leon himself kissed me. Here." Carlos tapped his right cheek. "Like Judas, another betrayer I learned of in the Spanish Bible. He bade me go in peace, hand raised like Christ Himself. He promised no harm, I said the same. He gave his word.

"That night my sentries awakened me. Oh, yes, I had the mother wit to post sentries between our two camps. The Spaniards approached with the sounds of the pigs that they were, clanking their armor and cursing. We stood to our feet, groping for weapons, but long before we were formed in battle line they were on us, breastplates flashing in the firelight, muskets barking into our straw huts.

"But they didn't kill us all. A remnant of men and boys fled into the darkness of the rain forest. The Spaniards fed on the ones we left behind, our old men and our women and children. My own wife and daughters were among them.

"We fought them from the trees, picking them off one by one. The young men still wanted to attack. They were beside themselves. You can imagine. I asked them, have you seen how their muskets knock a warrior down with a blow like ten arrows? Have you seen what happened to our people in the village? Wait. Hide. Kill. They obeyed."

"How many of you?" asked Manning.

Carlos let his eyes travel out of focus. "So many years ago, I can't. . . maybe fifty."

"Fifty! Against four times that many conquistadors," said Manning. "With superior arms and armor. They should have routed you."

Carlos lifted his chin a little. "We knew how to fight in the rain forest. The Spanish pigs knew nothing. They stood in ranks and sweated while we drifted in from the trees like the mist, enveloped, and then evaporated. Finally at mid-day I stood in a clearing and called a challenge to de Leon to come out, mano a mano. A duel. Do you know of it?"

"Someone told me. One of his officers. He said you tricked de Leon. . . ambushed him from the forest. He didn't have a chance."

Carlos spat onto the terrace cobblestones. "The same chance he gave our wives and children. De Leon fell, and the fighting spirit of those pigs fell with him. They left their dead and wounded behind to mark their retreat, and we took our revenge in the Spaniards we found still breathing. Finally we watched their great ships shake the sails from their masts and disappear over the curve of the earth."

"Never to return?" asked Manning.

Carlos put on an ironic smile. "Never to return and to return like locust. De Leon didn't return, of course. He sailed on to Cuba to die there, as you know. Other ships and other Spaniards found our shores. They returned eight years later. In those eight years we found women from other tribes. . . paid for them and fought for them. . . and began to rebuild our nation. Our boys grew into warriors.

We learned from other tribes the best sapling for the bow, the straightest birch for the arrow. And we learned, better than anyone has then or since, the art of poisons. A musket ball had the force to knock a man off his feet in those days. If it didn't kill him it took him out of the battle. Our arrowheads did the same after we dipped them in a potion boiled in the iron pots that the Spaniards had left to us.

"The poison," Manning said to Tomaso. "That stuff the woman you sent put in my milk. Aunt Dorothy. It was very old. . . used by Caribbean Indians." He turned back to Carlos. "That was from your tribe, wasn't it?"

Carlito nodded from his side of the table. "Very good. Yes. The woman who visited you was Tomaso's woman. We provided the Palytoxin. That is the poison's name. It's hard to detect. We like to make things look accidental. We have been making Palytoxin for a long time. It comes from seaweed. Ah, you know that. We first used it on the arrows that we put into de Leon. Did you know that?" he asked Tomaso, continuing without waiting for an answer, "Maybe without the poison the waters of the Fountain would have saved him. But he died, the snake." Carlito also spat onto the patio.

Manning kept still. There was no need yet to tell them of a cripple in a wheelchair in California.

"The poison and our warrior reputation kept the Spaniards at arm's length," Carlos went on, "but as time passed our hunting parties returned with greater frequency to report another wooden stockade, another stone fortress, always in the best valley, or astride the choicest river crossing. The Spaniards came with smiles and colored cloth to trade for furs and meat. 'We will live in peace, we are all brothers.' It always ended with some problem that seemed only to be resolved by sword or musket.

"We were stupid. I take the blame. I was slow to learn their ways. . . so slow to put down the furs and feathers of my fathers and take up the dark woolen pantaloons of Spain. For years we defended our lands. . . and the Fountain. . . with arrows and knives against musket and cannon. Our warriors died from Spanish bullets and our women and children died from Spanish disease.

"Finally I called the tribal chiefs together. Our 'nation' had dwindled to a hundred warriors and their families. The Fount had given us the gift of youth, but our pigheadedness had thrown that gift away in endless conflict. We must change, I said. We had three choices. We could fight bravely like idiots until the last Calusa fell in battle, or we could submit like women and live a twilight life as slaves of these men we hated. Or, we could become our enemies. They had the advantage of weapons, organization, and culture. We had the advantage of time. Endless time, to learn their language and their ways, to court and marry their women, and time to let each generation of our enemies age and die. In time we could emerge as European as they were.

"And so we did. It took three generations, but finally the Calusa 'Nation' became a secret society of American colonists that were perhaps a bit darker, a bit shorter, than their neighbors, but also a lot richer and smarter. We won the battle, in the end, without firing a shot."

"And the Fountain?" asked Manning.

"That was a battle we lost," Carlito said. "For six generations we left Florida and lost ourselves in the frontiers to the west. When we returned, Florida had changed. At least our part of it had. Farms and townships sat where our hunting trails had been. We couldn't find the Fountain."

"Couldn't find it?" Manning cocked an eyebrow.

Carlos looked out toward the square green garden. "Sounds silly, doesn't it? How do a people lose their way back to the central source of their power? Silly, but true. We simply returned to a different Florida, a White Man's world. In the two hundred years we were away the game trails had changed, the old trees we used as markers were gone. Florida never did have hills or mountains that we could use to navigate with. Even the swamps and bayous had changed. We were driven from the Fount of Life just as Adam and Eve were driven from the Tree of Life. We could no longer drink from it. But we have found the way back to Eden."

"Almost," said Carlito.

"Almost," Carlos agreed. "Fifty years ago we formed a team in Florida, on our old lands. An archaeologist, an historian, and a geologist. The best we could find. They have located the site of the Fountain. Soon, we will drink again."

Carlos winked at Manning. "Not a moment too soon, you are thinking." He pinched his own cheek with thumb and index finger. "You don't have difficulty guessing my true age now, do you? If you could have seen me even a month ago it would have been harder to guess. When the Fountain withdraws its powers the flesh loses no time on its journey to the grave. I was as strong and as quick as my great-great-grandson here." Carlos nodded toward the swimming pool across the lawn. "He and I would race each other in those waters. Ten laps." He wiggled his finger at Carlito. "Always I won."

"I see how you look," said Manning. "But I saw Henry Toledo, too, the night he died. He looked as spring-like as Carlito here."

Carlos raised a bony finger. "God plays by His own rules. He takes us either in the bloom of youth or the agony of old age. Two Calusa warriors, ones who had sipped from the Fountain, died this year of old age. One had congestive heart failure. The other lost the services of his kidneys and liver. Both went to their graves looking like teenagers. In contrast look at me. But keep in mind, I was more than one hundred when Ponce tasted the Fountain. I am the oldest man on the planet."

"But you are still standing," said Carlito. "God willing, you will drink from the Fountain again."

Carlos' chin went up. "And I am still Cacique."

"Is the whole tribe going to the Fountain?" asked Manning.

"Yes."

"And the children?"

"The boys, absolutely."

Manning wondered how the girls would take that. "How about Los Viejos? They need to drink, too."

Carlos brought his fist down on the table, rattling the pitchers. "I gave them a drink. They gave me the dead bodies of my people."

Carlito put his hand over the old man's fist. Manning said, "This Spanish army you are still fighting has dwindled to nine men, who are dying. Your quarrel isn't with them. It's with Ponce de Leon, who alone ordered the massacre."

It was the wrong thing to say. Carlos' anger focused on Manning. "You have become an irritant, Mr. Crenshaw," he said. "You should have stayed in New York." To Carlito: "Why have you brought him here?"

Carlito raised his eyebrows. "I thought he might tell us something we didn't know. I was wrong. He knows nothing.

"Take him back to New York and kill him there," Carlos said. "Leave a will. He will generously bequeath his considerable estate, Toledo's estate, to Tannenbaum."

"No, Cacique. Too dangerous, taking him through U.S. Customs," said Tomaso from the end of the table. "No need. I can find a homeless corpse on any street corner in Manhattan to serve our purpose. I can hire an expert to forge Toledo's signature as well as this man did."

"All right," said Carlos, yawning. "Kill him here."

They were talking about him in the third person, arranging his murder. He was no longer present. He had only one card left. It was time to play it. "What if I can give you something?" Manning asked. "Something even Tomaso can't give you."

Carlos narrowed his eyes. "We have talked enough." He looked out across the green lawn, then back to Manning. "Very well, what is it?"

Stay calm, Manning told himself. You may still be

able to ride out of here alive. "I have just said that your quarrel is with de Leon. Suppose I told you he was alive?"

Carlos looked at Carlito, who lifted his shoulders. He looked at Tomaso. "I buried him myself," said the Spaniard.

"Did you see him in the coffin?" asked Manning.

"No." Tomaso sounded uncertain, which helped.

"You buried an empty lead box. Ponce survived his wounds. I have met with him."

"And your proof?" Carlito asked.

"Tomaso can speak with him, on the phone. Perhaps Ponce's voice will be enough. Or Tomaso can ask him a question, one only de Leon can answer." Manning looked Carlos in the eye. "You can meet him too."

Carlos was very still. "How will you convince him to come here?"

"Not here. To the Fountain. Ponce needs to drink as much as you do. Suppose he comes? Suppose you could confront him again?"

Carlos' lips twisted up to show his canines. "Ya, Seguro!"

chapter 25

No Cards Left

"Yes?"

"Isaac, it's Manning."

"Where are you?"

Manning grinned into the telephone receiver. "I'm in Chiapas, with the Calusa. Remember them?"

Isaac skipped a beat, a rare display of astonishment. "You can still surprise me, Manning Crenshaw. Don Juan ran you off, remember? So you wouldn't hear what he had to tell me, that the Calusa were hunting us down, one by one, over the centuries. So what do you do? While I'm still trying to find a way to talk to them you find them yourself."

"Isaac, I need to talk to Don Juan. Can you reach him?"

"I'm with him. One moment." Manning could hear the two men talking away from the phone. Then Ponce was on the line.

"Don Juan, it's a long story. Cacique Carlos is alive, down here, with his people. Listen, he's found the Fountain. He's going back. He's dying, Don Juan, along with his people. He'll meet you there. He wants to confront you."

"He wants to kill me."

Careful. Keep calm. If you can talk him into this, maybe you'll live. "Okay. Maybe. Maybe not. I think he'll let you drink. And Los Viejos. You're dying too, you know that. What's the worst that can happen? You die a little early."

Manning could hear Ponce's low chuckle. "We received word back from my agent in Europe. Sir Harry. You don't know him. It doesn't matter. He talked to Toledo's doctor in Vienna. Enrique died of old age. What you say is true." He paused. "Very well. I'm putting Isaac back on. Tell him how we can meet Carlos."

Isaac's voice. "We're not coming. Carlos has been killing us off for centuries. He won't stop now."

"All I know is that Carlos says he won't kill Don Juan. He wants to confront him, but not kill him. I don't know if he's lying. De Leon takes his own chances."

"No. I won't risk Don Juan's life."

"You're risking his life if you don't. You're all dying, and Don Juan's going first. You can see that, can't you? Don Juan is ageing fast. He won't last the year. Here's a chance to return to the Fountain, to save his life and your own. Okay, maybe Carlos is still a little pissed. He's got good reason. But the other Calusa are ready to stop the killing, starting with his great-great grandson, Carlito."

Isaac was obstinate. "Too much risk."

"I'm an accountant. We have a saying: 'Risk is proportional to gain.' This is risky, but the potential payoff might be another five hundred years. Mind taking some risk?"

"Hell no."

"You don't mind?"

"No. I mean hell no, we ain't coming."

One last card. "Here's Tomaso. Talk to him." Manning handed the phone over.

"Hello, Isaac?" Tomaso shut his eyes. Manning could hear murmuring from Isaac. Tomaso said, "I came with Crenshaw. But I've been here before. I'm working with the Calusa."

Angry tones from the phone. Tomaso shut his eyes again, jaw working. He said, "Save your judgment. You might need it. I haven't killed any of our comrades. The ones who died all died of old age. I told the Calusa that I killed them, yes. I lied. I took Spanish money and arranged to send it to the Calusa. I stole. But I haven't killed any of our friends."

More strident sounds from the phone. Tomaso spoke again. "Because the money went for good. The Calusa are helping oppressed peoples with it. And I did you and the others a favor. While the Calusa were focusing on Spaniards who were dying anyway they weren't hunting down the rest of us." He listened, closing his eyes a third time. "You can think what you want of me. I went to them because I am dying. We're all dying, Isaac. They have promised me the Fount. They promise you all the same. They can be trusted."

Nothing from the phone for a long time, then more murmuring. Tomaso hung up. "They will come."

"You say you haven't killed. How about the attempts on me?"

"You were different. Carlito had begun to suspect me. He suspected that the Spaniards I claimed to have killed could have died naturally. I had to show him proof of a killing. You were not one of us. I could kill you to show Carlos a bona fide corpse. When the hit and run didn't work, I sent a woman whom I had used before."

"Aunt Dorothy."

"Yes. But first she was to find out, for me alone, about how Enrique died. Of course, you didn't know anything. That only confirmed my suspicion that he died of old age."

"And my brother? Carlito didn't think he was a Spaniard. You didn't need to prove anything to Carlito by killing him. Why did he have to die?"

Tomaso couldn't look at Manning. "It was a mistake. A mix-up. We had a man at Citibank. We knew you would come to take your money sooner or later. That morning, we expected you. Your brother came instead. Our man in the bank told our. . . told Howard Sergeant about the change, described your brother. He simply applied. . . the contract. . . to your brother. The men who entered the taxi with your brother and took the money were Calusa. You or your brother, they didn't care."

"And Adam was your victim."

Tomaso looked up with those odd two-colored eyes. "It won't do any good to say I'm sorry."

"It won't," Manning said, "because you're not. These Indians, they were looking for Toledo to settle an old score, not me. You came after me. . . and my brother. . . to save your own skin. It's you I want. I should have killed you in San Diego."

Tomaso only smiled. "Strong words. Noble words.

Now you need to back them up."

Manning didn't answer. He had no cards left. Tomaso said, "You have purchased a few more days of life while you assure a meeting between Carlos and de Leon. Then, I will kill you myself. No loose ends."

"How about Howard Sergeant," Manning asked. "Isn't he a loose end?"

"He's been taken care of," Tomaso whispered.

Howard Sergeant jumped at the buzz of his intercom. He wasn't over his visit from Maxwell.

"Phone call for you, Howard," said Ellie, his secretary. She was genetically incapable of calling him "Mr. Sergeant" or inquiring as to who the caller might be, or what he wanted. She was, however, able to keep her mouth shut.

It was Andres. "We have work."

"I don't know. I don't think I'm taking any more jobs." Howard looked at the brown stains on his leather desktop that no amount of scrubbing would remove.

"The money is good."

"How much?"

"More than ever before."

Howard met Andres at their usual spot, a public parking structure in Queens. They parked next to each other on the top floor, which was usually empty. Andres got into Howard's Cadillac and locked the doors. The Cadillac's windows were heavily darkened. "It's a simple job. Quick."

"I'm getting out," Howard said. He had thought about what to say to Andres all the way over and for an hour in his office. He still didn't know what to say, exactly, because he didn't know what to do. Maxwell and Toledo had meant business. Still, one big score. . . "Maybe," he said finally.

Andres looked at him. "The money's good. You don't have to do anything."

"Whose is it?"

"Hank Aaron."

"Hank. . ." That was the last thing Howard wanted to hear. Andres didn't know about Howard's hit on Toledo's brother. No way Howard was gonna tell him either.

Andres was still looking at him with that porcelain face. Howard struggled to keep calm. Make some conversation. "Who's the mark?"

Andres handed over a manila envelope. Howard opened it. No bio sheet on the mark. No photo. There was only a single white sheet with two block words printed: You're it.

Howard didn't get it at first. When he did, he didn't want to believe it. Then he saw Andres's eyes and knew. "No. Wait, wait. . ."

"We talked about Toledo, remember?" Andres said. "No touchee. He has some goods on me. I gave him my word."

"Andres. . ." Howard said, mind racing. Andres put his pistol under Howard's chin and fired upward. He rolled Howard over and lifted his wallet and wristwatch. Then he got out of the car, and then leaned back in to put a second bullet between Howard's eyes. He clicked the car's door to "lock" and closed it. He pulled off thin leather gloves and put them, the wallet, watch, and the gun into a flight bag. The bag was for the East River.

"I told you you didn't have to do anything," he said to the darkened windows.

Andres went to a health club in Manhattan three hours later to pick up his money. He inserted a key into a bank of lockers in the men's room and lifted out a plastic flight bag. He opened it in a toilet stall. A hundred grand in old bills and a small gift-wrapped package. Andres nodded, pleased. Hank Aaron sometimes stuck in a present on the really big jobs. He opened a leather carry-on bag and wrapped the money carefully in his packed clothes. Then he stuffed the flight bag in the trash under all the used hand towels and headed for Kennedy airport. He had tickets under different names for flights to Winston-Salem, then Chicago, on to Greece, to Athens. He was making a career change.

He phoned Felicia in Athens, waking her up, to propose marriage.

Felicia Ponti stood on tiptoe scanning the passengers departing United Flight 314. Look at me, a thirty-seven year old schoolgirl. She hadn't slept all night—up at five, finally, to motor from her villa to Athens International Airport two full hours early. It really must be love.

Then, there was Phillip, as slim and handsome and wonderful as ever, with a lopsided grin and casual wave.

They held hands, then kissed, and she got dizzy. She looked up at his broken nose and laughing eyes. Yes, love, definitely.

They walked down the long corridor holding hands, the Italian widow and the New York financier. Felicia felt as though everyone in the terminal were smiling at them. They had made the intercontinental romance work, against the odds.

"How was customs?"

"Simple," smiled Andres, thinking of the fix. He had phoned a friend in Athens, calling in an old debt. Someone had escorted him in a wide loop around the customs inspectors' booths.

"Do you have many bags?"

Andres held up his leather carry-on. "Just this. Traveling light."

Felicia smiled, puzzled. Phillip was full of surprises. "What happened, that you're here?"

Andres shrugged. "My life has become too complicated. I want a simple life. With you. Any complaints?"

"None at all. It's just so. . . sudden."

"Look, we'll talk about it at the villa. Right now I want the Greek sun on my face and the most beautiful girl in the world on my arm." He kissed her on the cheek. "Did you bring your Bugatti?"

"Yes."

"Good thing I packed light, then. Your car is as beautiful and impractical as its owner."

Felicia laughed with a sound like tinkling bells. They stepped from the terminal entrance into the parking lot.

One of Felicia's windshield stickers allowed her to park in the nearest row. Andres put down the top and took off his jacket. "It's warm. I had forgotten Athens' weather."

He opened his bag to stow his jacket and Felicia spotted a wrapped package. "Phillip. . . is that for me?"

"Perhaps." It was the gift from Hank Aaron. "Let's open it and see."

The gift turned out to be a slim, elegant Nikon. "It's adorable," said Felicia.

"For you," Andres said smoothly.

"Let's get someone to take our picture," Felicia said.

"I'll take you." Andres' rules still prohibited photos of himself. He arranged his fiancée like a fashion model, leaning onto the car with one knee raised. "Hold it. On three."

The explosion was a small one, so Felicia was unharmed. Andres, on the other hand, held the camera to his eyes and died instantly. Felicia was a widow before she was ever a bride. Her smile turned into a scream just before she passed out. It was a week before she was able to utter a sound, and another week before she could bring herself to answer questions for the police, and a month more before the nightmares stopped, and another month before she opened the leather carry-on and discovered her tax-free inheritance.

chapter 26

The Fount

Green Valley is a 90's development on Florida's West Coast, following a formula that has worked for retirement communities for 50 years:

- Lay out an attractive golf course easy enough to give a seven-handicapper a shot at making par;
- Surround the fairways with a thin crust of pink and orange stucco "executive town homes";
- Provide pool, spa, tennis courts, a fountain where children can throw pennies, and a clubhouse with a mahogany-veneer bar and cheap drinks;
- Spend money on an imposing entrance with security guard.

The security guard at Green Valley was named Ernesto, a Cuban with excellent English. He had two jobs and three children at Florida State. He peered into the first of white limousines in column and identified the driver as a recent addition to the "ecology team." He didn't know much about the team. They had been poking and digging on the premises for months. None of Ernesto's business. He waved the cars through.

Carlito drove the lead limo. He had been in Florida for five days. Carlos sat next to him. Tomaso and Manning were in the back seat. These three had just arrived from Chiapas the night before. By boat, at midnight, so that the gun Tomaso held on Manning could be kept from customs. The other cars were full of Calusa backup.

The cars made a three-quarter circle at the big terra cotta fountain with all the pennies in it and followed the blacktop road past streets with names like "Misty Knoll" and "Sunrise Lane." The condos ended and the cars drove on out to the end of the golf course, to the eighth fairway, which stretched into a par four meadow, secluded and quiet in the early morning. The cars parked.

Carlos got out first, opening slowly like a rusty jack-knife. He bent over his cane and stared at the van parked across the street in a cluster of sedans one hundred feet away. Isaac stood nearby with tiny Martinez and strong, square Pablo Cisneros. The other Viejos stood behind them in a circle.

Manning saw how Tomaso and the Spaniards avoided eye contact.

A gurney at the rear of the van lowered a wheelchair and there was Ponce.

The two old warriors faced each other. Manning hardly recognized Ponce as the man he had met only a week before. He had aged in the same way as Carlos—perhaps faster. His hair and beard were chalk-white. Age had eaten all the meat off of him so that he looked like an El Greco painting. He wheeled his chair toward Carlos.

Carlos watched him come. He took a shuffling step toward the wheelchair and would have fallen if an Indian on each side had not caught him.

Ponce wheeled to a stop three feet away from Carlos. The two men faced each other silently. The Spaniards and Indians moved in as well to form a circle around the two old men.

"?Como esta?" asked Ponce finally. "How are you?"

"Bien. I am well," said Carlos evenly. The silence returned. Carlos broke it. "You gave me your word."

"I know."

"You dishonored it."

Ponce swept his right hand around his head. "This place reminds me of the clearing where we fought each other."

Carlos' eyes followed the hand. "I should have killed you."

"You seemed to be trying."

"So were you."

"I would have run you through," said Ponce, "if you hadn't struck like a snake from the trees."

Carlos snorted. "With that woman's hat-pin you call a sword? If our arrows hadn't arrived you would have eaten my spear for lunch, Spaniard."

"But they did arrive, from ambush," Ponce said. "You used hidden archers. 'Just you and me,' you shouted to me. Who broke his word that afternoon? Who fought like a woman?"

"You speak of women? Who struck at night to slaughter our women? Our children?"

Ponce patted the blanket on his lap. "You lost your women. I lost my legs. We are even, scorpion."

Carlos raised his cane over his head, hands trembling with fury and age. He brought it down on Ponce's head, snapping the wood at mid-point. The blow toppled the cripple from his wheelchair and he sprawled on the grass. His robe fell away. Uncovered, he was a pitiful sight. Two white stumps of legs stuck out awkwardly from white boxer shorts that looked much too large. The legs ended in ugly folds of skin sewn together by a clumsy medieval surgeon.

Manning thinking: this is the legend that school children read about?

Ponce rolled onto his stomach and raised himself on his arms, shaking his head groggily. Blood streamed from a mean gash high on his forehead down his nose and into his beard.

The Spaniards, Martinez and Cisneros leading, took a step forward with pistols in their hands. The Indians produced their own guns, everyone pointing firearms at everyone with Carlos and Ponce in the middle. A bad gangster movie, Manning thought.

Looking back on it, Manning didn't remember moving. One moment he stood behind the Indians, looking around for a soft spot to dive to. The next he was behind Cacique Carlos holding his arm, bending the broken cane shaft away.

And the very next moment he held both of his hands to his left side, where a pain like nothing he'd ever felt before staggered him. More than that, he could remember a sharp gunshot that seemed to come too late to be connected to the pain, but Manning suspected that it probably was. It was only the second gunshot he'd ever heard, he realized. When was the other? Oh, yes, Audrey shooting Andres. Audrey. Would he ever see her again? He fell.

He fell on his back on the hard ground. Blue sky and white clouds filled his vision. The pain was overwhelming. This is what it's like to die, he thought. But I'm already dead, and cremated. He smiled to himself.

By turning his head, he found that he could look across the clearing. He saw Isaac and Carlito above him, back to back. Isaac was in a crouch, hands up, looking like Bruce Lee. Carlito stood tall, hands also outstretched. They faced the circle of men pointing all those guns at each other, Isaac shouting, "No. No fuego!" Carlito shouted even louder in the Calusa dialect.

It worked. The armed men held their pistols steady, but with no more gunshots. Just the one. One was enough, Manning thought. He peeked under his left elbow. Lots of blood on his shirt and on the green grass.

In front of him, the drama between the two old warriors played on. Ponce looked up from the grass. "You can kill me," he told Carlos. "It's all right."

"You broke your word," Carlos said again. He raised the stub of his cane again, still holding it, but Carlito caught it in the air, pulling Carlos off balance and into his arms.

"I kept it this time. I'm here." Ponce swung himself painfully to a seated position and leaned back on his arms in the grass. "I betrayed you, that time in Florida. I'm sorry." He reached up with one hand and took Carlos' arm.

"What do you want from me?" asked Carlos.

"Forgiveness."

"I can't," said Carlos.

"Oh, I think you can. Our Lord commands it. 'You must forgive. Seventy times seven.'"

Carlos was silent. Ponce rattled his arm. "Five hundred years watering this bitter root is long enough. Time to let it die. I beg you."

"Hey," Manning shouted, "Hey, I'm dying, here." It seemed like he shouted. Listening, he realized that no sound came out. No sound, because he wasn't breathing right. The pain like never before stopped him from taking in any air. He lay on his back looking up into tree branches. I really am dying, he thought. Audrey's face appeared—wide blue eyes, wide smile. I never told her I love her. Do I love her? Does it matter? Will she ever learn how I died, here on some crummy developer's golf fairway?

He closed his eyes, and when he opened them again a fat Spaniard's great bulk squatted next to him. Paco, he guessed. The fat man's fingers were busy inside his shirt. Manning to a slow, careful breath. "Is it bad?" he whispered.

Paco glanced at him. "Not too bad." Manning wondered what that meant. Wasn't that what they told the cowboy or the infantryman just before they died? Paco did something with his fingers and Manning almost did die.

Paco held up a gray lump. "Here's the bullet, my friend. You may have broken a rib or two, but the slug never went inside." He threw a disgusted look toward Martinez. The small man stood downcast, his gun at his side. "Martinez has always insisted on a twenty-two caliber. I have told him many times, no penetrating power. Something heavier, I tell him."

"Whose side are you on?" Manning thought but didn't say, not with Paco's fingers still busy under his shirt.

He looked at the two old men. Ponce still held Carlos's arm. Carlos shook his arm loose. Carlito, still holding him up, said, so quietly that Manning strained to hear, "Ancestor, we have come a long way. Your wife and children died at the hand of this man five centuries ago. So did my wife and son. I have buried them, in my heart, long ago. Can you do the same?"

Carlito looked from Carlos to Ponce. "How long can two men hate each other? This Spaniard has given up his hatred, I think. Will you carry yours to your grave? That's next, you know, unless we do the thing we came here to do." He pointed to the edge of the fairway. A flat rock stood there. Green moss covered it now, but the pink stone was visible underneath. The vertical outcropping still stood like a soldier after five centuries.

"There it is," said Carlito. "Both of you need its water to live. We all do. Shall we share it, or do you want to slap each other around until you both pass out? We can bury you together under a headstone that says, 'These two learned nothing in five hundred years.'"

Isaac lifted Ponce into his chair. "He struck first," Ponce said stiffly.

"The words of a child, Jefe," Isaac said. "Carlito has spoken the only sense I've heard this morning." He held Ponce's eyes for a second, then turned to Carlos. "Are you going to beat your enemy senseless with the stub of your cane, old man? You have killed us, one by one, over the ages. Are you happier now for all of that? Are your people better off? Until last week you didn't know this man was alive. Must you kill him?" He took the right hands of the two old men. "Will you, can you, turn all of this hatred into victory?"

"For the sake of my people, I can not," said Carlos.

"For the sake of your people you must," said Carlito. He took Carlos' other hand. "Come with me, come on. Let's see if you can refuse a drink to these old enemies of ours." He took Carlos' arm and the two Calusa moved slowly toward the flat rock, with Carlos leaning heavily on his great-great grandson. The other Indians followed them, then the Spaniards

Manning still sat on the grass, leaning on one arm, the pain just as bad, not entirely sure Paco knew what he was talking about. He watched Tomaso lean toward Carlito and whisper something. "Him?" Carlito answered, looking over his shoulder toward Manning. "No. We shall let him go. He took Cacique's bullet."

Is that what I did? Manning wondered. Then Pablo Cisneros knelt next to him and slipped his powerful arms under Manning's legs and armpits. "This may hurt," he said, and picked him up like a child. He was right, but Manning already hurt. The pain wasn't that much worse, and Manning really wanted to see the Fountain. Pablo carried him after the procession of Spaniards and Indians.

A shallow culvert had been dug in the soil next to the rock. "Our team found this site," Carlito said in a soft voice. "It matched the description we gave them. The geology and soil samples of the area indicate an historic swamp, but it has receded. The team took core samples, and dug here. Clear water flows out from under the rock at this site."

Carlito led the old Calusa Chieftain to the edge of the culvert and both men knelt. The others circled them. Manning leaned over Carlito's shoulder and could see a small stream of water trickling from under the rock into the green grass of the meadow. There was a kind of deep collective sigh from the Spaniards and Indians.

"The last time we drank from our Communion chalice," said Isaac. "It was a sign of unity, and devotion to our Lord. Is there any reason why we shouldn't do the same again?" No one spoke, so Isaac produced from a small leather bag the old silver chalice that Manning and he had admired in the Great Man's house. Los Viejos and the Indians looked at each other and at their shoes. Then beginning with the Spaniards, they all knelt in the grass.

"Don Juan," said Isaac, "will you begin?"

"Dear Lord," Ponce said, "we thank you again for this miracle. We pray that all who drink together today can live together in peace."

"Amen," said Carlos, to everyone's surprise.

Isaac filled the chalice and everyone drank. Manning was last. He took a swallow. The water was cool and sweet. He stood waiting for some feeling that didn't come, although he imagined that the pain in his side wasn't as sharp as before. Some of the Indians and Spaniards were filling plastic bottles with Fountain water for their comrades who were absent. Then everyone stood uncertainly. "Perhaps a prayer," suggested Pablo Cisneros.

Ponce crossed himself. "Our thanks to Almighty God for this second chance." At what? thought Manning.

The men walked to their cars. The tension was broken. Everyone smiled, and easy conversation started. The cars wound their way back toward the stone fountain and the main gate.

Andrew Trotter watched it all from a hillside through binoculars.

Stuart Davenport found The Great Man and Andrew Trotter at a table at Stan's Lounge in Fort Lauderdale. They shook hands and sat down together. Davenport was puzzled. A casual business pal from California had phoned that morning. Mr. Anthony Webb wants to meet you. He's a heavy hitter. Subject unknown. Today.

"Drink?" asked The Great Man.

"I'm fine. What's so urgent?" Davenport had jerked his entire day around to drive to this meeting.

"Right to the point. Good. You own Green Valley golf course. I'm interested in purchasing it."

"What makes you think it's for sale?"

"Everything's for sale, for a price."

"What price is that?" Davenport sat back in his chair and stretched out his legs. This was interesting.

Trotter handed a sheet of paper across the table. "This is a history of golf course sales in the country for the past two years. Average price is about four million. Mean price, three point nine. Highest price, twenty-four million, and that's for thirty-six holes, Southern California. What, in your opinion, is a fair price for Green Valley?"

Davenport scanned the page in front of him. Some of the sales were familiar. The data looked right. He kept a poker face while his mind raced. "Green Valley is a prime course. It's worth substantially more than the average on your sheet. We have no reason to sell. However, we couldn't let it go for less than seven million, even if we were interested. I'll talk to my associates and get back to you."

The Great Man passed over a large envelope. "You have no associates, Stuart. You own Green Valley all by yourself. You've lost money on it for the past three years. The only reason you have a positive cash flow is condo sales on the property, and you've sold the last parcel out. There's a bank draft in that envelope for thirty million. There's a sales agreement in there too. It'll work. Show it to your lawyer. The bank draft expires at five P.M. local time tomorrow. So does the deal. Call me by then."

Stuart looked at the bank draft. He looked at The Great Man. "Maybe I will have that drink."

Six men stood on the pink rock three days later, the usual suspects: Carlos, Carlito, Ponce de Leon, and Isaac faced the Great Man and Andrew Trotter. The Great Man was explaining his ownership of the Fount.

"How did you find out about it?" asked Isaac. "I know you knew about its existence. Don Juan gave you that knowledge to set up our initial meeting. But how did you find out it was here, on this golf course?"

The Great Man nodded to Ponce. "Easy. I bugged his room and his phones."

Ponce twisted in his wheelchair. "I had my room

swept. . ."

"You had your room swept for bugs every other week," The Great Man interrupted. "Who did it for you?" He studied his fingernails. "Actually, it gave me a chance to make sure all the mikes were still working."

"I pay your salary, Tony," Ponce said. "You don't have thirty million."

"You made me eat manure every day for fifteen years, but you taught me how to raise money." The Great Man rubbed his hands together. "Took some arm twisting and some groveling. I did it."

"Big risk," said Isaac.

"Big risk, big payoff," said Trotter. "We live in a youth culture. How much will the world pay to live forever?"

"How long will it take the world to swallow a fairy tale about the Fountain of Youth?" asked Isaac.

"Ah, that's where you four come in," said The Great Man. "The news that Ponce de Leon, and his soldiers, and his enemy the Calusa, are still alive will make every paper, every newscast on the globe. The world will want. . . need. . . the Fountain's waters the next day. And I'll be ready."

"And we are going to do this, perform for you, because. . ?" asked Carlito.

"Because you want free access to the Fountain for yourselves and for your families forever. That's my offer." The Great Man smiled broadly, winking a gold molar.

The Spaniards and Indians looked at each other. "It's an interesting offer," Carlos said.

"It's an offer you can't refuse," said Trotter.

"We refuse it," said Isaac.

All five men turned to look at him. "You can speak for yourself," said The Great Man irritably. "The others will have a different answer."

But Isaac had stepped off the rock and knelt down in the grass. "Look," he said to Trotter and his boss, pointing down. "Look closely."

Everyone looked. The streambed was dry. "You've diverted it!" Trotter burst out, furious. "It won't work. We own it. Our attorney. . ."

"You own a golf course," Isaac replied calmly. "That's all. Yesterday I spent some money of my own. I paid the groundskeeper. . . your groundskeeper. . . to isolate the golf course's sprinkler system. Your 'Fountain' had dried up by evening." He smiled at The Great Man. "The Fountain has been dry for some time. Who knows how many centuries? All you have is an underground water leak. Better fix it. You can't afford any extra overhead if you expect to make a profit on your thirty million dollar investment."

The Great Man was on his knees digging in the moist soil with his fingers, hoping for a miracle, but he had been around long enough to know better. He looked up at Ponce with bleak eyes. "Mr. de Leon. . ."

"Save your oxygen, Tony." Ponce stared down at him. "You're a great deal-maker. The best. No deal this time. I made you and I'm about to un-make you. Your creditors, whoever they are, will get a phone call tomorrow. When they hang up they're gonna put some screws to you like you never knew existed. You'd better find a good bankruptcy lawyer, or a country that doesn't extradite."

The Great Man glowered at Trotter, trying to find

someone to pin this on. He was hung out to dry, and he knew it. Finally he strode off, trailing Trotter. He stopped and turned. "You'll hear from me."

The four men on the rock watched them drive off. They didn't think that they'd hear from Anthony Webb. None of them smiled. Each had his own problems. They looked at each other and at the wet dirt under the pink rock.

"It did seem too easy," said Carlito.

Cacique Carlos leaned into Carlito's arm. He stood facing west, toward the sea miles away. He pointed. "A great tree stood there, Carlito, remember? The chiefs sat at council under it."

"We boys sat in the tree limbs listening to you old men grunt," Carlito said. "I remember a game trail behind that tree. You took me to it when I was a boy. You made me lie motionless with no sound. You could snare a rabbit with your hand."

Carlos smiled. "You too. You learned fast. Can you remember any other lessons I taught you then?"

"You said to me. . . a man can't control what he receives, only what he brings."

Carlos nodded. "God made us a gift of the Fountain only once, I guess. We can't control that gift." He looked around at his companions. "When we first drank from it, so long ago, tell me, how did you feel?"

"Contentment," said Carlito. "Fulfillment."

"Gratitude to the Lord," said Ponce.

"Peace," said Isaac.

"Contentment, gratitude, peace," Carlos repeated.

"We can't determine how we receive these, but we can bring them with us." He let go of Carlito and turned in a wobbly circle unaided. "I came here hoping to come to the Fountain. Instead I came home." He winked at Carlito, crinkling his face like a paper bag. "Go back, Cacique," he said, "lead your people. I'm staying."

Carlito looked puzzled, so Carlos said it again. "You're Cacique now, grandson of my grandson. Get used to it. It's been a long succession period. Go back. You have your hands full. The old ones need to be told that they have only a short time to live. The young ones have to learn the traditions and history of the Calusa, and you have only a few months to teach them."

"You," Carlito began, "Who will care for you?"

Carlos smiled and shook his head. "I've taken care of me for a long time. I don't need a hospice team." He swept his hand around. "I know this neighborhood."

"Maybe you'd like some company," Ponce said.

Carlos looked at him in astonishment. "You?"

Ponce raised his white eyebrows. "Me. I have some stature here. Don't forget, I gave this state its name. And I can always get us handicapped parking."

Carlos laughed in a clear baritone. "Why not? Why not indeed? A dried up old Indian and a crippled Spaniard. We'll haunt the rain forest and the shopping malls." He leaned on Ponce's wheelchair and filled his lungs. The Calusa song flowed from him like a brook, as haunting as a bugle call. The sound of it filled the meadow. When he stopped to take a breath Carlito took up the melody. They sang in duet like two violins. Isaac thought that he had never heard such music. He turned to Ponce to whisper something, but the old Spaniard was smiling to himself with his eyes closed.

The song trailed to a sweet ending and flickered out. Carlos reached over and took Carlito's hand. The two men touched the other's cheeks. Then Carlos took Ponce's wheelchair handles. "Come on, old enemy. We have a lot to talk about. I'll push you along and wipe your behind for you."

"And I'll bury you," said Ponce. His eyes sparkled.

"Did I say anything about being buried?" asked Carlos. He made a show of looking around. "Did anyone hear me talk about a burial?"

The two Indians and Ponce moved slowly to the car Carlos had come in. Isaac watched them drive off then he walked alone to the other car. He had things to do. Los Viejos needed to meet again, perhaps for the last time. The others had to hear the bad news, that there will be no reprieve from the governor.

epilog 1

Pupule Man

The funeral ceremony and procession three months later were the most elaborate that San Christobal de las Casas had ever seen, and the strangest. The natives wondered at the long line of dark men and women who walked though the slanted, hilly cobblestones behind Father Jose-Maria and the figure of the Virgin to the slow beat of a cowhide drum. Each man a red cotton shirt over white cotton trousers. Each had a single long black feather braided into his hair that pointed down to the back of his neck. A crow feather, some townspeople said. Others said no; it came from the eagle. The villagers wondered as well at the soft undulating song the men sang—keening notes that leapt like butterflies from low baritone to lilting contralto, filling the corridor of buildings and echoing from the low adobe walls.

"They are from Bolivia, from the rain forest," guessed one. "No," said the local barber, "I recognize Mr. Perez from the valley. He comes to me for the haircut."

The procession wound from the cathedral through the central plaza, but not out to the city cemetery on the hill. Instead, it walked the long way through the pine trees toward Santa Maria Valley. So the barber was right, and the men were los ricos from the valley. The townsfolk shrugged. Los ricos did as they pleased. Life went on.

A much smaller and quieter ceremony took place that same night in Havana. Nine men gathered in the soft rain at midnight on an old cemetery hill overlooking the harbor. Eight of the men had shovels and they dug silently, in shifts. Very soon they had excavated an ancient gravesite.

Manning stood to one side. He had wanted to help dig, too, but Los Viejos said no. They had discussed it three days before in Miami. Some said, open the Ponce de Leon monument in the cathedral at San Juan and place him there. Paco suggested the plan that they finally agreed upon. "We put an empty box into the ground long ago," he said. "We should fill it." Just as well. Manning was wrapped in bandages around the chest. He couldn't have dug in dry sand.

They struck the casket at four feet and dug around it until the lid was clear. The casket was remarkably preserved, but then it was made of lead.

They carefully laid the body of Don Juan Ponce de Leon into the box, sealing the lid with epoxy. Then they climbed from the hole and stood looking at each other.

"Perhaps a prayer?" suggested Pablo Cisneros, standing with his broad shoulders hunched in the rain.

"Something better," said Isaac. He produced a silver chalice—the chalice—and some wine and bread. The men ate and drank. Manning joined them.

"Lord, thanks for the gift of knowing him," Paco

said.

"Thanks for our long lives," said Esteban.

"And for the friendship of these good brothers," said tiny Martinez.

"And for your mercy and grace," said Santiago.

"And for salvation," said Isaac.

"Amen," said Manning. Everyone looked at him.

"What's next?" asked Manning back at the hotel in the center of Havana.

"I'm off to Hawaii, to my place, God willing," said Isaac. "Come on out."

"I've got some things to launder up," said Manning, thinking of Toledo's estate.

"In a few weeks then."

"Why Hawaii?"

"Well, it's my favorite local address. You like it too. After we spend some time there I'm off to Israel. That's where I want to end up."

"End?"

"I've been coming down with a headache lately," said Isaac.

Hermano Tomaso opened the door to his penthouse suite at the Meridian Hotel in West Palm Beach. "Hi," said Manning.

"Come in." Tomaso turned and walked to his glass and chrome bar. "Drink?"

"Thanks. Vodka martini." Manning had downed two already. He was feeling jazzed.

Tomaso poured. "How'd you find me?"

"You keep asking that. Same answer. This is where you stay in Palm Beach. Registered as Richard French. The same name you used at the Hotel del in San Diego. You're predictable."

Tomaso sat down with his own drink. It looked like iced tea. "I'm going to have to do something about you."

"Not tonight."

Tomaso looked him over. "Why not tonight? What is it this time? Do you have a thermo-nuclear device strapped to your chest?"

Manning smiled. A joke. He shook his head. "Not necessary. I'm no longer a threat to you, nor to the Calusa, nor to the Bimini Boys. None of you has a secret to protect any more. You don't even have fortunes to protect. You probably can't spend the loose change in your checking accounts in the time you have left."

Manning saw that he had scored some hits. Tomaso looked into his dark glass. "That's a bit. . . strong."

"You mean cold-blooded?" Manning swallowed his drink, watering his eyes. "A lot less cold-blooded than the way you murdered Adam. You know why I didn't put two or three bullet holes into that brocade jacket from your doorway? Don't need to. You're dying. Soon. I want you to think about that every day." He stood up. "Every night when you can't sleep. That pays Adam back better than a bullet." He walked to the door.

"Wait a bit." Tomaso looked up with hunted eyes. "You're right. I can't sleep. I'm not a bad person. . ."

Manning grinned and shook his head. "You're not a

bad person, I'm not a bad person. You killed my brother, I killed my brother." He stood with one hand on the open door. "Isaac told me about you. 'He's afraid to die,' he said. It's why you told me about the Calusa, why you led me to Carlito. You didn't want to die. I didn't care. Still don't."

Manning turned in a circle, pulling his shirt free from his trousers, showing the bandages still around his ribs. "Look, no gun. I'm through with 'em. Tossed 'em all away." He stood facing Tomaso. "You can kill me. It's what you do. Shouldn't you saddle a different horse? Isaac said you left the Church centuries ago because death seemed so far away. It's back. If there's a God up there, shouldn't you be telling Him you're sorry for all the killing and lying, and starting over?" He walked out the door. "Start now."

Manning shut the hotel room door behind him, thinking, I can't believe I said that.

Audrey Cobb's intercom bleeped. It was Stinky, Winnie's boss. "Miss Cobb, will you come up?"

Audrey straightened her skirt, smeared on a new coat of "Scarlet Letter" on her lips, and took the back stairs two at a time. When Stinky called her "Miss Cobb" something had hit the fan.

Stinky was seated at his imitation maple conference table with Winnie, and there was Manning, looking like a Mormon in black suit and tie. Audrey's heart skipped one or two beats.

"Mr. Toledo, here, wants to file a harassment suit," Stinky said. He had on his Intrepid Bureaucrat face. Winnie, as usual in situations like this, was sitting at the far end of the table with his mouth shut, hoping to avoid collateral damage.

Audrey ignored Manning. "You will recall our investigation of Mr. Toledo," she started. Keep calm. Keep smiling. Keep dancing. "Mr. Toledo used a series of falsified birth dates over the years. He admitted fraud with his father and grandfather to avoid inheritance taxes. We reached an agreement. Mr. Toledo paid a very heavy fine. The case is closed."

Audrey sat back with her smile still painted on. She actually looked down to see if her pounding heart was visible through her dress. The story was on record in IRS files, and it was pure manure. It was what she had promised Manning. Why was he here? What was going on?

"Okay," said Manning.

"Pardon?" said Stinky and Audrey in unison.

"It's okay. I just wanted to make sure I wasn't still under investigation." Manning stood and shook Stinky's hand. "You run a very efficient organization here, Mr. Simmons. Ms. Cobb has been courteous, professional, and intriguing." He reached for Winnie's hand. "Mr. Churchill, a pleasure."

Sunlight seemed to flood the room through the fluorescents. Stinky and Winnie were grinning like schoolboys. Now Audrey really didn't know what was going on. "Ms. Cobb, may I have a moment of your time in private?" Manning asked.

Audrey looked at her two bosses, who were still nodding and smiling. Winnie led her and Manning to Conference Room A. His smile wasn't as broad as before.

Audrey closed the door. "Intriguing?"

"Well, you are. It's why I came to see you again. You inhabit my dreams."

Audrey sat on the edge of the conference table. "Manning, what the hell is going on? I said goodbye to you in LA. Do I need to write it out for you in block letters?"

"Call me Henry, please. This conference room may be bugged."

"This isn't Moscow. It would serve you right, though. How did you get in here? Why is Stink. . . Mr. Simmons treating you like royalty?"

"Because I am royalty. My congressman made the appointment."

"Your. . . from Congress?"

Manning nodded. "Henry was a frequent contributor to his re-election fund." He sat next to her on the table. "How's it feel to be back in your cubicle? Any more tax-evading bachelor millionaires to run down? Don't you miss the old days? Red convertibles? Cruise lines? Hawaii?"

Audrey slid down the table, keeping her distance. "We talked that over, remember? Last time. You're my worst nightmare. . . all the things Mama warned me about. Old, divorced, lying, uncaring. . ."

"I care a lot." Manning slid down the table after her, wincing a little. His ribs still hurt.

"You left me with kidnappers while you were off playing Jay Gatsby. All the while you were feeding me a line. You fed me a lifetime's worth of lines. I can't trust you, Manning." Audrey got up and sat in one of the conference chairs across the table from Manning. The truth was, she did miss the old days.

"Audrey, a lot has happened. It's made me think. All this money, what good is it? 'Find someone to show it to,' right? That's what Isaac said. I want to have someone to show it to. Maybe you do too?" He looked at her, head down, eyebrows up.

"Manning, I'm. . . Winnie and I are engaged."

The air went out of him. "Right. Got it."

"I'm sorry. Maybe. . ." Audrey thought about how to end her sentence and shut up instead. Anything more would only make it worse.

Manning got up and walked out.

Audrey sat alone sucking on the second joint of her right index finger for all she was worth and tasting the salty tears that rolled down her cheeks into her mouth. Winston peeked in. "What did he do? Did he threaten you?"

Audrey got up and put her arms around him. "Winnie, be a dear. Shut up and hold me."

Manning found the elevator and punched "L." Audrey's image and the aroma of Coco by Chanel still filled him. When he left the building he looked for the nearest bar. Unfortunately, one was open right across the street.

Manning sat at Henry Toledo's carved teak desk playing computer solitaire. He had on pajama bottoms with a sweatshirt over his bandages. He needed a shave. He had needed a shave for a week. The apartment was a mess. Empty and half-filled vodka bottles lined the bar and lay on top of some old Domino's pizza boxes. Flies were working on the pizza.

Manning was a mess, too. He was massively hung over, with hands that shook so badly he had trouble working the computer to flip cards. He knew he would feel better soon. That was because he had started drinking as soon as he climbed out of his rumpled bed, two hours ago. The jackhammer pain behind his eyes was already kinder and gentler from the vodka and from the headache powders in Toledo's medicine cabinet. The booze and pills were doing wonders for the pain of his broken ribs, too.

Manning had pulled into his parking spot in the basement with his red Mercedes' trunk full of vodka. He wasn't exactly sure how long ago. He could only remember selected sound bites of his long, boozy drive up the East Coast from Florida. He remembered meeting with, and preaching to, Tomaso, and the disaster with Audrey. He remembered sitting at a stoplight somewhere in the pouring rain with the convertible top down. He remembered racing somewhere with police sirens blaring and lights flashing behind him, watching the speedometer point to 120 and wondering if that was miles or kilometers per hour. He must have escaped since he wasn't in jail. He remembered lugging the cases of Smirnoff up to his condo in the middle of the night, his ribs screaming at him, and locking the door.

Manning had decided to self-destruct. He was doing a pretty good job. He drank straight from the bottle and played cards endlessly on his computer. He was new to power drinking but had become a successful drunk in no time. The only thing that separated him from the stumbling wrecks in the gutters below, he knew, was his locked front door. He also knew, with alcoholic paranoia, that sooner or later someone would knock on that door. The police, or Henry Toledo's lawyer, or Agent Cobb of the IRS would expose him as the imposter, liar, and brother-killer that he really was. He would be evicted from Toledo's condo and join his fellow drunks in the mean streets. He twisted the cap off a bottle and continued his meltdown.

Then he was on his back on the rich carpet, and someone was knocking on the front door. This was it. He was found out. He was ready. He crawled on his hands and knees to the door while the room whirled. Knock, knock. He pulled himself up with the big gold doorknob and opened it. Pono, Isaac's man, was enormously in the doorway. "Mr. Talmud, he wanna see you."

Manning swayed. "How'd you get by the doorman?"

"Mr. Isaac say come get you. No doorman gonna get in my way." Pono stepped in and looked around. "Say, you livin' it up, pupule man."

Manning hung onto the door for dear life. "Tell Mr. Talmud that I can't come. I'm on my computer. . ." Manning discovered that he was going to be sick. Soon. He stumbled toward the bathroom. Pono got under his armpits and dragged him in. He made the commode just in time.

He threw up endlessly, winding up on his back again on the cool tile while the bathroom spun in wide circles around him. Pono re-entered. "Come on, pupule man. We gonna clean you up and get on the plane."

"What does 'pono' mean," Manning asked. "In

Hawaiian?"

"Pono means 'righteous.'"

"Perfect," said Manning. Pono was fiddling with the shower water taps.

Talmud's private jet sat at Kennedy International Airport. The Filipino pilot smiled his toothy smile. Manning crept aboard. He sank gratefully into a lounge chair. Everything hurt from his hair down. "Is there any coffee?"

Pono shook his head. "No coffee for you, pupule man. Unless you wanna be a make man."

"What does 'monkey man' mean?"

"Make. 'Mah-kay.' It means dead man."

Manning nodded. Sounded okay to him. "What does 'pupule man' mean?"

"Means 'crazy man.'"

"Perfect," said Manning. He fell into the plane's bed and slept like a "make man" for the 12-hour trip.

epilog 2

". . . Now Choose Life."

"A drink?" Isaac asked.

"Thanks. I've recently given up alcohol," said Manning.

"Not a moment too soon, from what Pono tells me. Coffee?" The sun and the blues and greens of Hawaii filled the great room of Isaac's estate. Isaac hobbled to the same silver coffee service Manning remembered from his first visit. Was that only a few weeks ago?

"Coffee, yes, would taste good," Manning said. So would some aspirin. Dr. Schmidt, his dentist, was back there somewhere behind his eyes, drilling. He watched Isaac pour. Manning was horrified by the change in his friend. Isaac's hands were gnarled, with knobs at the knuckles and finger joints. His skin stretched like old parchment over prominent cheekbones and pouched around his eyes in dark rings.

"What's happened?" Manning asked, but he knew.

"What we all expected to happen and tried not to think about." Isaac waved his hand in front of his face, brushing away imaginary flies. "Let's get on with it. I don't have time for pity. I don't have time for most things." He poured two cups, bracing himself upright with his left hand on the coffee table.

Manning crossed the room to get his cup and save his friend the trip. "Thanks. I can use this."

Isaac lifted his eyebrows. "So Pono tells me. What are you doing to yourself?"

Manning looked around the large open room as if the answer to the question might be hidden in a corner somewhere. "Paying the price of the prodigal, I guess. I made a mess of my own life so I took Henry Toledo's life and hamburgered that one up, too. Not content with that, I ended Adam's life for him. So I set out to kill Adam's killers or die trying. But in Chiapas I saw a way to do some good. . . I thought. Get you and the rest of your Spaniards to the Fountain again, restart your clocks. Make peace between you and the Calusa." He shook his head into his coffee cup. "It went sour, just like everything else in my life. The Fountain of Youth turned out to be a sprinkler system. Even the peacemaking was a bust."

"Nothing wrong with peacemaking," Isaac said quietly. "Jesus calls the peacemakers blessed."

"But all the players are dying," Manning ticked off his fingers. "De Leon, Carlos. . ." He stopped and looked up.

"Now me," Isaac finished for him. "People you like die. Get used to it. I have, in five hundred years. I didn't want you as a friend, remember. . . only to outlive you. That's no longer a problem, is it? Now we can be friends."

"Is that why you flew me back here? To tell me you love me?"

"Quit feeling sorry for yourself." The iron was back in Isaac's voice. He walked stiffly to a wall safe and opened it.

He removed a small glass bottle and handed it to Manning, who turned it in his hands. It was round and squat, shaped and colored like a purple onion. He guessed it was blown by hand long ago. The glass stopper had been fused to its neck. Manning shook it. Liquid sloshed in the bottom.

Isaac looked at his friend with eyes yellowed by age. "Can you guess what I have in here?"

Manning nodded.

"I've kept it all this time. Once it was almost a liter. The ages have taken most of it. There's enough for one swallow. Four and a half centuries ago I had a master glass blower from India make this container. He melted glass around the top to prevent further evaporation."

"How do you know it's still. . ."

"Good?" Isaac smiled again. "Well, of course I don't. I could drink some, but what would that prove? I already have the gift. No, someone else must test it."

"Nonsense, Isaac. You pinched this as a refill in case the magic ran out. Well, it's run out. You've got a second chance. Use it." Manning handed the bottle back.

"Use it," Isaac repeated thoughtfully. He set the bottle carefully on an ornate card table and shuffled to his wine rack. He selected a dark bottle covered with dust. "Pinot noir, from the hills along the Moselle. Bottled in 1840." He rubbed the dust off with his sleeve. "Do you think it's still good? Let's see."

He found a corkscrew and pointed it at the purple bottle. "You're right, my friend. I did take that water as insurance. I was on guard that night in Pascua Florida, remember? I had a half-full bottle of fine Madeira from

Portugal that I pulled on from time to time to keep the blues away. I sat that night and sipped from it until it was gone, and just before dawn I crept to the bayou and filled the bottle from the Fountain. I hid it in my rucksack. I told no one. . . until today, Manning."

Isaac inserted his corkscrew into the wine bottle he held in his hand but the cork crumbled around it. He poured the dark wine into the bar sink. "No fizz," he said. "Like me." He lifted a second bottle from the wine rack and pointed its neck at Manning. "I kept that precious water hidden for years, and when I could have used it wisely I didn't. Do you remember what I told you, the time I told the story of my beloved Maria Magdalena's death?"

"You said you would have given anything to save her." Manning stopped to think. "No. You said. . . almost anything."

"Very good." Isaac held up the small bottle. "I could have opened this and saved her. Instead I told myself, well, it's been so long in the bottle, it won't work. But then, why have I kept it? Because I love myself more than I loved Maria. So now, when I finally can use it, I find that I can't. I have dedicated it to her. . . too late."

Isaac worked on the second wine bottle with his corkscrew. It came out with a healthy "pop." "Better," he said, pouring for them both. He lifted his glass by the stem in a toast. "L'chaim. To your good health."

"And yours." The two men held their glasses up, staring at each other. They put them down, untouched.

Isaac smiled and shook his head. "God gave me a great gift when I drank from the Fount. It wasn't just long life. It was life long enough to learn what He wanted to teach me. He taught that five centuries are still trivial compared to eternal life."

"Eternal life," Manning said. He guessed what was coming. He wasn't sure he wanted to make the trip.

"Psalm 36 reads, '. . .The fountain of life is with you.'" Interesting, eh? Not a magical fountain in Florida. Something more valuable. The chance to live forever."

"Words in a book. Coincidence. Now is not the time to go metaphysical. Now is the time to open your bottle and save your life, Maria or no Maria."

"Solomon wrote in that same book, 'There's time to live and a time to die.'" Isaac held the purple bottle out to Manning. "Five centuries are enough. Take it, only be careful. God gave the Fountain as a blessing, but Satan uses it too. It led Tomaso to murder. Los Viejos hoarded life and riches like penny merchants. Me too."

He leaned against a table, spent with all his talking. "Carlito and the Calusa put away their savage ways and used their wealth and knowledge to pull the world's rabble out of the mire. The savages became Christians. . . at least my definition of Christians. . . better Christians than us Catholic Spaniards. Now God is calling in His markers. It's my time to die. I'm sorry for my sins. God forgives me."

Manning snorted. "Is that how it works? Forgiveness is easy. All you do is ask. That's too easy. You have to do something."

Isaac shook his head. "Doing stuff is how you miss it. Just believe. God does the rest. I'm ready for the rest. . . the other life, the eternal one."

"How can you be sure?"

"That there's an eternal life? Good question. An excellent question." Isaac pulled a thick leather-bound book from the bookshelf built into his wall. He hefted it, looked at it for a moment, and to Manning's surprise, kissed it. "Here's the answer."

Isaac gave the book to Manning. "Take this and the bottle. I have no further use for either. You can drink from the bottle or not, you decide. Believe me, please, when I tell you that it's no big deal whether you drink or not. But for God's sake. . . no, for your own sake, read the book. On pain of eternal death, I beg you, read the book. You'll find Christ's words in there. 'What does it profit a man to gain the whole world and lose his soul?' God gave all of us plenty of time. . . time to choose. Tomaso, the Franciscan, chose death. Isaac the Jew, the agnostic really, chose life."

Isaac pointed to the bottle and the Bible. "You choose."

Manning looked at the old leather Bible. "I'm not sure that I can choose. That book doesn't mean much to me. I mean, I'm sure that it's full of wonderful philosophy but so are lots of writings. . . religious. . . secular. . ." He looked at Isaac and his voice trailed off. This is what I say to a friend on our last day. . . maybe his last day?

Isaac cocked an eyebrow. He held up the bottle. "You remember how skeptical you were about the Fountain? What I told you?"

"You said something about seeing is believing."

"Not quite. I said that most people believe it when they see it. I said you would see it when you believe it.

When you believe what good news is in this book, well, then you'll see what I'm talking about."

Manning held the book and bottle in his hands. "What can I do for you?" he asked.

Isaac looked at his twelve toes. "Nothing. As folks say these days, I'm history. It's been a long history, my friend. I've got a flight to Israel. I'll spend my last days there."

Manning leaned forward. "Stay here. You have so much to teach me."

Isaac moved his great nose slowly from side to side. "I've watched too many people I loved whither away. I haven't the stomach to go through that with you watching."

Isaac picked up a phone. "I'm ready," he said. He smiled at what he saw in Manning's eyes. "Don't fret for me. I'm going to heaven. I'll be with all my old friends. . . with Maria, if she'll have me." Isaac's chuckle ended in a cough. "And with all my other wives. How will I referee among so many women?" He put a hand on Manning's arm. "I want to see you up there, too, my friend, some day. Fifty years or five hundred, it's all really just the wink of an eye. It's up to you."

Two Filipina entered with a wheelchair. Isaac sank into it gratefully. He smiled up at his friend. "Goodbye, Manning. Or are you Henry Toledo? You'll have to decide about that, too."

"I don't want to be either. Manning looked at his own bare feet. "I'm an equal failure as Crenshaw or Toledo. I don't know who I am."

Isaac kept his smile. He leaned from the wheelchair

and collected a file folder from his coffee table. "Here's something to help you decide. I have a trust registered and administered on the Isle of Man. Fifty million, more or less." Isaac winked. "Low corporate and personal taxes on the Isle of Man. No inheritance tax. No capital transfer tax."

He handed the folder to Manning. "I willed it all, this house. . . everything. . . to a man named Manning Crenshaw. Will you tell him that, if you see him?" He winked again at Manning's suddenly frozen face and wheeled himself out of the room. The Filipina left with him.

Manning looked at the empty doorway. After a while he took the Bible and the bottle and walked out to the lanai by the sea. He could hear the distinctive hum of Isaac's Rolls in the drive. The sea had flattened to a smooth jade green for the summer. A lone black sea bird with white breast circled high above its surface, wings motionless. An iwa bird, Manning remembered. "Ee-vah." Isaac had taught him how to pronounce the Hawaiian name.

There was one dark squall-cloud on the seaward horizon with rain trailing from it like a veil. The sun behind him painted rainbow hues onto it. Didn't the Bible have a story in it about a rainbow? Manning opened the book in front of him to search for Noah and the Flood. He found it in the front, in Genesis:

> So God said to Noah. . . whenever the rainbow appears in the clouds, I will see it and remember the everlasting covenant between God and all living creatures of every kind on the Earth.

All living creatures. Manning closed the Bible and put it on a round glass table in the sun, next to the glass bottle. He stared at them both, deciding. He was still staring when Audrey came in two hours later.